I0740022

Motherline

Lisa Rosen

ISBN: 9780989370103

Morgan and Dawson Publishing

4101 Lake Boone Trail

Raleigh, NC

27607

MorganandDawson.com

Cover design by David Paul Wyatt Perko

Acknowledgments

I have to thank the people who helped birth this book, beginning with the string of babysitters and baristas who got me through the early part of the work. I couldn't have done it without the time and the caffeine. Later, as my ramblings began to look like they might actually turn into a book, my writing group friends encouraged me to keep pushing--you know who you are.

My sister Frances read a late draft and gave me thoughtful feedback, for which I am grateful.

My husband Lee provided crucial tech support, listened to my endless dithering about how to invent people, and convinced me to keep writing. Most importantly, once upon a time, he helped me give birth to two actual babies. He's a good guy to have around.

And finally, my children, Toby and Delaney, who've been hearing about this book ever since they can remember. Aren't you glad it's done, now that you're old enough to be embarrassed by it?

Chapter 1

Maggie opens her eyes in the wee hours and wonders if it's really happening this time. This is the third night in a row that she's dreamt of wetting the bed. She pats the sheets to be sure her water hasn't broken and sighs, not wanting to get out of the warm bed.

She can tell that her husband's hand is still tucked under the edge of her pillow; they'd fallen asleep talking—again—about the plan of action if she went into labor during the night. She lies still for a moment, nuzzling Sam's arm, then hauls herself out of bed and stumbles to the bathroom. The cat thumps to the floor. Sam stirs and asks, "Are you okay?"

"Shh. I have to pee. Go back to sleep."

"Are you sure?"

"Shhh." It's comforting to know that he's so excited, even half awake, for their baby to come, but she still hates to disturb him. At least one of them should be well-rested when it starts. He mumbles something, then starts snoring almost immediately and Maggie chuckles, wishing she could get back to sleep that quickly. Instead, she hauls herself up and heads for the bathroom.

This business of having to get up every night is for the birds. At fully nine months pregnant and a few days more she has cultivated the habit of never fully opening her eyes during a nocturnal bathroom visit, but her brain is harder to fool. She tries not to think about anything, but her mind is in overdrive, by turns euphoric over the baby's impending birth, panicked over how the baby will fit into her busy academic life, and worried that she'll never fit into her normal clothes again.

She shuffles back to the bed and crawls in, rearranging the half-dozen pillows that help her sleep somewhat comfortably. She looks at the clock. Now it's 3:15 a.m. Anxiety licks at her; she's been tamping it down for days, but in the lonely hours of the night it threatens to flare up. Sam's breathing has settled and deepened. Maggie is alone in the dark. She wiggles into position, knowing that once her mind starts spinning, she'll never settle down. She breathes slowly in and out, but that meditative feeling of calm eludes her. Before she was pregnant, Maggie always slipped quickly and easily into restful sleep. Now she wonders how people with serious insomnia cope—this exhausting wakefulness is the most irritating thing she can imagine.

It's 9:15 p.m. in England. She could call her father, in London; he'd talk to her, keep her company. No. She wills the thought out of her head. Sleep is important. Talking—even Daddy's sweet, easy chit-chat—will just wake her up even more.

She would like to roll over, but it seems like too much trouble. She'll just stay here on her right side, staring at the pale green numbers on the clock and ticking off the minutes of this night. She drums her fingers on the mattress. Time to get serious. She mentally trots in a line of sheep, determined to get back to sleep.

The sheep are fleecy little things—lambs, in fact. She really does have babies on the brain, she realizes. The lambs are running around on a tree-less hilltop. She wonders if this is *gamboling*. That's an atmospheric old word you don't see every day. She contemplates it for a minute, and her mind leaps, unbidden, to the classes that she won't be starting on Monday. Hopefully she won't regret taking the semester off. She's good at her work, and without it she's already feeling diminished, as if she's not getting any-thing *done*. Everyone else will be getting back to normal after the holidays: breaking in the new archaeology grad students, applying for dig money, researching this winter's big project. And she'll be busy doing—what? When she tries to conjure up a picture of her life a week from now, all she sees is a looming grey blank, dotted with piles of those unimaginably tiny onesies. She reminds herself that she should be asleep, and squeezes her eyes shut. The lambs are still bounding about on their hilltop. She lines them up and brings in a length of fence. One at a time, over they go. At lamb number seven, her mind wanders off to remember the wet-bed dream. She brings herself back to the hilltop. At lamb number eighteen, the anxiety tries to worm its way in again, so she yet again enumerates the contents of the suitcase she packed two weeks ago for the hospital. That's too distracting; she gives up counting.

It's no use. She might as well embrace the wakefulness, since it appears to be unavoidable. These roller-coaster mood swings lately make her nervous. She can almost feel the hormones surging through her veins. She punches at the pillow under her head, pushing it into a small, lumpy ball.

I can do this. I am a perfectly capable human. People have babies every day. It's going to be fine, you hear that, baby?

It's normal, this worry, she knows intellectually, but she's still surprised by this latest surge of anxiety. None of the books—and she's read stacks—have really prepared her for this rising tide of panic, this sharp fear that her maternal instincts won't kick in. Maybe if she writes herself a note, she can stay on top of this thing, stay in control. She reaches for her book light, and feels a piece of paper flutter to the floor. Her nightstand is littered with sticky notes. She sighs. Sticky notes seem woefully inadequate.

I need my mother.

The thought surprises her. A memory hovers, teasing, a vague outline, the details buried in the depths of childhood: a wakeful night, an expectant household, the excitement of teetering on the edge of the unknown. She can't remember why she wanted her mother so badly that night, but the pull of that longing was deeply instinctive. She wants to be a mother like that mother, the one she can just barely remember, before everything fell apart—not like the distant, unpredictable mother she knows now.

§§§

Maggie's eyes popped open. Across the room, her sister's breathing was deep and steady. Maggie listened, secretly glad they were sharing a bedroom now. It felt cozy, having Dara right there all night long. Especially when she woke up.

She didn't feel at all sleepy. Even with Dara making her little snore noises, the whole house was so, so quiet, as if wrapped in a blanket. She wondered why she felt so awake. The little crack under the door was dark, so Mommy and Daddy must be in bed, too. It really must be the middle of the night.

Maggie pushed the covers down a little, so her ears could hear better, and listened as hard as she could. Someone was moving downstairs. She could almost feel it in her body: the soft clunk of a cabinet door closing, a whoosh of water in the sink. She wondered if it was Mommy or Daddy, and slipped out of bed.

Maggie peered around the kitchen door, blinking. The light over the breakfast table hurt her eyes. Mommy was sitting at the table, in the pool of bright light, the kitchen dark all around. Her belly was so big it pressed up against the edge of the table.

"What're you drinking, Mommy?"

"Oh Maggie! You startled me, honey." She held out one arm to Maggie, pulling her into the circle of light. Maggie snuggled up against her warm body.

"What is that?" she asked again, peering into the mug.

"Warm milk. Would you like some?"

"No, that sounds yucky. Why is it warm?"

"Warm milk helps me sleep sometimes. It might help you too. You can try mine, if you want."

Maggie looked again at the white foam; milk was supposed to be cold.

"No, thank you." She pressed herself up against Mommy's side some more; there wasn't room in her lap now, with the new baby taking up so much room in her belly.

"Did I wake you up?"

"I don't think so. I think I just woke up. I feel excited."

"Do you?" Mommy smiled. "I do too."

"Why? Is the baby coming?"

"Maybe. Plus, come here."

She held Maggie's hand and stepped into the darkness of the kitchen. She helped Maggie climb up onto the window seat by the mudroom. The air was cold by the window. Maggie shivered, and Mommy wrapped her arms around her from behind.

"Look."

Maggie looked out at the backyard. All the daytime colors were gone; the moon made the trees and the grass look all gray and white and shadowy. It looked like a magical version of her very own yard. Everything seemed to be glowing.

All of a sudden, it came to her: "It's snow! Mommy," she cried, craning her neck to look up at Mommy, "Did it snow? Is that it?"

She could feel Mommy's little laugh, jiggling her belly. "Yes, lovey. A couple of inches so far, I'd say." She leaned toward the window, looking up at the sky. "It's stopped for now, but it looks like we might get more."

Maggie put her hands flat on the window. "It's cold."

"It is. Hey—let's go outside."

"In our jammies?"

"Sure, why not? Come on, grab your coat."

"Mommy, you're silly."

"Yep. Sometimes it's fun to be silly, don't you think?"

Maggie giggled and jumped down from the window seat.

Outside, the yard was absolutely silent. The air felt damp against Maggie's cheeks, and tingly cold. When she breathed in she could feel the cold sucking into her throat. She coughed, and blinked, and squatted down to touch the snow on the ground. It was soft and wet, and cold like ice.

"Did it snow last winter?"

"It did, but not much. Don't you remember?"

"A little bit. I forgot what it feels like."

Mommy squatted down, carefully, and mushed a handful of snow into a ball.

"See how it sticks together? Here—catch." She tossed the little ball to Maggie, who caught it with both hands.

"Oh, it's hard! It looks like it might be soft."

"Snowballs can be deceptively painful."

"What does that mean?"

"It means they're small, but they can really hurt if you throw them at someone."

"Let's not play snowballs. Can we make a snowman?"

"Mm. Maybe we should wait till morning for that. There'll probably be more snow by then, anyway. Plus, Dara would be sad if she didn't get to help, don't you think?"

"Okay."

Maggie wandered over to the patio, poking her finger into the thick layer of snow on the arm of a chair. When she looked over her shoulder, Mommy was standing in the middle of the yard, waving up at the house. Her whole face looked happy. Maggie could see Daddy looking out the window. While Maggie stood still, watching, Mommy began to turn around, arms wide open, twirling in a slow circle. She looked funny, in her nightgown and rain-boots, her big belly poking out from her open coat. Maggie giggled and ran over to twirl next to her.

She went faster than Mommy, spinning, until her boots slid on the slippery grass, and she tumbled down.

"I'm all wet." The cold was beginning to sink through her jammies now, making her shiver.

Mommy chuckled, helping Maggie to her feet. "Goodness. You must be—your hands are like ice. Come on, we'll go in and warm you up."

"Aren't you cold?"

"Not terribly. Pregnant mommies tend to stay kind of warm."

"Oh. Is the baby coming soon?"

"You asked that a little while ago. Maybe. I'm kind of feeling like it might be very soon—that's what woke me up."

"Now?"

"Mm—it'll be a little while yet. Maybe tomorrow—today—in the daytime."

The kitchen was deliciously warm after being outside. Mommy helped Maggie strip out of her wet jammies and wrapped her up in Daddy's big coat, which she pulled from a peg by the door. They climbed slowly upstairs together, in the dark; Maggie held Mommy's hand, her teeth still chattering. Mommy reminded her to be extra quiet, so Dara wouldn't wake up, and they found dry jammies in a drawer, and Maggie hopped back into bed.

Mommy pulled the covers all the way up to Maggie's chin, kissing her forehead. Maggie snuggled up in the bed in a tight little ball, shivering, and fell asleep quickly.

When she opened her eyes again, white light filled her room. She bounced out of bed, straight to the window. Everything was white—the street, the yard, all the yards around—except for a deep set of tire tracks, black against the snow, leading right to their driveway. Her grandmother's car was parked in front of the garage door.

Maggie turned from the window, and shook her younger sister. "Dara, wake up. It snowed. And Yaya's here. The baby's coming today."

§§§

Unable to stare at the clock for one second longer, Maggie hauls herself over to her other side, facing Sam, and looks at his silhouette in the darkness. She thinks about waking him up so she won't have to lie alone in the dark, but he can't help, not really. He has too much faith in her. He's so close to his mother; he doesn't seem to understand that some women don't automatically know how to do the mommy thing. Besides, when it really comes right down to it, she's the one whose body is spinning out of control. He swears he'll be right there with her the whole time, and she has absolute faith he will, but there's nothing he can do to keep the indignity at bay. It's up to her to maintain control.

What have we done? I don't even know how to burp a baby—what happens if I do it wrong? Can babies explode from not burping? What if we screw this up? It's a person, not a cat. Maybe we're not ready.

That's ridiculous. They're as ready as anyone else. It's perfectly normal for a young couple (okay, thirty-something couple, but that's normal) to want to start a family. There was nothing accidental about it—they'd paid attention to her cycles, looking for that optimal moment that would result in a pink line on a dipstick. They'd waited together one morning, feigning nonchalance—he'd had to retie his tie three times, while she dribbled toothpaste on her blouse—until that line appeared, faint but distinct. She had looked at it, eyes wide, one hand on her concave belly, while Sam laughed. He laughed and laughed, until she chimed in, uncertainty lost in the giddy rush of excitement.

Her agitation seems to have awakened the baby. She presses her hand on the side of her belly, feeling the squirming and wiggling. The wild, soaring flips and turns of the second trimester are long since over. She can tell, now, that the baby is jammed into way too small a space and needs to spread out. Hard, bony little elbows and knees and feet push with a force that amazes her. She stays very still, absorbing the sensation, and searches for that feeling of connection.

Hi baby. I will do my best, I promise. Are you coming soon? When you get here, we'll go see Yaya. You're so lucky to have a great-grandmother. Not everyone gets one, you know. She's going to love you. They're all going to love you.

Maggie rubs at a bump under her ribs, thinking about the grandmother who had always glued her family together. Time and again, Yaya had picked up the pieces and kissed the boo-boos and dried the tears. She had set everyone back on the right track, even when her own daughter, Maggie's mother, had fallen apart and retreated from the demands of motherhood, finding it easier to escape into her work. Yaya knows how to do all the important things, like burping babies and changing diapers and making cookies. The knot of fear in Maggie's stomach slowly begins to loosen, and she rubs again, more firmly, at the hard bump in her side. It pokes back in response. She tries to visualize the baby—is that a knee, or a toe, or an elbow? She smiles in the dark, feeling slightly unhinged as her emotions careen from one extreme to the other.

She can't remember what it was like when her body was quiet. She felt invaded from the very beginning—long before that bizarre moment when she felt real movement for the first time. Those first tiny wiggles, so faint she almost missed them, made up for a lot. But not quite everything. It was a welcome sensation by then, but disconcerting nonetheless. She still felt as if she was sharing her very personal space with a stranger. Musing, she rubs at her side until the rhythm lulls her back to sleep.

When Maggie wakes up again, Sam is getting dressed. She sees him in the bathroom, tying a yellow tie, and yawns. She is careful to restrain her stretch; pointing her toes makes her calves cramp.

"Did I sleep through the alarm?" This is doubtful. She sleeps way too lightly now to miss an alarm clock.

"No. I just woke up for some reason. I think I'm stressed about getting everything done. I feel like it's the day before vacation and I've got to get two weeks' worth of work taken care of." Sam grins at her, a big goofy grin. An excited morning person is unbearable, Maggie thinks, yawning. But then, so many people and things and memories are unbearable to her these days.

"How'd you sleep?"

"Like crap."

"Yeah. You were thrashing around a lot."

"Sorry. Did I keep you up?"

"No—I was just worried about you. Anything happening?"

"Not that I can tell. I just couldn't turn my brain off."

Sam sits down on the end of the bed and wraps his hands around her right foot, rubbing each toe gently through the comforter.

"Excited?"

She shrugs one shoulder, and stares off into space. "I guess, but it feels weird—I'm excited, but the end-point is so vague."

"How do you mean? I thought the end-point was the baby."

"That's not what I mean—I mean the 'when.' You know? Like when you were a kid, that thing you were unbearably excited about—Christmas, or the last day of school—you knew exactly when it was coming. So you could sort of parcel out your excitement, pace yourself. I have no idea how to pace myself right now. I'm beginning to wonder where the top is. Is there a top?"

"You mean, is it possible to explode from excitement?"

Maggie squints at Sam. His great strength—the thing she fell in love with first—is the fact that he finds life uproariously funny. His blue eyes twinkle at her now, making it difficult, as always, to take herself too seriously.

"Stop laughing."

"Maggie, pumpkin. I'm not laughing at you I swear."

"You are too." She pulls the comforter up over her head.

"No, really. I'm not." Sam's voice is muffled now, and he has stopped rubbing her foot. His weight rises from the bed, and then he's tugging the covers away from her face.

"Are you upset about something, really?"

She hesitates. "Nah."

Sam waits, as if he knows she hasn't finished the sentence.

"I guess I've just got all the family stuff on my mind—baggage, you know?"

"Is your family ever not on your mind? That seems pretty normal to me."

"I guess I was hoping that all those years of therapy would kick in now, and help me not to get too wound up. I don't like getting agitated about crap I can't fix. I'd rather be a little more Zen about it all, going into labor."

"Listen, for what it's worth, from where I'm sitting, you sound pretty normal. You're probably not the first woman in history to go into labor worrying about her relationship with her own mother."

Maggie takes this in, absorbing its accuracy.

"Fine. Go to work, smart ass—let me be miserable in peace."

Sam frowns at her. She knows he's not going to let it go that easily.

"You're stressed. It's fine. I am too. The only reason I knew you were agitated during the night was because I'm all keyed up too. You're going to be a great mom, you know."

Maggie gives him half a smile. "Maybe."

"Definitely. What's on your agenda for today?"

"Um, childbirth?"

"You think? Are you feeling something?" His face lights up.

"No. I don't know. I don't think so. My back hurts so much. Maybe I should look up backache again—would you hand me the book, please?"

Sam tosses her the battered copy of *What to Expect When You're Expecting* from the top of a pile.

"Just the one?"

"This should do it. There's an OB textbook in the chair, but that's probably overkill."

"I suspect so." He smiles.

She begins flipping through the book, already distracted. "By the way, I'm going to have lunch today with Yaya."

"Oh good. That'll make you feel better."

"Hopefully." Maggie's grandmother is still, at ninety-three, going strong, relatively speaking, and taking a keen interest in the goings-on of her two grand-children—Maggie and her sister, Dara.

"Gotcha. Well, in the meantime, you ought to go back to sleep. It's only seven. I'll call you around lunchtime and I'll try to get home as early as I can."

Maggie looks down at the how-to-be-a-mom book in her lap. Sam leans over to kiss her forehead.

"Later."

"Mmm-hmm." She hears him start down the hall, and goes back to skimming for *backache, third trimester*. Maybe she should try *backache, labor*, or *pre-labor, symptoms*. But the book has no more secrets to offer; she's already read it from cover to cover, more than once. She curls onto her side, burrowing under the covers. Maybe Sam was right, and she should try to get some more sleep. This is the second day in a row he's gone to work and left her in bed, and it's beginning to weird her out a little bit. Lazing around is one thing on a Saturday, but she's not used to staying in bed while he goes to work. It makes her feel that she's losing control over her life.

She lies still for a few minutes, then hears rain starting. Yuck. Rain on New Year's Eve. How depressing. The pattering sound on the window and the tree outside is mesmerizing. She closes her eyes and goes inside, searching for the baby. It's a presence now, a companion, like Jamie used to be. When he was tiny he followed her around like a shadow, always there on the edge of her attention. When he was gone, the memories of him followed her in his stead. It was his hands she thought of most—grubby little-boy hands, fingers spread wide, pointing, touching, reaching. Always reaching.

She glances at the framed photo on her nightstand, taken when Jamie was born. She was six, and she was holding him as if he were her very own treasure. He had fallen asleep in her arms, and the photographer (Mother? Daddy? Yaya?) had caught her in a state of rapture. She still remembers the weight of her brother in her arms. She rubs her belly, thinking about that easy love, and willing her own baby to hurry up. Her stomach growls, so she pushes herself up to sitting and prepares to launch into the day.

CHAPTER 2

Maggie wanders into the kitchen in her bathrobe, too hungry to shower first thing. Ever since that morning sickness in the beginning, she's had to eat breakfast as soon as her feet hit the floor. There have even been a few times when she had to get a snack in the middle of the night. Pimento cheese at four a.m. might sound like a bad idea, but it really hit the spot. Not this morning, though. Toast sounds about right. Maggie puts two thick slices of oatmeal bread in the toaster and pours a glass of juice. She spreads one slice with butter, the other with peanut butter, and sits down at the table. The day stretching out before her seems to be daring her to embrace the languor and go back to bed.

Sam has left the newspaper on the table for her. She smiles, knowing he likes to take it with him; she had whined a little last night about how disoriented she's feeling since her maternity leave started. It's not loneliness, but more a sense that she's losing control over her days. Laziness is a disturbing temptation. The *Post*, damp from the rain and smelling of paper and ink is his offer of structure, of routine and normalcy. She scans the front page, then opens it to the second page. Hidden there, waiting for her, is a yellow sticky note, in Sam's bold, blocky handwriting:

SMILE. I LOVE YOU.

She does smile, then carefully peels the note off and sticks it to the tabletop. Her fingers trace the outline of the yellow square as she reads the paper, cover to cover. As she's finishing and starting to squirm in the hard kitchen chair, the phone rings loudly in the quiet kitchen. She jumps a little. Glancing at the caller ID, she sees that it's her sister and picks up the phone.

"Hi," Maggie says, a little more loudly than she meant to.

"Are you okay?"

"What? Yes I'm fine. Why? Is something wrong?"

"No, you just sound out of breath."

"I'm fine." She hesitates. "Okay—no. I'm kind of miserable. I can't get my back comfortable anywhere. And I'm worried. And bored being at home."

"I'm sorry. Is there anything I can do? Maybe we could go for a massage?"

Maggie blinks. "You know, that is actually a sort of horrifying thought."

"Oh, come on. It might make your back feel better."

"Think about it, Dara. How awkward would that be, getting naked in my condition?"

"You could leave your underwear on."

Maggie laughs out loud. "Yeah, that'd make all the difference. Lying on a table like a beached whale, in my granny panties. No, I'm good. Plus I don't think I want anyone touching me. If she accidentally rubbed me wrong I might have to smack her. Maybe after the baby comes. Is that a totally unrealistic goal, do you think?"

"Why are you asking me? I have no idea. As far as I can tell, babies come wrapped up in cute stripey blankets and go back on the shelf at dinner time."

Maggie laughs again.

"What? Is that not right?"

"Ahh. That's excellent. I needed a good laugh. So what's up? I'm guessing you didn't call just to brighten my day."

"Well, actually, I hesitate even to mention this, but I guess I can solve the boredom for you. I have a message from Mom."

"What do you mean, a message? Is she okay?"

"She's fine." Dara's voice takes on a soothing tone, which alarms Maggie even more.

"Dara, what's going on?"

"Nothing. Be quiet—let me finish. I called her just to check in when she was on her way to work. She asked me to relay the message, that's all. Anyway, the point is, she's got another project going. She dug up some rose bushes, and she wants you to go get them. She says Sam can transplant them to your yard next week. It's supposed to warm up a little."

Maggie thinks about this for a second, still confused.

"Why didn't she just call me?"

"Oh, who cares? She was getting out of her car when we hung up, so she was probably already thinking about work. Just go get the roses. I think maybe they aren't supposed to sit out in the cold."

Maggie grimaces, aware that all too often her mother's projects take on a life of their own.

"Maggie? She wants you to go get them today."

"Why can't you go? It's raining. And cold. I'm a whale. And I'm going to Yaya's."

"Sorry. Can't. I have a closing in a little while."

"Fine. Why on earth is she digging things up? Why would I want her roses? Why doesn't she want her roses?"

"Calm down—I have no idea. I'm just relaying the message. You know how she is. She's got some idea in her teeth and she's not going to let it go till it's done."

"Yeah I do know how she is. That doesn't mean I like it."

"You don't have to like it—you just have to go do it. Humor her. She's your mother."

Maggie rolls her eyes.

"I'll go. It's not a huge deal. I just wish…. Well, I don't suppose it matters."

"Oh, Maggie," Dara says. "I don't have a clue. Yes, it's bizarre. I don't know what else to tell you."

"Don't worry about it. I'll manage. They can't be too big, if she dug them up, right?"

"I guess not. Be careful. It's supposed to get icy today."

Maggie looks out the kitchen window at the thermometer, agitated. Thirty-eight degrees.

"Fine. There'd better be a reason for this."

"Like I said, don't hold your breath. Anyway I've got this closing, but I should be done by lunchtime-ish. Then my calendar is clear for a couple of days, so seriously, you really should go into labor. This is a good time for me."

Maggie smiles at Dara's excitement. "I'll keep you posted, but you shouldn't hold your breath, either. It's not like I have any control over it."

After they hang up, Maggie dials her mother's cell phone number, but she's not surprised when it goes straight to voicemail. She doesn't leave a message.

She shuffles over to the window. When she presses her hand against the cold glass, little halos of warmth condense around each fingertip. The bare bones of a Japanese maple shine black in the rain.

She heads upstairs to get dressed, lifting each foot and putting it down precisely. Her joints feel slack and wobbly. If she doesn't control her stride, her legs sometimes feel like they might fly off entirely. She turns on the shower, then hesitates, glancing at the clock. She ought to get going if she's going to make it to the Glenlake retirement community by lunchtime to visit Yaya. She calculates, then gets into the shower, telling herself she doesn't want to risk going into labor still wearing yesterday's odors. She has felt particularly ripe and a bit leaky in the last few days.

As the warm water courses over her, Maggie digs her knuckles into the small of her back. If she can just find the right pressure point, maybe the knotted muscles will relax enough to stop aching. She tilts her head back. The pregnancy has made her long hair so thick it takes a minute for the water to soak all the way through.

As she shampoos her hair, she mulls over her mother's request. Over the years, she's gotten used to these all-consuming projects and, as an adult, has learned to ignore them. They're just Katharine's way of taking a little break from reality. When Maggie was younger, though, she had felt a pang of loss, an aching emptiness, every time her mother threw herself into a new obsession.

§§§

Maggie lay in her bed, under the covers, not sleeping. Her room felt too big, almost as if it might echo if she spoke too loudly. She knew her sister was in the room right next door. She could knock on the wall and wake Dara up if she felt too lonely, but it wasn't the same. She could barely remember a time when they didn't share a bedroom, back before Jamie was born, and trying to fall asleep without Dara's wiggling and breathing sounds made Maggie feel very small, and very alone. It was too quiet in the nighttime, and their house made too many noises.

In a way, she was kind of glad they'd moved Dara into Jamie's old room, instead of her. She liked having the biggest room, since she was oldest. But more than that, she thought she might be scared—even more than she already was—to sleep in the room that used to be Jamie's. But mostly, she wished they could've just stayed together in this room, like before.

She'd come home from school that afternoon to find Dara's bed in the hall, and her mother painting the walls in Jamie's room. She had hovered in the doorway, watching Mommy paint the walls with Dara's favorite color: Hubba-Bubba pink.

"Mommy, you're covering up Jamie's sailboats."

Katharine had painted Jamie's room blue and stenciled it with sailboats when he was a baby. That had taken a long time; she'd painted on the weekends, when she wasn't at work, whistling along with the music on the radio, and stopping to make dinner for Ben and Maggie and Dara.

This was different. When Maggie had left for school that morning, her mother had been in bed still, the same as she had been most mornings since Jamie died. She and Dara had gotten good at dressing themselves and slipping quietly downstairs. Yaya would be there when they got home from school, a lot of days now, to make dinner and help with homework.

But at breakfast they mostly ate cereal with Daddy. Nobody really knew what time Katharine got up.

But she must've gotten up early that day. By the time Maggie got home, there were only a few sailboats left, high up by the window. They looked small and faded compared to all that pink paint. Her mother was working toward the last boats with a roller on a long pole. She looked up at Maggie, standing in the doorway and said, "It's time."

Maggie took in the entire room. It was completely empty. Her tummy felt like when she was going down the big slide, like she might get sick.

"Why is Dara's bed in the hall?"

"I thought you might like to have your own room." Her mother's voice sounded strange, almost squeaky.

"I don't think so."

"Don't be difficult, Maggie. You'll love having your own room. Besides, it's time. I'm going back to work."

"When?"

"Tomorrow."

"That's soon."

"Well I'm ready, and they need me. I can't stay cooped up in this house forever."

"Will Yaya still come over?"

Mommy picked up the paint roller and turned back to the wall. "I suppose. Go get changed out of your school uniform."

Maggie threaded her way through the furniture in the hall, and stepped into the bedroom that was all hers now. There was a dusty rectangle on the floor where Dara's bed had been. All the things that had been hiding under the bed were exposed on the floor: a crumpled tissue, a used Band-Aid with the ends stuck together where it had been wrapped around a finger. Three hairbands, and the missing grape-scented marker. Dara's clothes were piled on Maggie's bed, waiting to be carried down the hall to her new room. Holding her breath, Maggie opened the closet, the folding door sticking in its track like always. Inside, it didn't look the same. Maggie's clothes were spread along the rack, with too much space in between. She pushed the door closed again, so hard it rattled, and ran out of the room.

Racing through the living room and kitchen and mudroom, Maggie didn't stop to put on her shoes or her jacket. She barreled out the back door, not bothering to slam it shut behind her, and ran through the back yard where Dara was swinging. Maggie ran past the swing set, ignoring her sister, and crashed through the line of bushes at the back of the yard. Branches tore at her, scraping her arms. She stumbled on the thick, knotty roots, stubbing her toes, then caught herself and pushed through into the next yard. She veered into the first open space, heading for the street. When she reached the sidewalk, she ran as hard as she could, toes gripping the concrete through her thick school tights. She ran past Mrs. Hirsham's house, and Amy Oliver's house, and the house with the baby twins. A sharp pain stabbed her in the side, but she kept going.

She ran till she got to the stop sign at the corner, and then she stopped. She wasn't allowed to cross the street, and she didn't know where else to go, or what to do. She looked down at her feet. Her big toes were both poking out of holes in her blue tights. Mommy would be mad. She wished she'd thought to put on her roller skates, even though she wasn't supposed to skate in her uniform.

Dara was calling for her from their yard. Maggie stepped behind the trunk of a huge tree, hoping she couldn't be seen, and stood there watching the cars going by for a minute, until the panting slowed and she caught her breath. Dara was still shouting, "Maggieeeee! Come back!"

Maggie could feel dry dirt between her toes, worming up into her torn tights. She stepped out from behind the tree, picking her way through mulch and leaves, and walked back to the sidewalk, toward her own yard.

"Where did you go?" Dara was waiting by the mailbox for her.

"Nowhere."

"Uh, oh. You tore your tights."

"I know."

"What are you going to do?"

"Nothing."

"You could hide them."

"I don't care about the stupid old tights."

"You should put on your shoes."

"I don't care about stupid old shoes either."

"Don't be grumpy, Maggie. I'll hold your hand."

"No. Leave me alone. Just go inside to your stupid bedroom."

Dara looked confused. Maggie walked away, leaving her sister standing in the driveway, and flung herself across the seat of a swing facing the bare ground. She pushed off with her bare toes and swung back and forth, dragging her hair through the dirt until she heard her grandmother's car pull into the driveway.

CHAPTER 3

At 9:30, Maggie pulls up in front of the house she grew up in. She can see the roses on the wide front porch, a tangle of spindly sticks; she dawdles in the car, like a child, pouting. She is annoyed with her mother for dragging her out in the cold, but she's furious with herself for doing her bidding. Thank goodness her mother's car is not in the driveway; maybe she can get the damn plants and leave, without having to try, yet again, to interpret Katharine's behavior.

As Maggie gets out of her car, Mrs. Hirsham walks by, pulled along by the current generation of the three tiny Yorkies that yapped the soundtrack of Maggie's childhood. Her resentment fades a bit at the sight of them, bundled up in little plaid blankets. She had loved those dogs when she was little; there were always three, always wriggling and squirming and licking, and always indistinguishable. Her mother had hated their noise.

"Maggie?" Mrs. Hirsham peers at Maggie through thick glasses. "Oh, my dear! I had no idea—look at you!"

Maggie laughs and leans over for a hug. "Don't tell me how much I've grown!"

Mrs. Hirsham laughs too. "My goodness. You look a lot like your mother, the last time she was pregnant…" Her words trail off, and she looks as if she'd like to take them back altogether. "May I?" Her free hand reaches toward Maggie's belly.

"Of course. I didn't realize you didn't know." Maggie feels a pang—regret that she hadn't come sooner, hadn't shared this pregnancy with someone who would have so enjoyed it.

Mrs. Hirsham had doted on Maggie and Dara when they were girls; they had never known a Mr. Hirsham, or any Hirsham children. They had loved her chocolate chip cookies, and cupcakes on their birthdays. And there was an odd little statue inside her front door, a gnome. He always seemed to be hiding a bit of bubblegum, or a hard butterscotch candy in its crinkly yellow wrapper. Mrs. Hirsham's fingers graze Maggie's belly now, while the dogs bark and jump and strain on their leashes. She ignores them.

"Oh, my goodness. It's…you're…well, when is the baby due?"

"It's okay, Mrs. Hirsham. I'm a whale. I'm totally aware of it. Actually, I was due a couple of days ago, but soon, I hope."

"I'm so happy for you, dear. I'm sure your parents are thrilled."

Maggie cringes, not wanting to have to explain her mother's ambivalence about this first grandchild, but Mrs. Hirsham doesn't seem to notice. She glances toward the house and frowns a little.

"Actually, I was sort of wondering how your parents are? Your father doesn't seem to come around much any more, and your mother, well, she's as busy as always. How are they?"

"Oh Daddy's in London, on sabbatical. He's working on a book. I'm sorry—I assumed you knew. He won't be back in the States till late in the spring."

"Ah. That explains it. I don't see your mother much, but I did notice that she was digging up rose bushes over the weekend. Why do you suppose she was doing that? It seems like an odd time of year."

"I have no idea. But that's why I'm here—Dara said I was supposed to come get them."

"How is Dara?"

"She's doing pretty well, under the circumstances. I think this lousy real estate market has her worried, but she keeps selling houses, so maybe it's not too bad. I try to have lunch with her once a week or so, but she's busy. It seems like I'm the only one in the family who doesn't have some desperately important work going on." Maggie can hear the whine creeping into her voice, and grimaces.

"That's all right, dear. You'll be busy soon enough." Mrs. Hirsham's voice is soft. "And your grandmother?"

Maggie chuckles. "She's a force of nature. She's ninety-three now, you know. She looks a little frail, I think, but she seems very happy at Glenlake. I'm going to see her at lunchtime. I worry about her, but she's still going strong."

Mrs. Hirsham shakes her head and pats Maggie's arm. "She's lucky to have you worrying about her."

"This is going to sound silly," Maggie hesitates. "But—it's like she's my connection to Jamie, you know? When I was a kid, after Jamie died, nobody ever talked about him except Yaya. So many of my memories now of him, of all three of us, when Dara and I were small too—I'm not sure if they're really *my* memories, or if I'm just remembering stories Yaya told. You know?"

Mrs. Hirsham nods, looking lost in her own memories.

"I'm sorry, Mrs. Hirsham. I didn't mean to keep you standing out here in the cold. You need to get the dogs inside."

"Oh, we're fine dear. But I'm glad to hear about your family. I haven't been to see Amelia as much lately. I don't drive so well any more. Tell her I said hello, won't you? And your mother, too—when you see her."

They hug once more, and the little old lady follows her dogs down the street. Maggie, thinking about the elderly visiting the very-elderly, watches Mrs. Hirsham turn into her front yard. Then she walks up her parents' front walk, past the empty perennial beds. Her mother's garden is formal and perfect, always, but today the whole yard looks desolate, even for the dead of winter. She stands still, taking in the dormant shrubs and bare trees. A particularly bare spot catches her eye, and she frowns. Something clicks in her brain, and she sways on her feet, gasping for breath. She feels like she's been punched; she knows, even before she sees them, which roses have been dug up: the ones her parents planted when she was young.

She walks over to the empty bed. The root holes have been filled in and the mulch pulled over them. It's as if the bushes—six of them, two each for her, for Dara, and for Jamie—had never been there. She reaches out one hand to steady herself against the trunk of a redbud tree and stares around at the silent garden. Why would her mother do this? The rain is starting up again, more of a mist than a downpour, but she shivers, cheeks damp.

Maggie trudges up the front steps and knocks on the door, even though she knows no one is home. She knew even before she got in the car that her mother wouldn't be there. It's Tuesday. She would be at work, of course. Still, she peers through the beveled glass next to the door, unsure which would be more upsetting—the silent house, or having to face her mother's calm productivity. Always a little unpredictable, Katharine has been more distant than usual since Maggie got pregnant—a secret disappointment to Maggie, who had hoped the pregnancy might deepen their relationship. She knows, though, that nothing has really changed, and she has no idea how to truly bridge the gap between them. Perhaps they are destined to perpetually orbit each other like distant stars—nominally related, in the same universe even, but never really making that mythical intimate connection.

She looks down at the roses on the porch, bare sticks bundled together. The roots are covered in newspaper; there's a note tucked under the string. She sorts the tangle of branches into discrete plants and counts the root balls —how many? Six, just as she thought. A memory tugs at her. The day her parents planted the roses, the whole family was working together in the broad front yard, and they had christened them "the baby roses."

She looks down at the tangle of branches, flooded with sadness and frustration. Remembering the family they had once been breaks Maggie's heart all over again, every time she looks back. She wants to weep at the sight of the baby roses. Her childhood—her own birth, even—is being dug up too, just as she's about to have her own baby. She clutches the porch rail, and bangs her head slowly against a pristine white column. "What. The. Hell."

§§§

It had been a beautiful day in late fall—Maggie, at eight, was old enough to feel the bittersweet urgency that comes with the end of the growing season. The maple trees that marked the far edge of the lawn blazed red; Maggie, dancing with Dara across the bright green grass, felt like the whole world was glowing. She knew cold weather was coming— the geese had been flying over for weeks, calling to each other with honks and squawks. But today they all reveled in the warmth and light and color.

Mommy and Daddy worked together, Mommy deciding where the roses would go and Daddy digging the holes. Maggie noticed how pretty Mommy looked, with a bandana pulling her hair back. She touched her own hair; if she could find her bandana, she could look like Mommy. She left Dara to her dancing, and wandered over to her parents, wanting to help, to be pulled into their happy little bubble. She hovered next to Mommy, watching her look up at the trees and pace off each planting spot.

"Here, Mommy. How about here? This is a good spot, isn't it?" Mommy was making some mysterious calculation that Maggie couldn't understand; she squinted at the sun, trying to see what Mommy saw when she looked up at the sky, and poked at clods of soil with the toe of her sneaker, but Mommy just knew, somehow, exactly where she wanted the baby roses to go.

They didn't look like much; Maggie squatted and looked again at the little metal labels that identified each bare stick of a plant. The names were mysterious—Wife of Bath, Constance Spry, Windermere—and she mouthed them to herself, stumbling over the last one. Mommy had said it was Jamie's; hers and Dara's were pink, but his was white. She said rose plants didn't come in blue, so he couldn't have a boy color, but that he wouldn't mind white. Maggie wasn't sure about that as she watched her younger brother digging in the lawn with a beach shovel, imitating Daddy. He kept at it, tearing up the grass, until Mommy saw him, and swooped him up in her arms. She tickled him till he squirmed and smeared even more mud with his shoes on her jeans.

"Maggie, you and Dara come play with this silly boy, please."

"No! I want to help you plant our roses."

"Honey, please—it would help even more if you'd occupy Jamie. He's mangling the grass, and we really want to get this done before the weather turns."

Maggie frowned and looked up at the clear, bright sky, wondering why the weather mattered. She didn't want to play with Jamie, but she liked it when Mommy needed her. She looked around the yard for something to do with her baby brother. Dara was spinning in circles, arms out, head thrown back.

"Come on Jamie, let's do dizzies with Dara."

He scrambled up from where Mommy had dumped him on the ground, shrieking and laughing as he ran to spin with Dara. The three of them whirled like dervishes, arms flung out, careening off each other, winding themselves into a state of dizzied oblivion. Maggie spun until she could feel the dizziness take hold of her brain, then flung herself down on the ground, staring up at the sky. For a moment, her sensations were split—she could feel the earth solid and steady beneath her back, but her body still felt like it was whirling through space. The bright sky, studded with puffy clouds, spun and danced above her. She lay on the ground, watching the world spin, until she caught her breath, then jumped up and did it again.

Jamie, having barely outgrown his toddler clumsiness, kept tripping over his own feet, which sent Dara into fits of giggles. She tried to walk in a straight line, staggering and weaving like a drunk person. Maggie fell down again, laughing so hard she couldn't stop. She lay on her back, watching the clouds scud by and trying to catch her breath, till the sky settled into place. Her breathing calmed back down, except for the last few giggles. The sun glowed red through her eyelids as she lay there, feeling her body relaxing against the ground. A breeze swirled through the yard, twisting leaves from the trees and showering them down. Maggie laughed as one landed on her face.

"Dara, look! The leaves are spinning, too!"

At that moment, Dara tripped over Maggie, catching her in the stomach with a knobby knee, and forcing the breath out of her. Maggie flung out one arm, trying to push Dara off, and smacked her in the face. Dara was silent for a stunned second before she started to wail. Maggie shoved Dara's legs off hers so she could sit up.

She looked up to see Jamie bending over, peering at her.

"Whatsa matter, Maggie? Are you crying?" he asked.

"No. But Dara is, because she's a big doofus and she fell on me." Maggie kicked at Dara, still crying into the ground. On the other side of the yard, she could see Mommy watching them, hands on her hips.

"Do you have an owie? I can kiss it and make it better," Jamie offered, putting one grubby hand on each side of Dara's face, and leaning in to kiss the top of her head. He missed, and toppled into the pile. Maggie laughed, allowing him to push her back to the ground again. He was solid and heavy, and warm against her in the chilly air. He threw out one arm, reaching for Dara, who tucked her teary face into Maggie's armpit. Jamie wriggled around until he could kiss the top of Dara's head, then lay stretched across his sisters, one hand on each. The three of them lay snuggled together, staring up at treetops and the endless blue sky, as the breeze kicked up again. Maggie watched as more leaves floated down, landing all around them. One caught, flame-red, in Jamie's blond hair.

"Is everything all right over there?" Mommy called.

Jamie lifted his head and yelled back.

"I'm snuggling the girls, Mommy. I make it all better, see?"

Without even looking, Maggie could hear the smile in Mommy's voice.

"That's great, sweet boy. Thank you."

"Welcome Mommy. See? Mommy, do you see? We're snuggling in the leaves!"

"Yes, my darling. I see."

Jamie wiggled on top of his sisters, making them both laugh, and popped his head up to shout for Mommy's attention again. "Mommy! Are you watching?"

"Jamie, honey," Mommy called back to him, "I can't watch you right now. Daddy and I are trying to get these planted before it gets cold. Can't you feel how chilly it's getting?"

"Ooh, she's right; it's getting really cold. Wanna feel?" Maggie stuck both of her hands up the back of Jamie's shirt, planting them flat on his warm, soft skin and making him squeal and squirm. He reached over and put his cold hands on Dara's neck, making her shriek, too, and they both rolled into Maggie. Uncontrollable giggles bubbled up in her chest and burst out, infecting them all.

Arms and knees and feet and hair and voices all tangled together, till Maggie could hardly tell where she ended and Dara and Jamie began. They laughed until Mommy finally came over to see what was so funny. Maggie giggled some more, and Mommy laughed too, a ray of sun slanting across the top of her head, making it look like her hair was on fire. This made them all laugh more, so she threw up her hands and went back to help Daddy finish tamping down the earth around the baby roses.

When they were all planted, and Daddy was putting away the tools, Mommy called them over to see the little plants. They looked even scrawnier now that they were in the ground—just skinny sticks poking up, with a few thorns.

"Why'd you leave the tags on them?" Maggie wanted to know.

"Because that's what you do with roses. So you'll always be able to remember their names."

Jamie squatted down and looked at the plants. He looked very serious.

"Which one is mine, Mommy?"

"Here, these two. See? This tag says 'Windermere.' They're yours. They'll have big, beautiful white flowers on them in the spring."

"Will you remember their name?"

"Yes. See the tag? We'll remember. But we'll always know which ones are yours, because they'll be white. The girls' are pink."

"But you'll remember the name? Because of the tag? Can I have a tag, too, so you can remember my name?"

Mommy burst out laughing, then, and so did Maggie and Dara. Jamie looked surprised, but then he laughed too. When they went in the house, Maggie had an idea: she made three nametags out of construction paper and hung them around their necks. She and Dara took theirs off at dinner, but Jamie wore his until Mommy said he couldn't sleep in it.

"I hafta keep it, Mommy, so everyone can remember my name," he said, as she taped it to his closet door.

"Oh, don't you worry sweet boy. How could we ever forget your name, with you here reminding us?" Then she swooped him up and tucked him into his bed, like she did every night in those days.

§§§

Maggie looks up at the house now, remembering that silly nametag with a pang, wondering if it got thrown away when her mother cleared out Jamie's room in the manic aftermath of his death. She shivers in the December cold, trying to reconcile the mother of her memories with the mother who would spend a cold holiday weekend clearing out her garden—*getting things done*—rather than surrounding herself with loving friends and family. It's too depressing; she shakes off the memories.

After a moment, she gathers herself to the task at hand, and looks back down at the pile of plants. She'll have to make two trips. She carefully lowers herself to the ground, grabbing the doorframe for balance, and wraps her arms around the whole mass. She's glad for the thick fabric of her sweater protecting her arms. For a second, she's stuck, teetering on the balls of her feet, her unwieldy belly tipping her forward into the great clot of thorny branches. The plants seem rooted to the floor of the porch; she struggles with the weight of it all. She throws her shoulder into the doorframe, managing to leverage herself, and the bushes, upright. Her muscles are shocked. The unaccustomed strain ripples across her abdomen.

She wrestles the roses into the back of the brand-new, family-friendly station wagon (built-in car seat, thankyouverymuch), and pulls the note off the roses. She reads it before she puts the key in the ignition.

Maggie—

I think maybe, after all these years, it's probably time for me to downsize so I'm going to start looking for a condo. I do not, however, wish to abandon my roses, so I'd like you to put some of them in your yard, please. You may remember that we planted them many years ago, so be careful with them. They are early David Austins. I trust you'll know what sort of care they need.

    Mother

She blinks, and reads it again, trying to make sense of her mother's words. What in the world? She goes back to that first sentence, about the house, impatient with her mother's concern for the roses. Of course she knows what they need, but that seems sort of irrelevant. She wipes her cold nose on the sleeve of her sweater, and plucks a thorn from the wool. Heaven forbid the roses feel abandoned.

As she pulls out onto the quiet street, she calls Sam's cell phone. He answers instantly; she hears the question in his breath. Her throat starts to close, so she clears it, gathering herself.

"Maggie? Are you okay?"

"Yes. No." She sounds like a frog. She breathes for a few seconds, then, realizing what Sam must be thinking, speaks slowly, controlling her voice with each word. "I'm not in labor. Nothing's wrong. I'm just freaking out, and I don't know why." Her voice cracks a little. "Dara called. She said Mother wanted me to go to her house to pick up some roses. So I did. There was a note on them—she's moving to a condo." She pauses.

"Wait. I don't understand."

"Neither do I." She pulls a tissue from her purse and wipes a clear circle in the passenger window, peering out at her childhood home. "Tell me what I'm supposed to do about all this."

Sam sighs. "All of which?"

"All of my crazy family. How am I supposed to bring a baby into this mess?"

"Pumpkin, none of this is *your* mess. Maybe you should go see your grandmother and not worry about anything else. On the other hand, you could call your mother and have a straight conversation with her."

"Right. I'll give her a buzz and ask her what's up. Maybe she'll tell me she doesn't want to be a grandmother. Because I so want to hear my own mother say she doesn't like babies. No thanks."

"Sweetheart, you know that's not true. What makes you think she doesn't like babies? She loves you, but she's obviously having a hard time with this. It's like you've got some kind of Norman Rockwell image in your head of this perfect mother, and you know full well—Katharine is not it. But you know what else? No one is."

Maggie's stomach twists at Sam's words; she does know it, but she can't figure out how to let go of the ideal. She scowls. She's so tired, and it's so hard to explain the push and pull that keeps her tied to her mother, but always at arm's length.

"I know." She pauses. "I thought maybe now, with the baby…."

"Stop. That's the problem. That's exactly what freaks her out—when other people have some kind of emotional expectation of her. Besides, isn't it really the baby you're worried about?"

"I don't know. Yes. I'm just upset about everything. I feel like it's all getting away from me."

Sam pauses for a second, thinking about how best to not upset her even more. "Maybe it is, a little bit. Our life *is* about to change. But it's okay—you don't have to control everything. Maybe you should focus on one thing you can do that'll make you feel better. Go see Yaya."

Something clicks into place in Maggie's brain, and her sadness suddenly crystallizes, a small, bright point of focus in the middle of her confusion.

"You're right. That's exactly what I need to do. She'll know what Mother's up to; I can tell her—"

"Maggie, honey. That's not what I meant. You need to go be with her. She's ninety-three. She can't keep solving all your problems. Go sit with her, hold her hand, and tell her how much you love her. It's time for *you* to be there for *her* now."

Maggie listens to the faint roar of the cellular connection in the silence. She doesn't want to hear Sam's words.

"I know. I'm just not ready to do that—I need her." Her voice drops. "I'm scared."

Her cell phone crackles, and she realizes Sam didn't hear her whispered worry. She sighs. "I'm almost home; I'll dump off these roses and head out to Glenlake. Thanks for talking me off the ledge."

"That's what I'm here for. I love you, Maggie. It's okay. We can do this."

"I love you too. I'm just…tired. It'll be fine."

She clicks off the phone and drops it into the passenger seat.

It doesn't feel fine. Nothing does. Not even a little bit.

Chapter 4

When she gets home from the rose mission, Maggie goes straight to the phone to call her father. It's dinnertime in London; he answers on the first ring. Somewhere in the back of her mind, Maggie realizes that this is the first time in her life that almost everyone she knows has been dying to hear from her, and it's not even about her.

"Maggie? Did you have the baby?" The excitement in his voice is the polar opposite of the misery in hers.

"No. I'm going to be pregnant forever. I'm miserable. And…." The lump in her throat swells again, and she sniffles. Her father makes murmuring, clucking noises, the way she knows he would if he were here. But she won't let him fuss over her, not now. "Daddy, did you know Mother is planning to sell the house?"

For a moment, Maggie hears only the faint humming of miles between them. Then Ben clears his throat.

"I didn't."

After an empty pause, she presses on. "Is that it? You don't have anything else to say about it?"

"What do you want me to say? It's her house. Frankly, I don't know why she hung onto it as long as she did."

"Daddy! How can you say that?"

"Well, it just seems logical," Ben says, his voice mild. "Your mother is one person, rattling around in a five-bedroom house. If we had reversed things when we got divorced, I would've sold it immediately."

"And uprooted me and Dara from our childhood home? Just like that?"

"Of course. Kids are resilient, Maggie. You survived the divorce—which has to be a bigger deal, emotionally, than moving to a new home. You would've been fine. You will be now too—I would point out that you are an adult, with a home of your own, and soon a child of your own."

"I know, but … " She trails off, rubbing her belly. His logic is unassailable, but the words themselves are beyond her comprehension. She doesn't *feel* resilient, not any more than she *feels* like someone's mother.

Even this late in her pregnancy, with the baby's arrival imminent, she is startled to think of herself as the *parent*. That is Katharine's job—she's the mother. Maggie isn't quite sure how to visualize herself in that role, and when she thinks very hard about how it will go—when she tries to imagine herself as the mommy, knowing and doing the mommy things with all the mommy surety—things get hazy.

"Maggie? Are you there?"

"Yes, I'm here. I'm fine. I'll deal with the roses."

"That's my girl." His voice lightens, and takes on a cajoling tone. "Hey—you know what I did the other day?"

He's changing the subject. The overt diversionary tactic rankles, but only for a second. She's ready to be comforted; it's easier to let Ben steer the conversation back to softer ground. "No, tell me."

"I went to Stonehenge."

"Oh!" Maggie smiles into the phone, imagining her father, graying now but still tall and slim, his long legs striding over the rocky ground.

"It's changed. You wouldn't believe it. You haven't been back, have you? Since that time we all went together?"

"No," she chuckles. "Stonehenge? Um, Dad—it hasn't changed in a couple thousand years. Trust me—I'm an archaeologist, remember? I'd've heard."

"Well then. You'd appreciate what they've done with the place."

Maggie smiles into the phone, allowing herself to be distracted by the familiar silly banter. Ben goes on to tell her all about the walkways and barriers and general tourist trappings that now stand between visitors and the ancient standing stones.

"Oh—that old pub is gone."

"Which old pub?" That family trip, so long ago, is a blur to her now. An endless succession of pub lunches all runs together.

"The one with the pudding. Remember? When you had such a fit?"

Maggie chuckles. She can barely remember the joke now and Dara hardly remembers the trip at all. The day of the pudding joke had been particularly dark, and at the time it hadn't really been a joke, but it had since taken its place in the family mythology.

§§§

They were in the south of England, on what was supposed to be a spur-of-the-moment family vacation, but it felt more like an extended funeral to the girls. The English countryside in February was consistently gray—skies, trees, fields, roads. The legendary gardens were dormant, the forests were bleak; even the stone walls along the road seemed to weep. At ten, Maggie could understand her mother's grief. She even knew, on some level, that her mother hadn't been the same since Jamie's death, but it was beginning to seem like nothing would ever get back to normal. She missed her brother, and things would never be the same without him, but her young mind could look fear and grief in the face for only so long before she simply had to move on. She missed her grandmother, back home in Washington. Yaya had been holding the family together since Jamie's death, and Maggie felt unmoored without her steadying presence. She wasn't sure where the center was any more.

Maggie had tried so hard on that trip. The unhappiness that was suffocating her family was palpable. The mother Maggie used to know—the one who read to her and talked to her and patiently showed her how buildings are built—had disappeared. Katharine was tense and driven, pushing a sight-seeing agenda guided by a check-list. She seemed to take little joy from the trip, staring blankly at soaring cathedral ceilings, moving restlessly from one great monument to the next, stopping only to consume whatever meal appeared on a plate in front of her, then ready to press on.

When Ben tucked the girls into their hotel bed at night, Maggie could see the sadness in his eyes and knew instinctively that he was worried about them all. She saw him watching Katharine, who refused to talk about Jamie's death. Her stifled unhappiness cast a pall over the family but she seemed not to notice the girls for hours at a time, intent only on crossing off the next item on her itinerary. Dara prattled on, choosing, as children can, not to join in the orgy of misery. But Maggie couldn't escape it. The sadness pulled at her. Turning ten had been a milestone for her, and she wore her new maturity self-consciously. So when her mother's distraction made her feel flat and empty, she tried to think of ways to relieve the unhappiness.

So Maggie was scrupulously obedient. She held Dara's hand on every crosswalk and subway platform. She ate the soggy foreign vegetables that kept appearing with dinner. She brushed her teeth without being reminded, and went to bed in strange hotels without contriving to stay up later. She tried to be as still and quiet as a mouse whenever a museum guide was speaking. It seemed suddenly that stillness and quiet were the attributes that adults valued most in young girls. Mostly, though, she tried not to miss Jamie.

The day they visited Stonehenge had been the turning point. It had been six months since Jamie's death. They had gorged themselves on guilt and recrimination. They had wallowed in grief, until the day that Maggie finally melted down from plain old ordinary childish hunger. A long, boring bus ride had preceded a damp ramble through a mucky field. The evidence of sheep was everywhere, but even those hardy creatures had retreated from the raw chill. Lunchtime had come and gone by the time the tiny little group of tourists crested the windswept hill. She had tried not to whine as they trudged up the slope, but Dara had no such compunction. Now, as they all stood in silence looking up at the megalithic circle of stones, Maggie's stomach growled loudly. She squirmed, old enough to be embarrassed by her body's noises.

"Daddy," she whispered, instinctively reverent in this amazing place. "I need a snack."

Ben looked frustrated. "Maggie, I just told Dara for the tenth time, I don't have any snacks. Please be patient. We'll eat soon. But right now, we're paying attention." His words were clipped and forceful.

Maggie could tell no snacks would be forthcoming. She wished Yaya were there, with her bottomless purse that always held a pack of crackers or a stick of gum. She pouted for a minute, then saw the futility of the expression and gave up. She looked around. The ancient stones loomed over her, more breathtaking in their dominance of the landscape than any cathedral or stately home she had yet seen. She craned her head back to look at the top of the first stone, and saw it rising up into the endless, empty grey sky. She was mesmerized.

She wandered away from the tour guide, slipping unnoticed into the middle of the ring of stones. If she stood very still, and looked straight up at the sky, she could almost feel the earth turning. She tried to think very hard about how old the stones were. Snippets of the tour guide's speech reached her on the wind, and her imagination began to bring the tidbits of lore and myth to life. She focused on the nearest stone, nearly 15 feet high, leaning slightly toward its neighbor, the ground around it scattered with bits of the smashed stone that had once been a lintel connecting the two uprights. Maggie had always been a very quiet child, and today she disappeared as far into herself as she ever had. Her family might be crumbling, but her own imagination—her own mind—was a place where she was in charge.

She sat down with her back against the cold stone, and tried to think herself into its past. She registered the damp seeping through the seat of her pants and the rich animal smell of sheep dung mixed with earth and rain. She rubbed the stone with her fingertips, feeling the tiny ridges and pores and bumps that had been carved out of the earth so long ago, and tried to imagine what that much time must mean.

She picked up a chunk of the rock that had crumbled on the ground and examined it studiously. The edges were sharp and solid; bits of mineral glittered. She could feel the heft and weight of the stone behind her back. Clearly wouldn't break easily, or be moved easily. She was solidly sheltered in the cleft between stone and earth. She wondered about the people who had put these stones here, trying to imagine them coming and going, bringing the hilltop space to life with their presence. She couldn't visualize the whole of the circle awash with humans, so she focused on her own little patch of ground. She looked to her left, at the empty spot next to her, just big enough for another child to sit pressed up against the rock with her.

Her young mind worked hard to put another child into that space. She saw the details of his face—it was smudged with dirt, and freckled. His eyes were brown, like Jamie's, and wild, curly hair hung almost to his shoulders. He was eleven, she decided, taller than her, with a big smile. They huddled conspiratorially together in the lee of the rock, hiding from the grown-ups who would make them do horribly difficult chores. She couldn't visualize much below his face, having no idea what his clothes might have looked like, so she saw something vaguely toga-like, assumed it would be dirty, and focused on his face. A whole scenario came alive in her head, involving a smuggled picnic and wading in the nearest stream (there had to be one nearby, for the purposes of her fantasy).

A loud, plaintive bleat, close to her ear, broke into the reverie, and she looked up to realize it was a real, live, modern-day sheep. Its narrow black face, grimy with mud, hovered so close she could feel its breath. It was as big as she was and, standing over her, it looked huge. She screamed, scaring both herself and her visitor, who promptly ran away. By the time Ben got there, Maggie had wedged herself into a ball between the two giant stones. He squatted in front of her.

"What's wrong, baby? What happened?"

"A sheep."

"What about a sheep?"

"It baa-ed in my face."

"I see. Are you hurt?"

"No. But I'm hungry."

"Well, then, come on out. Let's get a snack."

"But you don't have any snacks." She looked directly at him, aware that she had caught him in an almost-fib. Her father gazed at her for a moment, then he looked back over his shoulder at the tour group.

"Okay. Here's what we're going to do. We're just going to be rude. We're going to collect Mommy and Dara, and we're going to abandon the tour. We'll walk into the village and find somewhere to eat. But now, understand." His voice took on a warning tone as Maggie wriggled out of her cold crevice. "We'll have to walk a long way. Dara's not going to like it. You will absolutely have to cooperate, or else we'll all be too grumpy for words. Okay?"

"Okay, Daddy."

As Maggie looked back on that walk she remembered an eternity of cold, hungry trudging down damp country roads. The reality was only a couple of miles, but they were difficult for a hungry child anxious for approval. She found it difficult to stay pressed close enough to the hedgerows to please her mother, who was jumpy and irritable. Dara ignored commands to stay out of puddles, then gave up trying to have fun and whined. Ben had to carry Dara part way on his shoulders, annoyed at the mud her shoes smeared on his jacket. Maggie tried valiantly to keep up, but was vexed by pebbles in her shoes, thorns that snatched at her from the bushes, unsure footing on the wet road, and rapidly increasing fatigue. She also had a vague feeling of uncomfortable responsibility somewhere in the back of her head. She wasn't sure why, but for some reason she felt that this grumpy afternoon was all her fault, and the growing guilt made her uneasy. All in all, it was a group on the verge of meltdown that finally pushed into the tiny little pub at the bottom of the High Street.

An elderly gentleman shuffled to the table with a pot of tea. Maggie was appalled and amazed at his lack of teeth, but happy for the steaming hot drink. She ordered a cheese sandwich, disappointed to find that it wasn't grilled, nor was it American cheese. Thick, dense slices of white bread were smeared with butter and stuffed with slabs of a pale, crumbly cheddar. Hunger prompted her to pull out the cheese, which, surprisingly, she liked, and to carefully tear the crusts off the bread before nibbling at it.

She tried to eat the boiled potatoes, knowing how much Jamie had loved any kind of potatoes, but they did not appeal. Dara whined for peanut butter, but was placated with a ham sandwich. Finally, revived by the hot tea and sustenance, the entire family began to perk up a bit.

Ben turned to Maggie. "So tell me again why you started screaming up on that hill."

"A sheep baa-ed me."

Katharine cocked her head toward her daughter. "Just like that? Out of the blue?"

"Yep. Right in my face. It smelled nasty."

"What were you doing?"

"Sitting. I was having a story in my head."

She caught the look that passed between her parents, but plunged ahead. She launched into an extended retelling of the story that had so engrossed her earlier. Katharine, however, was not engrossed, and Maggie talked faster and louder, trying to hold her mother's interest. She could see her mother's eyes following Dara, who was wandering around the empty pub. Katharine, long since finished with her lunch and ready to move on, fidgeted in her seat and turned halfway around to watch her younger daughter. Maggie looked toward her father, to make sure someone was still listening to her tale. He was sipping his tea, gazing at the ceiling.

"Daddy, are you listening?"

"Yes, but it's getting a bit long, don't you think?"

"I'm almost finished."

At that moment, Dara, on the other side of the room, fell off a bar stool with a crash and a wail. Ben bolted out of his chair. Maggie glanced toward her mother, who sat rigid and pale, clutching her elbows tight. Maggie sat very still at the table, craning to see Dara, but unwilling to leave her mother alone at the table. She didn't want Dara to be hurt, but even more, she didn't want Dara's shenanigans to have upset their mother any more. Ever since Jamie's accident, she'd been especially unpredictable whenever one of the girls got hurt.

Maggie watched as her father squatted down to talk to Dara, and was relieved when her sister stood tearfully up and helped him set the stools to rights. Maggie shrank back in her chair, a bit cowed by the intensity still radiating from her mother, even as her shoulders started to slump. Ben and Dara returned to the table, where Ben's soothing murmurs seemed to renew her mother's agitation. Maggie could feel the tension growing at the table, but couldn't figure out how to relieve it. She tried to resume her earlier narration, but she could tell no one was listening.

Katharine drummed her fingers on the table. Ben stared hard at his wife over Dara's head. Dara's sniffles calmed into hiccups, then finally settled down altogether. Suddenly, she sat straight up and demanded the candy bar that had caused her to fall in the first place. Katharine, at the same moment, scraped her chair back from the table and announced that it was time to go. Tempted by the thought of irresistibly sweet chocolate, Maggie cast her lot with her sister, and turned pleading to her mother.

"Oh, please, Mommy. Can we have candy bars? Please? We'll eat them fast." She realized, as the words came out of her mouth, that her mother was the wrong parent to petition. Ben often gave in to his daughters' wheedling, particularly in recent months, but Katharine had grown increasingly spartan since Jamie's death. She looked sternly at Maggie.

"No, you may not. Lunch is finished. It's time to go now."

Ben looked at his wife for a minute, then got up and walked over to the bar. When he came back and sat down, the girls clamored for candy, while Katharine puffed up with impending outrage.

"Don't worry, dear." Ben spoke clearly and firmly. "I didn't get them candy bars. Girls, I ordered you each a pudding. That's what this pub serves for dessert."

Katharine hissed at Ben, "Why would you do that? It's time to go—I cannot sit here for one more second!"

The girls, familiar with their mother's controlled rage, quietly scooted their chairs until they were sitting right beside each other, on the far side of the round table across from her. Ben folded his arms, tipped back his head, and settled in to wait out his wife's tirade.

Maggie hated it when her parents fought. She didn't like to see her mother yelling or, in this case, whispering angrily. She didn't like to see her father look tense and distant. She particularly didn't like to feel scared and nervous and always vaguely guilty. She wondered if they would ever be a normal like before, when Mommy laughed more and Daddy smiled a lot.

She leaned in closer to Dara, until their shoulders barely touched. They watched and listened, exchanging glances, relieved when the pub owner shuffled over with two bowls of dessert. Dara gleefully grabbed a spoon and tucked in, but Maggie, distracted by the argument, proceeded a bit more slowly. She was appalled to see something that looked nothing like pudding. Instead of the smooth, creamy, chocolate she was used to, the substance in the bowl was altogether wrong. It had raisins. It had some sort of white sauce on top. It looked as if it was made of wet cake. It was not a chocolate color at all. She looked up from the bowl in disbelief, to see Dara shoveling the glop into her mouth.

"Dara! What is this? Are you eating it?"

"I don't know, but it's yummy."

"But it's not pudding!"

"No. But it's yummy. Can I have yours?"

"No! It's mine. Don't touch my bowl!"

In one of those fits of childhood irrationality, Maggie felt a desperate need to own the pudding that she didn't want, just because it was hers. Everything had been taken from her: her brother, her happy parents, the normalcy of home. Dara *could not* take this horrible dessert from her. She could feel Dara eyeing her bowl. She could also feel Katharine's steely tension battering up against her, Ben's sadness and confusion swirling around her and, through it all, the sharp, keening black grief for Jamie. All those scary, painful feelings threatened to overwhelm her, and no matter how she cast about, she couldn't find a rosy, happy place in her mind. The pudding was the final nudge.

"Mommy! Dara is trying to take mine!"

Her mother didn't hear her.

Maggie took one tentative bite. Distraught, she tumbled over a mental precipice, no longer able to hold her ground against the onslaught of unfiltered emotions. She spat out the bite, tears rolling down her face. Dara paused, spoon in midair. She looked up at her parents, a little nervously, then back at Maggie's full bowl. One little hand snuck across the table, and inched the bowl toward her. Even through her tears, Maggie sensed the threat and finally howled, all the pent-up feelings of the day, the trip, the past six months fueling a complete meltdown. It didn't matter what a good girl she'd been—nothing would ever be the same.

Maggie's catharsis was intense, but effective. The pub owner looked on, stiffly appalled, as Ben scooped her up and carried her outside. He found a stone bench on the village green and sat with Maggie crumpled in his lap. Her sobs quieted to occasional wracking shudders. The damp air was cool on her hot, sticky face. Ben hummed and rubbed her back while her breathing slowly settled to normal. When she had calmed down, he squeezed her shoulder.

"What's wrong, baby?"

A pause, then a mumbled reply: "I don't know."

"Maggie, try harder. We need to talk about it."

"It wasn't pudding."

"What?" She could hear the confusion in his voice, and buried her face further in his damp shirt, frightened by the surge of her own feelings. He rolled Maggie part way around so he could peer into her face.

"What are you talking about?"

"The pudding. You said we could have pudding. It wasn't pudding. It wasn't even chocolate."

"What was it?"

"I don't know." She sniffed a bit. "But it wasn't pudding. Ask Dara. She liked it."

She hid her head again, trying to absorb her father's calmness. She could feel him waiting for her to sort herself out and explain what was going on. With one ear against his chest, she could feel the steady rhythm of his breath; slowly, the storm in her subsided. A bird twittered. Dara's chatter carried faintly on the breeze, but all around Maggie and her father was a pocket of quiet. Maggie knew her father would give her as much time as she needed. Bare branches rustled, and she became slowly aware that a highway hummed somewhere in the distance. Eventually, she looked up at her father.

"I don't like the food here. I want to go home."

"Do you mean home to the hotel, or home to Washington?"

Maggie hesitated. "Both."

"I see. Why don't you like the food?"

"It's brown. And mushy. And I don't like the way it tastes. And you said we were going to have pudding—that wasn't pudding."

"Maggie. Pudding is the English word for dessert. No, it wasn't choco-late pudding like you take to school sometimes. It looked more like bread pudding, didn't it?"

"Maybe. But I don't like bread pudding."

"What are you talking about? You love bread pudding at home."

Maggie pouted. She didn't like being tripped up by her own logic, but her father caught her in her own words every single time.

"Jamie wouldn't like it either. He hates raisins." She knew the words would upset him—they upset her as she said them. But she couldn't stop herself. Ben looked at her with sad eyes. She buried her head in his chest again, until the urge to cry some more went away. When she looked up at her father again, he gave her a small smile. In his hand was the candy bar that had caused the debacle to begin with.

The chocolate was perfect—creamy and sweet. By the time Maggie finished hers, Dara had reappeared and was making a grand Cadbury mess. Later that evening, as the Lamberts left their hotel room in search of dinner, Ben announced solemnly that dinner would, under no circum-stances, be deemed yummy by any party present. Katharine raised one sarcastic eyebrow, and headed out the door. The girls giggled doubtfully, but Maggie knew when she was being teased. She wasn't sure exactly what the joke was, but she knew it was theirs. Her father had heard her, and understood. He wouldn't let her starve.

CHAPTER 5

After Ben says good-bye, extracting her promise to call as soon as the contractions start, Maggie trudges back out to the car to unload the roses. The note from her mother is still in the front seat; she starts to open the door to get it out, but is distracted. Something doesn't feel right. A new ache has crept into her consciousness—an ache where? She stops, breathes as deeply as she can, and listens to the whining misery of her body, trying to pinpoint the exact location. It seems to be her pelvis. But it's hard to say; streaks of leaden exhaustion seem to course down the backs of her legs, and her back throbs. She wonders if she should call Sam again. She rests a thorny bundle on the bumper of her car, massaging her back for a second, trying not to get her hopes up. She's been expecting to go into labor for two weeks now, and it seems like it's never going to happen.

She glances at her watch, trying not to get her hopes up. Rush hour is well over; by this late in the morning, it ought not to take more than about twenty minutes to get to Glenlake. She still has plenty of time to get to the nursing home by lunch.

But then the baby squirms hard, distracting her. She looks at her belly; even through her sweater, she can see it undulate. It looks alien, bizarre, but it feels so much *of her*. It can't be a baby—it's only her body, after all these months of lush growth, reaching the limits of endurance. She can't reconcile this aching, leaky breathlessness with the stroller, the crib, the little diapers piled in the nursery upstairs.

When her maternity leave began two weeks before her due date, Maggie welcomed the chance to rest for a few weeks, tidy the house, and gather her thoughts before meeting her baby for the first time. That's how she thinks of the birth—as if she needs to compose herself, and put her best face forward, so as to impress the child into wanting to stay with her. The exact definition of *good mother* eludes her, but, in her academic fashion, she has determined to do the research, analyze the sources, and synthesize the mothering material into a workable set of goals. The potential for flaws in her approach has only recently begun to occur to Maggie, as her hormone levels increase. She realizes that her control over the situation is illusory, at best. A small, sharp kick to her bladder grabs her attention. She decides to pee before she gets back in the car to go to the nursing home.

When Maggie sits down on the toilet these days, she often has a flashing image in her head of the entire contraption tearing away from the wall, unable to hold her enormous weight, and dumping her, and its contents, all over the bathroom floor. She knows in her head that this is irrational, that yes, thirty pounds is a lot to gain, but she still doesn't weigh nearly as much as Sam. And the toilet holds him just fine, with nary a groan or creak. Still. She sits gingerly, lifting her belly with one hand to try and open a passage of relief for her miserable bladder.

At nine months' gestation, with the weight of a full-term baby squirming constantly, it's tempting to stop drinking altogether, to try and reduce the number of trips to the bathroom, at least at night. But Maggie knows this is a bad idea, so she has dutifully drunk all the water and milk the books say she should, both for her own health and that of the baby. It's getting old, though, she thinks, as she glances down at the toilet paper.

There's blood.

She feels as if her heart has stopped. For a moment she can't think straight, and her mind drops down an empty shaft of panic, coming up hard against memory. The residual fear of bleeding, so wrong, so impossible in that avenue of blooming cherry trees, takes her breath away. She feels like she's falling, remembering dizziness, weakness, fear, drug-induced grogginess, and the soft scent of daffodils mingled with the sharp iron odor of blood.

Then a new pain in her belly startles her into a moment of clarity. With an effort, she pushes aside that visceral flashback and looks carefully at the smear on the tissue. The doctor asked her last week if she'd had any bloody show, and she breathes deliberately as she tries to remember what the books said about bleeding in labor. Maybe this dark brown smear isn't immediately life-threatening—she decides to call the doctor instead of the ambulance.

After exactly four-and-a-half minutes of pacing slowly back and forth across the kitchen on hold, Maggie gets a nurse on the phone and tells her she thinks she's in labor but she's not sure. The nurse asks a series of questions about the contractions, none of which Maggie answers in a way that she feels will meet with the nurse's approval. Finally, when the impatient voice asks if she's had any show, Maggie fairly shouts "Yes!" This is a concrete question for which she has a concrete answer: *Are you bleeding? Yes, I'm bleeding.* She swallows her panic.

"Yes, I've had some show, a few minutes ago. And I'm certainly uncomfortable, but it's hard to define the parameters of the discomfort."

There. Maggie is satisfied with this, a clinical, intelligent statement accurately describing her assessment of her current condition. She doesn't like to sound emotional, bumbling through I-don't-knows and I'm-not-sures and I-can't-tells. She has a suspicion that this particular nurse has never cared for her, and has probably believed all along, through all those office visits and tummy checks, that Maggie isn't cut out for motherhood—not strong enough to pop out a baby in a rice paddy, not woman enough to nurse with one hand and stir the soup with the other.

The nurse tells her the doctor can see her in half an hour; can she get to the office by then? Maggie looks at the clock, torn. She'll miss Yaya's lunch. Thinking about that blood, she rubs her belly, and is disturbed to feel it tighten under her hand. She tells the nurse she'll be there.

Maggie hangs up; maybe half an hour won't stretch into an hour and a half this time. She'll go straight to Glenlake from the doctor's office. It's probably a false alarm anyway. She heads for the car, balancing book, purse, bottled water, a file of work she needs to look at, and a bag of clothes to go to the cleaners. Getting in is a challenge—she feels as fragile as an egg, as if unnecessary bumping or jostling might crack the shell of her tight belly, causing its contents to spill out messily. Maggie thinks, as she does every time she gets behind the wheel these days, that her inordinately long legs are finally paying off—never much good at basketball, as everyone used to say she would be, she is indeed very good at driving with the seat pushed far back enough from the steering wheel to leave room for her stomach. Small consolation for an entire childhood towering over her peers, but better than none.

Sitting in the waiting room, the half hour does, indeed, begin to feel like an eternity, and her anxiety grows. Maggie realizes she's read the same page three times. The sharper stabs of pain have subsided into a dull ache that wraps around her lower back and belly, causing her to shift uncomfortably in the only comfortable chair in the waiting room. A quick visit to the bathroom reassures her that she's not about to bleed to death, so the cessation of immediate physical panic leaves her mind dangerously free to wander. She resolves not to think about her parents.

She remembers that it's December 31; for the first time in recent memory, she is beginning a new year without the familiar excitement of a dig on her calendar. The unpredictability of the months stretching out ahead of her makes Maggie nervous. She'd love to be out in the field right now, she thinks, squirming. Even the hardship of camping in the jungle would be better than being trapped in this unwieldy body. She closes her eyes to conjure up a scene that will distract her—a trick she's relied on her entire life.

Her first dig—an optional summer study, between her junior and senior years of college—was in Belize, and she knew, from the very first day, that this was what she needed to be doing. The site pleased her, with its straight-lined quadrants and clearly defined procedures. That tiny little square of earth was her own to explore. Each small, careful pile of dirt that she sifted through contained the potential of a lifetime, a century, a millennium. She had found herself in a trance of repetition, the edges of her consciousness blurred by the breathtaking intoxication of discovery. The excitement of finding a pottery sherd almost as long as her thumb had kept her awake for two days. Lying in her cot at night she had recalled rough edges as her fingers closed around it, brushing away the dark earth. With a soft, small brush she had revealed the clay, the echoes of paint faint on one end. In that moment, she knew—could feel, in her bones—the lives that lay buried in the earth, waiting for her to uncover them, bring them back into the light, into reality. She knew what she was doing in the field, never second-guessing herself or doubting her own judgment. That confidence buoyed her days.

The door chimes, and Maggie looks around, realizing she's not squatting in the dirt, but wedged into a waiting-room chair that is barely wide enough to accommodate her girth. She shakes herself now, turning off the daydream. Fantasizing about digs won't help; if anything, it'll upset her more. She needs to focus on what matters today—getting out to see Yaya, before she really does go into labor. She can't quite accept that this vague, mundane discomfort might be it—isn't labor supposed to be more dramatic, more sudden?

She looks at her watch. She's accustomed to having to wait for her appointments, but this is ridiculous. She taps on the receptionist's window.

"I've been waiting forty minutes."

"I'm sorry, but Dr. Morgan had a delivery this morning. She's a little backed up."

"I know, but I'm getting really uncomfortable."

The receptionist glances past her at the waiting area. "Like I said, I'm really sorry. We'll get you back as quickly as we can."

Maggie hesitates, and lowers her voice. "I'm not sure, but I'm kind of wondering if I might be going into labor."

The receptionist eyes her for a minute, looking doubtful. "How far apart are your contractions?"

"I don't know, exactly." Maggie feels her face flush.

"Well, let me know if they get worse. I promise she'll see you as soon as she can."

Maggie turns back toward her chair, certain everyone in the room is staring at her. She fiddles with her purse; when she sees her cell phone, she wonders if she should call Sam to let him know where she is. But she's been convinced labor was starting for three weeks now and she's starting to feel a little foolish. Besides, he'll want to know if she's called her mother yet, and the thought makes her cringe.

She rearranges the papers and files that she brought in from the car, and finds Katharine's note about the roses stuck in the pile. She re-reads it, trying to interpret her mother's words in a way that doesn't make her want to cry. It doesn't work; no matter which way she looks at it, she feels like her family is splintering apart while she frantically clutches at the pieces, trying to hold the whole mess together. She starts to get a fluttery, panicky feeling in her chest, so she shoves the note into her purse, all the way down to the bottom, trying not to think about it. She'll go see Yaya in a few minutes; that'll make her feel better.

She looks around the room and realizes that she's in a holding pen, surrounded by remarkably young, glowing pregnant women. She doesn't glow, she's not radiant, and she's utterly sick of being pregnant. Her back is still hurting, and her lower abdomen is starting to feel a bit crampy. Another protruding belly enters the room, this one with a husband in tow. She contemplates this, the phenomenon of husbands who attend every doctor's visit, who carry copies of the ultrasound pictures in their wallets, who caress and talk to their wives' swollen bellies, trying to make contact with their own flesh and blood. She wonders what it would be like to be the guy—watching, waiting, so integral to the process, but really out of the loop entirely. When Sam looks at her belly, she sees something like hunger in his eyes. She wishes he were here now, but she's glad he's not. He'd be too antsy.

She shifts in the chair, unable to cross her legs, and glances at her cell phone again. Maybe Dara's closing would be over by now. It seems like this is a pivotal moment in her life, one she should share with someone close to her heart. At this thought, her stomach flips, and she carefully avoids the image of her mother and whatever oddness she is up to now. Maggie chews on her lip and rubs her side; a little knob (foot? knee?) is poking uncomfortably into her ribs. It wriggles under the pressure of her finger. Relieved at this evidence of the baby's wellbeing, she pushes back. Her emotional pendulum swings in the other direction, nudged by the ferocity of her connection to this odd little creature. She forgets, occasionally, that her body is not just exploding of its own accord. Forgets that the end result will be a real, live person. Every now and again the umbilical cord tugs her back to that essential reality, and she is able, for a moment, to touch the baby's life, to feel its *self* alongside her own. In those moments, she feels alone with the baby, and the jumble of people and relationships that ordinarily fills her mind quiets to a dull background roar.

The wiggling sensation is deeper inside now, where her fingers can't reach it. Just as quickly, she is alone again, in an uncomfortable chair, back to contemplating whom she can call for support. She checks her watch, then pulls out her phone, punches three on the speed dial, closes her eyes, and waits for Dara's voice.

"What's up? Baby?" Dara skips the preamble.

"Can you talk?"

"Yep. Closing just finished."

"I'm at the doctor's office."

She hears Dara's sharp intake of breath. "What's happening?"

"I'm still waiting." Maggie glances around at the nearly full waiting room, dropping her voice.

"When I peed a while ago, there was some kind of nasty-looking glop. I don't know. It kind of scared me. Maybe it means something. Who knows."

"Ew. Is that normal?"

"I think so. Hopefully she'll see me soon."

"Are you excited?"

"Excited's not really the right word. I feel kind of yucky. Plus...."she hesitates.

"What? *I'm* excited!"

"No—it's just... I went and got those roses from Mother's. She left a note on them."

"Okay. What?"

Maggie reads the note out loud, her voice going husky on the last sentence. She blinks back tears in the silence when Dara doesn't respond.

"Dara? What's going on?"

Dara blows out a breath. "I don't know. I guess she's just ready to sell the house. She didn't talk to me about it, if that's what you're thinking. I'm not going to worry about it."

"You mean about who's going to be her agent? No—I didn't mean that. That's up to the two of you. No, I was thinking about the roses. She dug them up, Dara." She pauses. "The roses she planted for the three of us. Our baby roses. I don't even know how to feel about that."

"Why do you have to feel anything?"

"I don't, I guess. I just…it just feels sort of personal, that's all."

"I don't know that it is, necessarily. Lots of people are downsizing their houses—you know that. Maybe digging up the roses is just her way of being preemptive. Or maybe she was bored and wanted a project. You know how she is."

"I know. It just hit me kind of hard. The garden looked so bleak and empty. It was depressing." She blinks, not wanting to cry here in the waiting room.

"Wow, you really are being a downer. You should shake that off—I'm not going to worry about Mom's wackiness. We've got more important things to do. Like having a baby."

"I didn't realize you were volunteering to do that part. Feel free." Maggie grins in spite of the gathering tears.

"Oh! I meant to tell you—I'm wearing my scarab."

"Seriously? I didn't realize you still had it."

"Well, I had to dig a little to find it—get it? Dig?"

"Haha." Maggie rolls her eyes. Her family's digging jokes, trotted out at every opportunity, have long since ceased to be funny. They're just another thread in the fabric of her daily life.

"I noticed you wearing your amulet the other day—you know, the one you got in Mexico." Maggie winces at the reference, but Dara, oblivious to her embarrassment, continues. "And it occurred to me that the scarab is kind of similar. So I found it in the bottom of my jewelry box. I've been wearing it." Shyness creeps into Dara's voice. "Y'know. For good luck."

Maggie rubs the small stone amulet, hanging on a thin leather cord around her neck, and smiles. She often goes days without thinking about the necklace she always wears, but then she'll feel its warmth on her skin, and the thrill of the find, the connection, will rush over her again.

"Thank you," she says, touched.

"All righty, then. Let me know what the doctor says, okay?"

"Right. Bye." She ends the call, and slips the phone back in her purse.

Chapter 6

The waiting room door opens and the nurse calls back another patient. Maggie frowns. She's never going to make it to lunch if things don't move along. She fiddles with her phone, looking for a distraction, and thinks about Dara wearing that stone scarab necklace. She's touched that she even still has it, never mind wears it—she never would've guessed that Dara would be the type to save something so worthless. It was just a cheap little souvenir that she picked up on her high school senior trip. Those two weeks in Egypt had made the rigor of her academic high school worthwhile. Yaya had slipped her an envelope of extra spending money before she left, so she made a point of buying trinkets for everyone. She had been in a state of constant embattlement against her family in those days, full of contentious teen-age girl hormones, but from five thousand miles away, Maggie was able to see her sister through sentimental eyes. Looking back on that trip now, she has a vague sense that it changed something inside her.

§§§

Maggie had been over the moon when her high school's history department put together a trip to Egypt. But she had come up hard against her mother's reluctance to let her go. It was too expensive, too far, she'd miss too much school. She was too young to appreciate it. The last, stinging argument had been about archaeology itself—it was a bad choice, Katharine had said. Not a real science, not a viable career. Maggie was crushed. She had run screaming to her room and refused to come out for the rest of the day. The next morning, heartsick, she had slipped into the empty kitchen and found an envelope on the kitchen table, with her name written in Yaya's loopy hand.

I know how much this trip means to you, and I know that your mother is having a hard time getting used to the idea. So I would like to send you. That way she doesn't have to decide, and you still get to go.

There was a check to cover the full cost of the trip, plus a little bit of spending money.

Her mother hadn't tried to stop her, once Yaya offered to pay, but she hadn't been enthusiastic, either. So it was her father who saw her off at the airport. Maggie strode down the jetway without looking back. This was her first real trip without her parents, and she intended to enjoy every second of grown-up independence.

Several days into the trip, after they'd recuperated from the flight and gotten their bearings, the group (twenty equally bookish students from her senior history class, two teachers, and four parent chaperones) went to the Egyptian Museum for a private tour. In the gift shop she had bought one of the souvenir sheets printed with the English alphabet, then translated into Arabic and hieroglyphs. She'd learned enough in class to know that the ancient Egyptian language didn't exactly work that way, but the posters were amusing anyway. She thought Yaya, with her love of reading, might find it interesting. Then she saw the scarab, dangling on a chain on a rack of "Egyptian"-looking souvenir necklaces, mostly pyramids and sphinxes and pharaoh heads. She bought the scarab, pleased with herself for recognizing the ancient Egyptian symbol of creation. The clerk wrapped it in tissue paper, and Maggie tucked it in her purse, feeling expansive and benevolent. Dara would love it.

Their museum tour lasted three hours, and by the end Maggie's head was reeling with dates and dynasties and the provenance of artifact after artifact. Finally, they made their way into a small, dimly lit room with a large glass case in the middle. Maggie was at the front of the group; the docent stood back to let them all file in. It was hard to see in the low light, so Maggie bent her head very close to the case to examine the dark, lumpy figure inside. As her eyes adjusted, she realized that she was looking into the face of yet another mummy—an early one, a body that had been simply buried in sand, without the wrappings and paraphernalia of the later, more celebrated burials. The body of a child, curled on his side, had dried nearly beyond recognition. It looked like desiccated leather pulled taut over a skeleton, nearly black with age. She stared into an empty face. The lips curled back to show small, brown teeth. The nose was sharp; the cheekbones protruded under hollow eye sockets. Maggie was horrified. She stumbled back onto Steven Arnette's foot.

"Ow!" He thumped her in the back, and she lurched toward the case, face to face with the gruesome dead child. She turned and ran from the room, shaking. One of the teachers, Mrs. Trask, came running after her. She caught up to Maggie in a room full of shimmering gold, masks and jewelry, delicate and ageless and impossibly bright.

"Maggie! Where are you going? You can't just leave the group like that. What's the problem?"

She was shaking. "That mummy was horrible. I can't go in there. I'll wait out here."

Mrs. Trask looked back toward the mummy room, where they could hear the docent's cheery voice rising and falling. She looked back at Maggie, sitting at the foot of a statue, fiddling with her necklace. She crouched down next to her. "Are you sure you're okay?"

"I'm fine. I promise I'll wait right here. But I'm not going back in there." She knew Mrs. Trask knew her parents; she thought her dad might be friends with Mr. Trask. Hopefully she'd leave her alone.

"Is there—do you want to talk about anything? Is anything bothering you?"

"No. I'm fine. I just didn't like it in there. Really. It's too dark. I'm tired."

Mrs. Trask looked back toward the mummy room again, clearly torn. "All right, then," she relented. "You can stay right here. But don't move. We have to get back to the hotel on time if we're going to make the boat this afternoon."

"Yes ma'am. I'll be here." She hugged her knees to her chest as the teacher turned back to the group. Her insides had turned to ice. She could see the outline of the mummy in her mind; she willed herself not to think about the tiny fingers, the gaping mouth, the vulnerable curve of the body. She didn't understand why *this* ancient body—just an anonymous child— troubled her so, when she'd already seen so many. There was an echo in the image; she closed her eyes, desperate to shut it out, to think of something else, something happy.

She conjured up an image of Brian, the boy who sat behind her in Honors English. His cologne was so strong that she could smell it in the air around her all day, even after she'd changed classes. She wondered what class he was in now. She looked at her watch, trying to decide what time it was at home—six hours back; everyone's asleep still. She closed her eyes again and settled back against the pedestal under the statue, and began a systematic daydream about how desperately Brian must be missing her during her ten-day absence. Her mind wandered around the English classroom until Mrs. Trask was back, urging her to her feet, shepherding the class out toward the bus.

They were going to an island this afternoon, somewhere in the Nile Delta. They were taking a river bus. The teachers acted like it would be a marvelous treat; apparently, this was where the locals all went to hang out at the beach. What a notion. Here in this endless desert heat, to want to go lie in the sand. She filed down the dock with the rest of the group, swiping at the strands of her hair whipping in the breeze. The boat was old and awkward, and already nearly full. It sat low in the water, and the corrugated metal gangway wobbled as they lurched across. They couldn't find seats together, so Maggie followed Grace Andrews up to the open section of the upper deck. They squeezed in at the end of a cafeteria-style bench, the hard plastic kind with the high back. The river breeze tempered the hot sun, but when the engines rumbled to life, clouds of diesel smoke wafted over the top deck. Maggie wrinkled her nose at the smell, but then they were moving.

The river was crowded. Feluccas and river taxis and barges and small cruise ships vied for position. An amazing yacht glided by so smoothly that it barely seemed to break the water's surface. The feluccas, tiny little sailboats, bobbed like toys. Maggie stood up and made her way to the rail, stepping over children playing a dice game on the floor.

She leaned out over the rail, staring down at the water foaming by. A plastic drink bottle churned up from under the boat. The water was too brown for her to be able to see much, but she gazed down into it. If she stared at one spot long enough, it seemed that the boat was standing still, while the water swirled around them. Grace elbowed her. Maggie tore her eyes away from the waterline of the boat and looked out toward the opposite shore.

"Do you realize that this is the Nile?"

"Well, duh." Grace looked at Maggie as if she'd taken leave of her senses.

"No, really. Think about it. The Nile. How long have we been learning about the Nile River? I think it was the first river I ever learned the name of. It's been here forever."

"Maggie, pretty much most rivers have been here forever, haven't they?"

Maggie made a frustrated noise in her throat. "You know what I mean. There weren't any pharaohs sailing up and down the Mississippi. They were here. Those mummies in the museum—they were real people. And they were here, on the Nile. It was the same river, even that long ago."

"Well, there might have been pharaohs on the Mississippi. How would we know?"

"Well, that's just it. Anywhere else, we wouldn't know. But here—they did all this." Maggie's sweeping arm encompassed the entire shore, toward the city. "Well," she amended, looking at the mass of roofs and skyscrapers sweltering in the smoggy heat, "you know what I mean."

Grace grinned. "Yeah. It's pretty amazing. I didn't want to come on this trip, but my parents really wanted me to. My brother got to go to Germany when he was a senior, and I thought that would be tons more fun. But it's kind of cool here. It is *so* old. I'm glad I came." She turned and leaned her back on the rail. Maggie followed her gaze, looking around at the crowded deck: couples nuzzling, families looking for a day off at the beach. A group of high school girls giggling in the front corner were approached by two beautiful dark-haired boys smiling and strutting. It was interesting to see—a ritual that she knew instinctively, played out in words that she couldn't even begin to understand.

"Yeah, me too. I'm ready to go home, though." Something about ordinary life going on all around her, but completely out of her reach, made her long for home—for bickering with Dara, and avoiding her parents, and hanging out with Yaya.

They made their way back to the bench and sat together in silence for a while, lulled by the noise of the passengers and the boat's motion. Grace leaned back and closed her eyes. Maggie looked at the childish heads bent over the game at her feet, two light brown, one blonde, and one with dark, shiny hair. Another little boy sat back slightly, watching the game attentively. One of the players spoke to him, and he nodded, apparently waiting for a turn. A smaller child, with a near identical face, jumped on his back from behind; he shrugged him off, annoyed. The littler boy scooted around the edge of the group on his backside, coming to a stop where Maggie's feet blocked him. He curled up to watch and, after a few minutes, was leaning against her legs. She could see his face in profile. One dark blonde curl hung over his forehead; the rest of his hair, damp with sweat, was matted to his head. His eyelashes were dark against flushed cheeks. His eyes fluttered open every few minutes, but he was clearly struggling to stay awake. His little body was heavy against Maggie's calf, but she wasn't sure what to do with a strange boy sleeping on her leg, so she sat still. His nose turned up at the tip. His ear was so tiny. She looked at the curve of cartilage, the downy soft lobe, the specks of dirt in the bowl of the ear canal.

His eyes fluttered open, looking up at her, and in that moment, she saw Jamie looking back. His eyes had stared at her in her dreams for months after he died, but eventually they faded. Now, ten years and most of her adolescence later, she had managed to stuff that image so far into the back of her mind that she had mostly forgotten about her younger brother's eyes. But here, floating down the Nile, so far from home, this little Egyptian boy who bore no resemblance to Jamie at all was looking at her with Jamie's eyes. Her gasp startled Grace awake.

"What's wrong?"

Maggie tore her eyes away from the boy and stood up quickly. "Nothing." She scanned the shore over Grace's shoulder. "Let's go downstairs and see what everybody else is up to. Maybe it's air-conditioned."

Grace shrugged and followed.

§§§

Chapter 7

Finally, after she's given up a cup of urine, several drops of blood, and the amazing ticker tape that traces the lifebeat inside her, Maggie is permitted to shed her gigantic maternity pants in favor of a little paper gown. Any illusion of dignity has deserted her; she shivers, which causes her uterus to tighten uncomfortably again. It's a disturbing sensation—the idea that her labor might really be starting makes her suddenly feel she's not ready. She looks around the tiny exam room, trying to distract herself.

The walls are nearly covered with framed photos of babies, many of them in Dr. Morgan's scrub-suited arms. Interspersed with the photos are full-color posters, cross-section drawings of a baby in utero, one for each month of gestation. She moves to stand in front of the full-term drawing—something she hasn't allowed herself to linger over until today—and nearly trips over a basket of sanitary pads. It's odd to think she hasn't needed them in nine months; she wonders idly if her period will stay gone for a while. That would be nice. She's never been the kind of woman who could really get enthusiastic about her body's monthly rhythms.

§§§

Maggie looked at the box sitting in the middle of her bed. She had made her bed before school this morning; Dara still got yelled at sometimes for forgetting, but Maggie didn't like to come home from school and do chores. Ever since she had started junior high last month, she'd had homework every single day. She was already tired of it. She wished she could stop and climb trees on the way home, like Dara, but then she might not get her math done, and the thought of getting a demerit, and having her name on the board, in yellow chalk, for anyone to see, made her stomach clench. She had to get the homework done right away.

She dropped her bookbag and picked up the box. It was brown cardboard, with labels and packing tape. She never got boxes in the mail, but her name was right there on the label. The return address said Kimberly-Clark. She didn't know who that was. Mama wasn't home yet; she wasn't sure if she was allowed to open it. But it wouldn't have been on her bed if it hadn't been meant for her.

"Yaya?" she called from the top of the stairs. "Can I open this box?"

"Of course, dear. It's for you."

She scrabbled at the tape with her fingernails until it tore on one side, then she pried the box open. There was a pamphlet on top; a photo of a girl about her own age, with shiny blonde hair and blue eyes, smiled up at her. "Being a Girl," the title proclaimed. Maggie frowned, and pulled the booklet out to see what was under it.

A collection of smaller boxes was fitted in like a jigsaw puzzle. She pulled them out, one at a time, reading the labels. Pantyliners, adhesive pads, and a tiny pouch with a little elastic band inside. She unfolded the band, examining the pointy tabs, one on each side. Irene had gotten her period twice already, but she hadn't said anything about a belt. It looked strange, and sort of old-fashioned. Maggie dropped it and opened a small box of pads. Each one was wrapped in pink plastic. She dumped them out on the bed—there were six. In the bottom of the box were more pamphlets. She sat down on the floor with all the papers in her lap.

A few minutes later, as she was looking at the drawing of the ovaries again, trying to imagine how they didn't just rattle around loose in her body, Yaya tapped at her door. She shoved the papers under the bed and scrambled to her feet.

"Everything all right?"

"Yes. Fine." She sat on the edge of the bed, blocking the pile of supplies from her grandmother's sight.

"Are you sure?"

"Yep. Fine."

Yaya hesitated. "It's okay, honey. The box was for you. I just wanted to check and see if you had any questions. It's okay to talk about the pip."

"Oh. No, it's fine. I know about it. But where did the box come from?"

"I ordered it. So you'll be ready, when it's time. It has different things in it, right?"

"I guess." Maggie shrugged.

"That way you can try different ones and see what you like. Then we'll get you more."

She nodded. "Irene already started."

"I thought she might have. She's a little more mature than you are."

"Oh." Maggie looked down at her scuffed shoes; her cheeks were hot, and she was afraid she was going to cry.

"Oh—no, honey. I don't mean like that. Not in a bad way." Yaya sat down next to her on the edge of the bed. "I just mean her body is changing, that's all. Yours will too, when it's ready. Everybody changes at their own pace."

Maggie nodded, still looking down at her shoes. The front of her white uniform blouse was wilted and rumpled from the school day, but even if it had been perfectly starched and ironed it would still look as flat as Dara's. Several of the girls in her class—Irene included—were wearing bras every-day. Real bras, too, not the little trainer ones. Amy Oliver had one of those, and had shown it off in the bathroom one day, but Maggie knew it wasn't the same as a real grown-up bra. It seemed silly, but right now, she didn't even need that. The mysterious supplies in the box were interesting, even fascinating, but seemed to belong to a world that didn't include her.

"Maggie?" Yaya touched her hand, and Maggie slid over to be wrapped in her wiry arms. "Do you want to talk about it, honey?"

"No, I know how it works. We had a class last year, at school."

"Oh, good. I wasn't sure if the school had told you or not."

"Yeah. It was kind of dumb. It …" She hesitated, not sure how much to confide.

"Why was it dumb?"

"We … most of us already knew. We had a book. Everybody read it."

Yaya nodded. "I bet that was interesting. What book was it?"

"*Are You There God? It's Me, Margaret*. Stephanie's mom bought it for her. It's not bad, I promise."

"I've seen that book. I'm sure it's fine. I don't remember seeing you reading it, though. Did it make sense?"

"Yeah. I read it in my room. Then I gave it back. We all read it." She remembered standing on the edge of the group of girls, at recess. Someone had brought in a thin, folded piece of paper, instructions for inserting a tampon. She couldn't see it clearly from where she stood, but she could tell enough from the whispers and giggles that it was something disturbing. She hoped there weren't any tampons in the box on her bed now.

She pulled free of her grandmother's arms, and stood up. "Thanks for the stuff. I'll look at it."

"Be sure and read the materials, okay? Let me know if you have any questions. I know it might be a little embarrassing, but it's better to ask than not know." She stood up and put one hand on Maggie's head. "Okay?"

Maggie just nodded, and Yaya closed the bedroom door behind her as she slipped out.

That night Yaya made cubed steak for dinner and stayed and ate with them, like she did most nights lately. Mama got home just in time to sit down with them, still wearing her gray suit with the tiny stripes. She ate carefully, trying not to get anything on her silky white blouse. Maggie wondered how she kept it looking so tidy all day; she couldn't keep her school uniform clean no matter how hard she tried.

Mama was telling a boring story about zoning. She told a lot of those stories. Maggie knew vaguely what zoning was, but didn't understand how there could be so much to talk about. Either you could build a building where you wanted to or you couldn't. She cut her chop into little squares, keeping them lined up in one quadrant of the plate. The grown-ups kept talking, ignoring the girls.

Dara took a spoonful of mashed potatoes, then another, piling them into a mountain, then poured a puddle of rich brown gravy over the top.

She hummed to herself as she mixed it all up, pushing the peas and chop to one side of her plate. The humming resolved itself into words.

"There's a place in France, where the naked ladies dance …"

"Dara. No singing at the table," Mama said.

The words dissolved into humming again, but no one spoke.

"Dara. I said no singing."

"I'm not singing."

"No humming."

Dara pouted and turned to Maggie. "What's that stuff on your bed?"

"What were you doing in my room?"

"Looking for you. What's that stuff?"

"None of your beeswax." Maggie looked intently at her plate, spearing a pea on each tine of her fork.

"I know what it is." Dara's sing-songy voice held a taunt. Maggie glared at her.

"Hush, girls. I'm talking." Mama didn't like to be interrupted.

"Wait—is something wrong, Dara?" Daddy asked.

"Maggie has girl pads."

Everyone was quiet for a second, looking at Maggie, then Daddy pushed his chair back from the table, mumbling something about work upstairs.

As his footsteps clomped down the hall toward the stairs, Dara grinned at Maggie.

"*I* know what they are. Becky's sister has them. They mean you're on the *rag*."

"You shut up, Dara!"

"Maggie? What is she talking about? What's on your bed?"

Maggie could feel the blush creeping up her cheeks, but Yaya rescued her.

"I bought her a sample pack of Kotex."

"*You* did? Wait—Maggie, have you started your period?"

"Mom! No!" Maggie slid further down in her chair, tugging at the edge of the tablecloth. "I hate you," she hissed at Dara.

"Then why are you buying her pads?" Mama glared at Yaya, her mouth small and angry.

"Because she'll need them soon."

Mama didn't speak for a second, but when she did, her voice was quiet. "That's not for you to decide."

Yaya looked Mama in the face.

"Nor is it for you to ignore."

"Don't you dare—"

Yaya shook her head, almost imperceptibly, and cut her eyes toward the girls.

"I'll handle my family, thank you very much." Mama glared at Yaya for another long second, then got up and walked out of the kitchen, taking her suit jacket and briefcase with her. The three of them—Maggie, Dara, and Yaya—sat at the table, listening to her stockinged feet on the stairs, the slam of her bedroom door, and the rise and fall of her voice, mingled with the low murmur of Ben's.

§§§

When the doctor walks in, Maggie is leaning against the exam table, rubbing her belly to try and relax the muscles.

"Good morning, Maggie. How're you feeling?" Dr. Morgan is talking even before she enters the room. Her style is a bit too jovial for Maggie's taste, but she's supposed to be the best, so Maggie has steeled herself for nine months. This time she can't really muster a smile, still rubbing her stomach through the gown. She has found the largest lump, the baby's bottom, and unconsciously circles it with the heel of her hand.

"I'm tired. And hungry. And cranky."

Dr. Morgan looks over the top of her glasses at Maggie. "I can see that," she says drily. "What did you have for lunch?"

Maggie frowns, looks at her watch. It's already noon. "I haven't eaten yet. I've been here all morning."

Dr. Morgan nods. "I'm sorry you had to wait so long. I was at the hospital. Hop up here for me."

"Hop? Really?" Maggie gives the doctor a dubious look as she eases herself onto the bed; she can feel the paper cover popping and ripping under her bulk.

Dr. Morgan chuckles. "You must not be too miserable yet if you still think that's funny. I had a mom growl at me yesterday when I asked her to roll over."

"You're kidding, right?"

The doctor grins as she places Maggie's feet in the stirrups. She keeps up a steady stream of chatter as she examines Maggie, fingers reaching further into her vagina than should be possible, oblivious to her grunts and grimaces.

"Your monitor strip says you're definitely contracting, but not very often. Let's see what your cervix is doing. That's fantastic—you're nice and soft. Seventy-five percent effaced, and I'd say about two centimeters dilated. Well, I was hoping to make it to the opera tonight. But it looks like I'm going back to the hospital instead." She laughs again; she doesn't look especially put out by the change in plans.

Dr. Morgan strips off her gloves, and helps Maggie sit up. Maggie tries to pay attention to what the doctor is telling her, but has trouble focusing. She thinks irrelevantly that she could bring some opera to the hospital with her. Puccini might be tolerable during labor. But she's hearing the doctor through a fog; the only reality is what's in her body. The external world seems to be slipping away. She feels panic rising in her throat. The timing is terrible. There's something else she needs to do. She looks again at her watch, trying to comprehend the passage of time.

"All right?" Dr. Morgan peers at her. "Maggie? Hello?"

"Oh. Yes. I'll call Sam. Now." She tries to look sane, and alert. She scoots carefully off the front of the table. "No, I'm fine. I am. Okay. I'll go straight home. We'll meet you at the hospital in an hour."

"Are you sure you're all right?"

"Yes. A little nervous, that's all, since the miscarriage."

Dr. Morgan frowns, turning back on her way to the door. "We talked about this, right? Chances are this is going to go just fine, but all the notes are in your file. I'm going to call the hospital now and let them know you're on your way. You don't need to be worried. I'll be there soon to check on you."

"I know. I think I'm just scared of the pain."

"How are the contractions?"

"Honestly? I thought maybe I was imagining them. Maybe that's not what I'm nervous about—well, it is, a little bit, but…well, the whole thing, I guess. I'm fine, really. I promise." She takes the deepest breath she can, and tries to muster some confidence.

Dr. Morgan eyes her. "Do you need to call and get someone to drive you?"

"No, I'm okay. Really." Maggie forces a smile, and turns to get dressed.

When she gets into her car, Maggie turns on the heat and sits for a minute to organize her thoughts. She sips on the box of apple juice that the nurse gave her on the way out, as if she were a six-year old who had earned a treat. Ordinarily very pragmatic, for some reason she's having difficulty with basic sequencing today. First order of business, she thinks. Going to the hospital. She thinks about this for a minute, turning the fact over in her mind like a wrapped parcel, examining all of its angles and possibilities.

She thinks back over all she's read about childbirth. The books all say to stay home as long as possible, laboring in familiar surroundings without the intrusion of hospital staff and procedure. And then there's Yaya, and the promised lunch. She chews on this for a minute, not sure which of them is in greater need of the time together. Surely she can hold off for a while before she goes to the hospital—would it be too peculiar to be late to your own labor? She calculates how long it would take to get to the nursing home, eat, then get to the hospital. She doesn't want to get stuck giving birth at Glenlake. That would be very bad. She snickers, and is glad no one can hear her thoughts—she sounds like a crazy person, even to herself.

Her belly contracts again, for a few seconds, and she can feel fear pushing up in her chest, barely contained. *Yep. Definitely time to get some help with this. Too scary to do it alone.* A lump begins to build in her throat as she dials Sam's number, but she gets control of her voice by the time he picks up the call, and simply tells him the pertinent facts. He says he'll meet her at home, and she hangs up. She pulls up Katharine's work number, then hesitates, and finally tosses the phone on the passenger seat and puts the car in gear. One thing at a time.

When Sam strides into the kitchen, Maggie is pacing. Their house is a renovated 1940s shotgun-style bungalow, and the long middle hallway barely gives her room enough to stride and turn with a rhythm that keeps both the pain and panic under control. Movement feels industrious, so she keeps going. She had put her packed suitcase by the door, but its square presence disrupted the flow of the hall and made her nervous, so she put it out on the porch. She gives Sam a tight smile, but keeps walking.

Sam catches her gaze as she walks back toward him, and his face splits into a giant grin. "What are you doing? What did the doctor say?"

"Like I told you. I'm in early labor." Her laugh is not normal. "I'm not so sure about this. If this is the easy part, I'm thinking the hard part's not going to be much fun."

Sam looks concerned for a moment, then moves into problem-solving mode. "What are we supposed to do?"

"Meet her at the hospital. I thought about waiting a while, but I guess that's silly."

"All right then. Where's your bag?"

"On the porch. But what do you think?"

"I think the porch is an odd place to put your bag."

Maggie rolls her eyes. "Don't be dense. It was in my way so I put it outside. But what do you think about the hospital? I don't want to go if it's too soon. Plus—what about Yaya? I'm not sure what I'm supposed to do."

"I think we should go on to the hospital, if Dr. Morgan's waiting for us. Yaya will understand. Maybe someone can bring her over later, or tomorrow."

Maggie thinks for a minute, still pacing, and finally stops by the door. The idea of getting Yaya to the hospital seems nearly impossible, but it's too hard to explain her complicated list of concerns, so she shrugs assent. She hadn't realized it would be so hard to know what to do at this point.

"I don't think this is how it happens in the movies. I'm supposed to say, 'Honey, it's time,' and you're supposed to rush around like a crazy person, and then a few minutes later we have a baby. I'm thinking that's not the path we're heading down."

Sam makes an odd little noise.

"Did you just *giggle*?"

"What if I did?"

Maggie rolls her eyes, and heads for the car.

On the drive to the hospital, Maggie has two contractions, Sam asks her three times how she's doing, and his cell phone rings four times. Between the second and third calls, she reminds him to call their families. The list is in her suitcase, and she's still explaining her system of prioritization as Sam is speed-dialing his parents.

"Hi, Mom. We're on our way to the hospital!" As always, Maggie is mildly shocked by his lack of preamble. She always feels she has to identify herself when she calls her own mother; she's never quite certain Katharine will recognize her voice, and doesn't want to test her. Of course, her mother is in a busy office full of people all day, and Sam's mother is home arranging flowers or having a pedicure or something. Ellen would never not know Sam's voice—Maggie secretly thinks she lives for his calls. Maggie realizes with surprise that Sam is handing her the phone as he merges onto Wisconsin Avenue. "Hi, Ellen. Yes, I can talk. No, it's not a problem between pains. But during, I kind of have to be quiet." Ellen gushes, and Maggie's mind wanders.

She likes the word "pains"—it sounds more elegant, more intuitive than "contractions." It's also more the essence of the thing itself. Her fingers graze the amulet again, searching for the serenity it usually brings her. Ellen's voice jangles her breathing, so she hands the phone back to Sam.

As Sam talks into his headset, thrilling his mother with his attention, one hand maneuvers through clogged D.C. traffic while the other fiddles with the multitude of buttons on the dashboard. Maggie feels her seat warming beneath her, and the soothing strains of a Chopin piano concerto fill the car. How considerate, she thinks. At least it's not a Sousa march, or some sort of relentless drumming routine. She tries to settle her body into the soft leather of the seat, and stares out the window at the glassy cold streets. She rubs her belly, and a line about the bleak midwinter drifts through her mind. She can't quite remember what it's from, or what the rest of the line is—a Christmas carol, maybe? But the image seems fitting. Even the busy city seems to be closing itself up against the chill. She closes her eyes for a minute, and can feel her frightened muscles begin to relax, lulled by the warmth and Sam's voice. She can feel the contraction begin, and she breathes slowly, trying to hold on to the moment of peace. To her surprise, it works. She breathes right through to the other side, and the tension releases her. Amazing. Maybe this is going to be bearable after all.

CHAPTER 8

When Sam finally arrives in her tiny triage room, Maggie is on a gurney, hooked up to the monitor again, wondering what took him so long. Sam nods at the nurse, and moves over to look at the monitor strip. He examines it with an air of total authority, then asks, "How's she doing? Is everything all right?"

"Everything seems to be fine. Not a whole lot of contractions, but enough. We're waiting for a bed to be ready in labor and delivery, then we'll move her upstairs and let Dr. Morgan take over. In the meantime, you two can just sit tight here. I'll check back with you in a bit."

Sam drops his body into a chair and rubs his neck as the nurse steps out of the room, leaving the door open.

"I'm fine. Thanks for asking," Maggie says.

"Is something wrong? Why are you snapping at me?"

"I'm not. I just don't want to do this by myself."

"What are you talking about? All I did was park the car."

"Fine, but don't leave me by myself, okay?"

"Of course not. We're a team, remember?"

"I know you keep saying that, but I'm starting to think this is going to be a lot worse for me than it is for you."

"But I'm here. I'm with you, every step of the way. Anything you need. Speaking of which, did you realize it's after one? I didn't eat. Are you hungry?"

He is dialing before the words are even out of his mouth.

It crosses Maggie's mind that no one has told her she can't eat, so why not? He's talking to his mother, rattling off an order.

He looks up at her. "Do you want soup?"

She is nervous about breaking rules, but nods, and when he gets off, he holds up one hand to ward off her words. "Don't even go there. You're lucky I caught her before she got here. She's going to stop at Krugel's."

Maggie finds his competence both comforting and nerve-wracking. If he would just keep his voice down. She contemplates him for a moment, but chooses to let the moment go. "Have you called anyone else? We probably ought to start letting people know we're here."

Sam gives her a hard look. "Have you called your mother?"

Maggie fidgets with the hospital ID bracelet on her wrist.

"When was the last time you talked to her? Thanksgiving? Just because she's behaving badly doesn't make it okay for you to. You should call and tell her the baby's coming."

"I guess. Maybe in a while. I told you what that note said this morning. I'm having a little trouble wrapping my brain around it." She looks up at him, blinking, "I feel like the house is a big chunk of my childhood and she's just throwing it away without even consulting me. Or Dara—she didn't know anything about it either, for the record."

Sam runs his hands through his hair. It is an endearing habit, Maggie has always thought, one that makes him look both wild and vulnerable in equal measure. Right now he is clearly exasperated, scrubbing at the top of his head as if he can shake the answers out.

He mumbles something. Maggie catches the word *craziness*, and glares at him. He shrugs.

"I guess you won't suck it up and tell her how you feel?"

"Yeah, right." Her stomach does a sad little flip, so she goes back to her original train of thought, pushing the confusion aside, with an effort. "Anyway, you should call everyone else."

He frowns, holding out the phone, but Maggie cuts him off, ticking off the names on her fingers. "Dara first, then Daddy, but you probably won't be able to get him, your sisters if you want, Melissa is *dying* to hear, but Rachel's in Colorado."

"Mom's already called them. All of them. Everyone on your list, plus probably about fifteen other people. She's in total panic mode. Brace yourself."

"Great." Something clicks in her brain, like a kaleidoscope turning, causing all of her perceptions to shift enough to challenge her balance. "Wow. This isn't really going to be our baby, is it? All these people, they all want a piece of it. What if I don't want to share?"

Sam's brown eyes hold hers for a minute. "I think that's a good thing. I mean, I think in the long run, we'll be glad Mom's around and into being a grandmother. As opposed to, you know, *your* mother." Maggie winces. "It takes a village, right?"

Maggie gives him a wry smile. "Which is great, except that our village is populated by lunatics."

"Anyway, I think everyone's been called."

"Except Yaya."

Sam clears his throat. "Yeah. I wasn't sure what you wanted to do about letting her know. Do you want to call now, before that nurse comes back?"

"I guess. I hate talking to her on the phone; I feel like she can't hear half of what I say, but I guess I have to at least try, since I'm clearly not going to make it over there today."

Sam hands her his cell phone, she calls the nursing home, and is put through.

"Gabrielle? It's Maggie. Can Yaya talk?"

"Sure—wait one second. She's just finished up her lunch; I was gathering up her tray. Hold on."

Maggie waits, hearing the faint sounds of her grandmother's post-prandial shuffle across the room, her reedy voice sounding weak from this distance. Guilt squeezes her heart—she should be there, helping Yaya tidy up after lunch, fluffing the pillows behind her back, holding her thin hand while she drifts off to her afternoon nap.

She hears fumbling on the other end, then Gabrielle's voice in the background. "It's Maggie." Silence, then faint, scratchy breathing. "Miss Amelia, it's Maggie, your granddaughter. Tell her hello."

"Where's Maggie?"

"Here, Yaya. I'm on the phone. Here I am."

"What? Where? Oh. Maggie. What was that?"

"Yaya—it's me, Maggie. How are you?" Out of the corner of her eye, Maggie sees Sam get up to push the door closed. She's shouting, but she can't help it. She has to make Yaya understand. "Yaya, I'm sorry I didn't make it to lunch."

"I already had lunch. I don't know what… what was that we had?" Maggie hears Yaya's voice drift away from the phone, and realizes that Gabrielle, there in the room with her, is more real to Yaya than Maggie on the phone is. She's little more than a disembodied, distorted voice. Yaya's hearing aid is probably lying on the nightstand. Her heart squeezes.

"Yaya! Come back. I'm here, on the telephone."

"There, Miss Amelia. Talk into the phone. Talk to Maggie."

"What? Oh! Maggie, honey. How are you?" For a second, she sounds like the old Yaya. Tears spring to Maggie's eyes.

"I'm fine Yaya. I think I'm in labor."

"In what? I can't hear you, honey."

"The baby is coming!" Maggie's really shouting now. Sam looks a little alarmed, eyeing the door. She shrugs at him.

"Oh, that's nice. I'm going to take a nap now, though. It seems like I'm mighty tired today. Maybe you could come later."

Maggie realizes that her grandmother hasn't heard a word, and wilts a little. "I love you, Yaya."

She hears more fumbling, then Gabrielle speaks. "Don't worry. I'll tell her. You go have that baby now, and have someone call and tell us when it comes, okay?"

"Thanks, Gabrielle. I will." Maggie hangs up the phone, and hands it back to Sam, blinking hard.

"Was that as bad as it sounded?"

"Worse, I think. She sounded really out of it. I know she can't hear on the phone, but that seemed like more than just bad hearing. I worry she's starting to get confused.." Something occurs to her. "You know what you said earlier, about maybe bringing her over here?"

Sam hesitates. "I know I said it. I'm not sure though. Do you really think she's up for coming all the way across town?"

Maggie leans her head back against the pillow. "I don't know. Probably not. It's awfully cold. Maybe with lots of blankets? Doesn't your assistant drive an SUV? He could bring her." She pauses for a second. "No—never mind. Not Seth." She goes on quickly when Sam rolls his eyes. "I bet Dara knows someone with an SUV who could bring her over here. Just for a few minutes. Maybe after the baby comes?"

"Maybe. Let's wait and see. There's no telling what time that'll be."

Maggie glares at him. "What's that supposed to mean?"

"Nothing. Just…you know. It's not exactly looking like we're in a big rush or anything."

Maggie doesn't reply, lost in thought. It might work. With a wheel-chair at each end, and plenty of help lifting her in and out of the car, and lots of blankets to keep her from getting chilled. She wonders if she should go ahead and call Dara, and ask her to make it happen. She realizes Sam is eyeing her.

"Seriously, Maggie. Let's wait and see. If she doesn't get over here today, we'll go see her as soon as we get sprung. I promise."

Maggie pouts at him. "Fine. I guess we'll just sit here and wait for the baby. Slowpoke." She squirms, to the extent that she can. "Nothing's happening. See on the strip?" She frowns for a minute, then turns as the nurse opens the door. "Can I take the monitor off yet? I have to pee."

The nurse unhooks the tight strap around Maggie's belly and points her to a tiny bathroom. As the door thunks closed, Maggie looks around. She hesitates. There is a small, white plastic bowl resting across the top of the toilet, blocking her access. There are no instructions that she can see; she's afraid to look stupid, but equally afraid to do the wrong thing. She's terrified that she might SCREW UP—how can she raise a child if she can't even figure out how to use the hospital toilet? She considers her options. She could pee in it, but what if she's not supposed to? What if it was someone else's, and it's contaminated? On the other hand, if it was someone else's, she doesn't want to touch it. And if she moves it, and the pee that was intended for the bowl goes into the toilet instead, will some crucial piece of evidence that will ensure the health of her baby get flushed? Most importantly, will that efficient nurse yell at her? Will she fail motherhood, before it even starts, by not knowing what to do with the white plastic bowl?

She can hear her heart beating, and wonders if Sam and the nurse have noticed that she's not making peeing sounds. She's beginning to feel warm, and her belly aches. And she still needs to pee. She finally takes a deep breath, opens the door, and with an air of assurance, announces, "Excuse me. Someone left a bowl in my toilet. Does it need to be removed?" No one is there.

Damn. She closes the door again, then thinks *executive decision.* Somehow this phrase helps when she has a crisis of confidence at the university, or (rarely) out in the field. It's as if the very words somehow invest her with actual executive powers, a decisiveness that at times she lacks. She uses the extra hit of confidence to hike up her gown, and void her bladder with a sigh of relief. Not much comes out, so she waits for a brief moment, to be sure, and her fingers wander up to rub the amulet dangling around her neck. She hopes no one will try to make her take it off; she needs all the good luck she can muster at this point.

She sniffs a little, feeling hormonal and sorry for herself, and carefully lifts her belly up off her legs, to try and clear a passage for more urine to escape from her cramped bladder. The baby's legs wriggle in response, and she feels the pendulum of her emotions swing toward euphoria. These moments of direct connection, of call-and-response, of action and reaction, have been few during her pregnancy, but dramatic—and welcome.

With the fingers of her left hand, she can feel a hard, nearly vertical ridge that begins above her pubic bone. Maintaining the pressure with that hand, she slowly traces her right hand up the ridge, up the swell of her belly, pushing with her fingers to maintain the contact. Finally, up by the right-hand side of her ribcage, she feels a very small, hard lump that scoots when she presses it, but her finger follows. She is playing, and laughing at her baby.

She tries to visualize the body parts: backbone, disappearing at the hip, femur tucked across to her left ribs, then fragile little shins pushing back toward the right. So the lump at the top left must be what, a heel? She looks down at the lump in amazement. If she looks precisely when she feels the kick, she can actually see her flesh bulge outward. For a second, the realization staggers her. The baby is right there, under her fingers. Nothing separates them except a thin, delicate layer of skin.

The wonder vanishes immediately. Maggie muses that while skin may seem like a minor barrier, labor seems insurmountable. The poking has irritated her sensitive abdominal muscles, and they respond now by contracting sharply. She is stuck on the toilet for a minute, breathing shallowly, waiting for the stab to pass. She dabs at her crotch with toilet paper, and stands up slowly. When the gown falls back into place, she is once again simply a waddling monstrosity. She glances at the pitiful little puddle in the plastic bowl, and opens the door.

"We were beginning to wonder if you'd fallen in, but we realized you wouldn't fit." Sam grins at Maggie, clearly pleased with his own wit.

"How droll. No, I had a contraction. I'm in labor, remember? You're not supposed to insult me while I'm actually in the process of bringing your child into the world."

"Well, it's a slow process. Can't you speed it up a little? I've got some phone calls to return."

Maggie makes a face at him, and heaves herself onto the bed. The nurse goes into the bathroom, and comes out to make a note on her chart. Maggie decides to assume that this means she was indeed supposed to pee into the bowl. She still wonders why the room was empty moments before, but it seems easier to let it go, so she turns to Sam with an air of expectation. "Okay. I feel better. So when is lunch arriving?"

"Any minute now. She's bringing sandwiches, too, if you'd rather." Sam stretches his arms over his head, confident in his management of the situation.

The nurse, frowning a bit, announces that Maggie really shouldn't eat a big meal—clear broth should be adequate. Maggie, who has anticipated this, wants desperately not to be cowed by what she perceives to be unnecessary hospital rules. So she hedges and avoids the nurse's gaze. On some level, she thinks that if she can avoid arguing with medical personnel, things will magically work out. She makes a sort of noncommittal noise, and wiggles around on the bed, trying to look busy.

Her stomach growls. She gets hungry so suddenly lately, and not just a little hungry, either. Panicked, low-blood-sugar, dizzy kind of hungry. She sees her purse, hanging on the back of Sam's chair, and remembers the snack bar she tossed in a couple of days ago. She sneaks a look at the nurse, whose back is turned.

"Would you hand me my purse, please?"

"What do you need? I'll get it for you." Sam pulls her unwieldy bag into his lap, and peers into the depths.

"Just give it to me."

"Come on—your purse can't be that complicated. Tell me what you want. I'm going in." Maggie rolls her eyes at Sam's joking.

"Please," Maggie snaps. "Hand me my purse." She stares pointedly at the nurse's back. She doesn't want her snack confiscated. Sam looks at her like she's gone around the bend, but he hands over the purse.

She scrabbles around in the bottom, coming up triumphant. She unwraps the bar as discreetly as she can and pinches off surreptitious chunks. It's gone in three bites; she sits chasing little bits of oats and seeds and almond skins around her teeth with her tongue. She realizes she's openly picking at her teeth, and looks up to see Sam suppressing a grin. She wads up the wrapper and tosses it at him. Trying to stretch a bit, she squirms around in the bed for a minute. She's getting restless in this tiny space.

She decides to occupy her mind by being calm and meditative. She sits up straight, closes her eyes, and wills all her muscles to relax. This is good practice, she thinks. It lasts for about five seconds. She looks down at her hands; her fingers look like stubby sausages. Her engagement ring seems like a distant memory—by the third trimester, the ring was uncomfortably tight on her swollen finger, so now it sits in her jewelry box, awaiting her body's return to normalcy. The only jewelry she wears these days—besides the watch she can't live without—is the amulet necklace. She touches it; the tiny piece of stone, warm from her body's heat, represents the only act of flagrant criminality she's ever committed. Sometimes she still feels a little guilty about the theft, but she can't imagine being without the amulet. Her fingers trace its smooth curves. With a pang, she remembers the thrill of discovery, the sure, easy confidence that she was where she was meant to be, doing the work that made her feel important.

Chapter 9

§§§

In 2003, Maggie had been doing fieldwork outside of Muyil, in the northeastern part of the Yucatán Peninsula. A Mayan pyramid, nearly two thousand years old, and close to collapse, was slowly being resurrected from the jungle. With acceptance of Maggie's grant proposal came affirmation of her work and her identity. The grant allowed her three months on the site, in decidedly rustic conditions. The mail came from Cancun every three days, more or less; sometimes Sam wrote, sometimes he didn't. He was accustomed to the immediacy of email and telephone. The relative difficulty of reaching Maggie by more traditional means stymied him, and he frequently gave up trying altogether. She missed him desperately, but was so immersed in the work that she didn't have time to dwell on her feelings.

She had stepped into another world, and withdrawn from modern reality. Her father, unlike her lover, did indeed write, as did Yaya (almost every day), and often those correspondences were the only regular reminders of the life she had lived in Washington. As she watched this pyramid rise up from the earth, and helped push back the urgent growth of the vines and trees that had covered it for many hundreds of years, she began to live more and more in the history of the people who had built it.

In their heyday, the Mayan people had been one of the mightiest of the ancient Central American civilizations. Relatively isolated on the Yucatán peninsula and down along the Atlantic coast of modern-day

Belize, Guatemala, Honduras, and Dominican Republic, the Mayan people were the only indigenous tribe to have survived European colonialism with relatively little diffusion of the gene pool. Whenever pressure was exerted by outsiders to conform, to convert, to submit, the Mayans had simply retreated deeper into the jungle.

As a result, the laborers Maggie oversaw in the heavier excavation work were clearly direct descendants of the laborers who had originally built this pyramid. Her historian's eye saw a poetic beauty in this—this incredible structure had been built by hand, and then abandoned, and now the men so patiently reclaiming it had the same mythology, even some of the same rituals and traditions, as the men who had originally quarried, carried, and placed every stone as a monument to some long-forgotten god.

The team of men working with her were grubby, sweaty, unkempt, and bedraggled after a day of carefully pulling chicle trees out of rocks by the root, hauling off buckets of dirt, and extricating vines from ancient, crumbling limestone. But in her mind's eye, she could see the long, white sacbe, the road that linked the sacred site to quarries and cities all over the Mayan kingdom, lined with quiet, patient men and women, each wearing the traditional tumpline, the fabric sling that distributed the weight of a huge stone squarely across the forehead of the worker who had carried it each of the many miles from the quarry.

As the pyramid's original shape began to emerge from the jungle floor, Maggie's work grew more painstaking. In a large, semi-permanent tent devoted exclusively to cataloging, Maggie, two colleagues, and three research assistants began the laborious process of carefully cleaning, identifying, and recording every item, sherd, and fragment removed from the ruin. Maggie handled each piece reverently, like a novice in awe of the Sacrament. A carved tile was the product of an artist whose life she could not begin to comprehend. A clay handle had once been part of a jug, filled for a feast by an unknown person who had flesh and blood and thoughts and feelings every bit as central as hers.

Each piece she examined sent her into a new reverie, for the first time overwhelmed by the immensity of a historian's work. The screen of time that hid the pyramid's secrets was densely woven of life itself. If she held a crumbling statue long enough, quietly enough, she could nearly feel the outline of another person's life, but it was muted by the tapestry of lives and time and events between them.

One evening, Maggie sat in the door flap of her tent, sweating. As the green light of the jungle began to dim, she scratched at the mosquito bites that scarred her legs. She was thinking about an intriguing piece she had uncovered that day, a tiny little statue of a woman ripe with child, squatting in the time-honored position of birthing. She had seen many renditions of similar images, both in the field and in collections. She recognized the ancient symbolism of a life arriving successfully, and safely, in the world. This piece was different from any she had seen, though, because it was so clearly a practical item. A tiny loop on top of the woman's head suggested that it had once dangled from a cord, and a smooth, worn path down one shoulder and across the rump looked for all the world like the rub left by a nervous thumb. She could almost see a scared young Mayan princess, about to give birth, knowing she might not survive the process, and pleading with her goddess for protection—or at least safe passage to the other side.

Maggie had been feeling an almost haunting kinship with this woman all day, carrying this presence with her like a secret friend. She mulled it over now, wondering why this particular piece touched her so much. She thought of it tucked away in its own little box in the cataloging tent as she took in the warm smell of moist earth, and the quiet chittering of birds settling into the night. The frogs here sang an unearthly chorus of clicks and chirps that mesmerized her.

She realized without regret that she had no idea what day it was. She wasn't even sure of the week. She had been working for some time on understanding the finer points of the Mayan calendar, but somehow that arcane explanation of the world's origins didn't have much bearing on her sense of having slipped out of the world altogether. Suddenly Maggie realized that time had snuck up on her indeed; she had forgotten that this was the weekend Sam was flying down to meet her on the coast. The thought of Cancun's busy tourist hotels and crowded beaches made her flinch.

This was a problem—her immersion in the ancient world and obsession with unearthing the pyramid just didn't leave room in her life right now for a tacky twentieth century mega-resort filled with loud, bikini-clad sunbathers.

Reluctantly, Maggie roused herself from her contemplation of rainforest insect sounds and went searching for Alex, her research partner from the university. She found him in the cataloging tent, surrounded by snapshots.

"What're you working on?"

"I'm trying to figure this out." He pointed to a preservation box on the floor in front of him. In it was a small statue, nearly intact, of a creature with a human body, clearly male but with a parrot's head.

"Hunh." Her brow wrinkled. She glanced up at him. "This isn't a Mayan god."

"I know. That's what I'm trying to figure out. Here, this one was found at Chichen Itza, but it wasn't in the pyramid. It was in that first dwelling they excavated off to the side of the courtyard." He handed her a photograph of a strikingly similar statue.

"This one here"—he pointed to the box—"was in that first big room to the left of the passageway. I was about to catalog it and put it away, but I realized I had seen another one somewhere."

"What do you suppose it is? Decorative, or ritual? And where did it come from? Oh, wow." Her mind reeled. "Alex. This is a big deal. We should talk to the team who found that…"

She started to drop to the floor, ready to hunker down for the sort of sleuthing she loved, when she remembered why she had come looking for Alex to begin with. "Oh, wait. I came down here to tell you—I'm leaving for my break weekend." He looked befuddled for a minute, as if she made no sense. He was as obsessed with the work as she was.

"So soon?"

"Well, remember last week the mail truck didn't come on time because of Cinco de Mayo? That makes today May 12. Sam's coming—I'm supposed to meet him in Cancun tomorrow."

"Then you'd better get a move on." He stood up and stretched. "Best of luck. I think I've done all I can tonight—my brain is fried. Have fun in Cancun!" She heard the sarcasm in his voice. The resort city held about as much appeal to him as it did for her. But Sam would be there.

Alex caught the look on her face and smirked as he left the tent. She looked around, smiling to herself, about to turn out the light when she saw the amulet on the table in front of her. She instinctively reached out to touch it but stopped, her hand hovering over the box. She only hesitated only a second. The box would go right back in the pile of empties; no one would ever know. She could even erase it from the dig record, just to be on the safe side. But no one would remember it, she was sure.

Her heart skipped a beat as her fingers curled around the warm stone. It fit snugly in her hand, the contours of the figure an exact match for the curves of her palm. She peered at the tiny face. It was carved, not painted, so there was little detail, but the shape of the eyes and the set of the mouth made her wonder about the woman it had been made for. Lying small and heavy in Maggie's palm, the amulet felt solid and strong, as if it could confer confidence upon its wearer. Before she could realize what she was doing, she slipped it into her pocket. Her heart pounded. She glanced around, but she was alone in the tent and knew no one had seen. Then she turned off the light and slipped back into the darkness, trying not to think about what she had done.

Maggie didn't have a car—hadn't needed one a single time in the six weeks that she had been at the site. She would have to scramble to get herself to the resort where Sam would be waiting for her. Only fifty or sixty miles down the coast, their little camp seemed, indeed was, worlds away from the striking modernity of Cancun. The nearest village was ten miles away, and part of that distance was traversed by means of a rutted track through the jungle.

When she started asking around the camp, she finally found an older man whose son-in-law would be driving into the city in the morning with a load of tourist trinkets to sell in the market—painted stoneware and embroidered blouses. She extracted a promise from him that José, the son-in-law, would pick her up at 5:30 a.m. This sounded awfully early, but she understood the need to get a prime spot to sell before the tourists woke up and hit the streets.

Packing proved to be more of a challenge. She had brought with her only what she thought she'd need for climbing pyramids and digging in the dirt, but as soon as she arrived she'd sent Sam a list of things to bring when he came to visit. She hoped he remembered them. She put her basic wardrobe into a large backpack and looked at it doubtfully: rugged, worn shorts, shirts, underthings, T-shirts and boxers for sleeping. None of it struck her as vacation wear, but it would have to do. She grinned to herself. She did at least have a bathing suit, but it had been wasting in her trunk for two months now.

The next morning, in the early dark, she looked around her tent once more, picked up a book, then two, then her hand hesitated over the pile of reports from Ixhil that she intended to read. She needed to visit the site soon, to see if the commercial and social relationships between the two settlements were readily apparent, but she knew that she would lose herself in the documents if she took them with her. Sam would resent her distraction. Better leave it for later. The two more general books would keep her entertained, but not completely unavailable.

She had heard there was a decent historical archive in Cancun; maybe Sam would play golf one day, and she could get over there to do some research. A couple of questions had been bothering her that required access to wider resources than were available out here in the boondocks.

Forcibly pulling her mind back to packing, Maggie turned off her torch, zipped her tent closed, and started the ten-minute walk out to the road to meet José. As she moved further away from the cluster of tents, the glow of the solar path lights faded, and she flicked on a huge flashlight. She chuckled to herself, imagining how Sam would react when he realized she had brought a flashlight strong enough to light up a football field, but no decent clothes. Some things, she had concluded, were necessary in life, and others weren't. The hard part was figuring out which was which—life could be deceptive. As she rounded the last turn in the path, she heard an engine chugging ominously, idling awfully loudly. The truck waiting for her on the dirt road looked to have been made before her birth. She groaned, realizing how long this morning was going to be.

Two and a half hours later, after bumping and sweating and trying to follow the mixed Mayan and Spanish dialect of her chauffeur, Maggie stepped out of the ancient truck in a cloud of exhaust fumes at her hotel. The bellman looked down his nose at her, her bag, and her ride, and made no move to help her. She hoisted the knapsack onto her back, squared her shoulders, and marched through the revolving doors into the cool hush of the hotel lobby. She squinted as her eyes adjusted to the dimness, and backed up against a wall to get her bearings.

The lobby was beautiful. As she looked around, Maggie realized how much she must stand out. A fountain burbled in the middle of the room, well-tended bougainvilleas and palms screened the plush couches and chairs, the marble floors gleamed, and brilliantly plumed birds preened in ornate cages. After a moment, an officious-looking gentleman with golden braids looped across the shoulder of his uniform asked if he could help her. Maggie was aware of her sweat-stained face, her grubby hands, her wind-blown hair, and her general air of nomadic ne'er-do-well.

"Check-in, please," she requested, with as much worldly confidence as she could muster. She was escorted to a polished counter, where she announced that she was Maggie Lambert, checking in with Samuel Franklin. The air in the lobby became palpably more welcoming.

A second later, Sam himself happened to step out of the elevator. He scanned the room and came bounding over when he saw Maggie. Suddenly, her trek through the jungle, the disruption of her work, all of it fell into place, and she was overwhelmingly relieved to see him. She fell into his bear hug, dropping her bag, wrapping her arms around his neck.

Sam kissed her, hard. Ah, yes. Dizzily, she remembered the joys of life in the here and now. Sam pulled back and looked at her.

"You look dreadful."

"Thanks," she grinned. "I'm glad to see you too. Don't worry—nothing a real shower won't fix." Waving off the now-obsequious bellman, Maggie shouldered her bag and leaned into Sam as he led her toward the elevator.

After a hot shower, complete with honey-scented soap and a thick white towel, followed by a room service salad and sandwich, Maggie felt like a new person. Or maybe more like her real self, she mused, lying in the chaise by the pool. It was an interesting dilemma. Her tired mind circled the words, the concept of a real self. Was she more real out in the jungle, consumed by an ancient world that lived on only in her mind, or was she more real here, in the noise and light and movement of the modern world, surrounded by the tangible, superfluous wealth of a culture that she often forgot existed?

The sun was lulling her toward sleep, but the teasing question of reality kept her from slipping out of the day entirely. It seemed there must be an answer, but the warmer she got, the harder it was to remember the question. It was difficult, even, from behind closed eyelids, to remember exactly where she was. The day merged with memories of other glittering, hot poolsides, other warm, sunscreen-scented afternoons, in the islands, on the East Coast, in Greece—along the profound, amazing banks of the Nile. Maggie melted into her chair, riding the sun into her dream-memories. Sam suddenly loomed over her, drips of cool water interrupting her reverie. In the pool, they dipped and dove and floated, touching and nuzzling and pulling apart again.

Later that evening, dressing for dinner, Sam was in high spirits. Maggie had bought a dress that afternoon, a panic dress, she thought, looking at it. It was exactly what she would not have worn ordinarily. The filmy silk swirled around her calves when she walked, an abstract swirl of pale pink and powder blue that clung through the top and flowed over her long legs. But not too bad, she thought, cocking her head and looking critically in the big mirror in their room. Sam was in the bathroom. She looked at her hair, long and stringy, and turned to her backpack, looking for something at least a little decorative to get the hair up off of her neck; Sam liked it up.

As she rummaged in the bag, her fingers touched a bulge in the inner pocket, and she remembered with a jolt the tiny amulet. Oh, no. What had she done? She pulled it out, and for a moment was filled with panic. But even as she berated herself for being such a colossal screw-up, she knew, on some deep level, that she needed it. A plan popped into her head, fully formed. She pulled Sam's sturdy black suitcase out of the closet, fumbled for the zipper of the inner pocket he never used, and tucked the amulet in. She stuffed a sock in with it, for good measure. She'd retrieve it when she got home. Sam would never know. She swallowed, and put the suitcase back in the closet. When Sam came out of the bathroom, she was stark naked on the bed. She didn't feel guilty all evening.

Two months later, when she finally dug the amulet out back in Washington, Maggie couldn't believe she had done something so out of character. But even as she started to question her own sanity, that same odd feeling of connection washed over her again. The tiny woman fit perfectly in her hand; she knew she should feel bad about absconding with the thing (she didn't even want to contemplate how badly she had jeopardized her career, or worse, how many international laws she had broken), but it felt like it was meant to be part of her. She strung it on a thin leather cord, long enough to tuck inside her shirt, and was never without it again.

§§§

Now, propped up in bed in her modern triage room, Maggie rubs the amulet and wonders if its ancient strength will work for her. The confidence she felt when she stole it—that brash intensity, so sure of what mattered in life, of what she needed—is barely a memory now. She doesn't even feel like the same person. Her single-minded focus on tracing the threads of history has given way to this wild ping-ponging between excitement and anxiety. She breathes deeply, searching for that old, elusive Zen.

Chapter 10

"Darling! How are you? My goodness—finally!" Ellen's peremptory cheeriness precedes her into the room, calling Maggie back to herself. She is a tiny woman, with blonde, smooth, perfectly coiffed hair. On this day, she has dressed, as always, with the necessary care and attention to detail. Her makeup is flawless, her accessories coordinated, and her figure trim and well-presented. She is confident of her importance in the world, convinced of her standing as the belle of one of Washington's oldest families. A smile lights her face as her eyes find Sam. "Lunch has arrived! Here Sam—help me with these bags."

"Oh, I heard from your father," she says to him over her shoulder. "He was able to get on an earlier flight; he should be here by dinner time." Sam gallantly rescues his mother from the burden of food she's carrying, and submits comfortably to her clucking and fussing.

Maggie watches their exchange for a moment, not sure whether to be offended or relieved at being mostly ignored. She gets up to rummage through the bags and boxes of food. The contractions are still far enough apart that she feels hunger in between, and she's beginning to tire. Soup sounds about right—she hopes it's that golden, aromatic chicken noodle that Krugel's is famous for.

Ellen is finally satisfied that Sam hasn't changed a bit in the week since she last saw him, and turns the full weight of her attention to the mother of her impending grandchild. "Maggie, darling. How are *you* feeling? You look tired. Should we have the doctor in? Are you sure you should be sitting up like this? You know, when Sam was born I didn't feel a thing. My doctor was marvelous. It's amazing, really, in retrospect, given what a *robust* baby he was." Ellen's chatter breezes past Maggie, with a flutter of hands and a gracious little laugh here and there for emphasis.

Maggie has heard the story of Sam's miraculous birth regularly since she married him, and chooses now to discreetly tune her mother-in-law out. She wonders irrelevantly where her father-in-law is. Surely not golf—it's too cold. She breathes through a contraction, sips her soup, and nods and smiles as politely as she can. Time seems to be settling into the rhythms of her body, slowing down to match the now-regular cycling of tightness and release.

As Maggie finishes her soup, feeling both revived and soothed by the rich broth, the nurse reappears. A room has become available in the birthing center, and Maggie will be moved now. Her heart flutters; she really can't change her mind and walk out now. The nurse sets about efficiently reconstructing the bed—rails up, mattress down, cords disconnected. Maggie starts to get up, thinking she should find a robe and slippers, but is thwarted by hospital policy—she will need to stay on the bed and an intern will wheel her to her room. This seems unnecessary, but she does as she is told.

Sam and Ellen are still chatting. As she is being pushed into the hall, Maggie has to interrupt them to remind them that they'll need to move all of her things to the new room. Does she really have to keep up with everything? They look surprised, but eventually the food and suitcase do indeed wind up in room 3-C, where they belong.

The nurses here on the maternity floor are much friendlier, Maggie thinks, as she settles into the new bed. It's bigger and even more complicated-looking. She is careful not to touch any of the buttons embedded in the side rail. The room is institutionally feminine-looking, with dusty pink wallpaper, flowered drapes, and generic pastel prints. But it's surprisingly cheery, with a wide window and a cushioned rocking chair. It's tiny, though, and when Sam and his mother arrive and spread out lunch on the corner table, the room seems full indeed. Maggie uses the bathroom (having been given, mercifully, very clear instructions on peeing into the white plastic bowl), then crawls back onto the bed.

The phone rings, and Maggie answers. It's Rachel, Sam's sister. Her cell phone connection is bad. She's apparently on a ski lift and Maggie hears chatter under the wind. Rachel is her usual bright, breezy self. She asks the perfunctory questions about how things are going, but is clearly distracted. She is gushing about something, laughing with someone. A contraction starts, and it seems too difficult to explain this to Rachel, so Maggie wordlessly hands the phone to Sam.

Not much later, Dara arrives, nodding to Ellen and Sam, and heads straight to the bed to lean in for a hug. Maggie lifts her cheek for the kiss, feeling the cold air trapped in Dara's long coat and little drips of melting ice fall off it to sprinkle Maggie's face. Dara is blunt, as always. "You look like shit. Shouldn't there be a doctor here?"

"Why does everyone think I need help? I'm fine." Actually, she's not fine; irritability is beginning to prickle over her skin. This regular suggestion that labor might be more than she can handle is beginning to wear on her. It occurs to her that she hasn't actually seen Dr. Morgan since she got to the hospital, and a warning note chimes in the back of her head, but she ignores it.

"Well. Glad it's you and not me."

"Gee, thanks for the support. You don't have to stay, you know. Especially if you're not going to be nice."

"Oh, sweetie, I can't anyway. I got a call—I have to show a house in half an hour. But it's near here, so I thought I'd check in."

"Well since you're here—I need a favor."

"Anything. What can I do?"

Maggie glances at Sam; he frowns a little, then shrugs. "Is there anyone at your office who drives an SUV?"

Dara draws back, looking surprised. "Adam does. He may be needing it, too. It's supposed to get icy tonight."

Maggie pauses for a second, contemplating this news. "What time?"

"How could you possibly care? You're not going anywhere."

"I know, but…when?"

"Not till after dark. Why? Are you plotting a prison break?"

"Sort of, actually. I was wondering if he could break Yaya out, and bring her over here."

"Maggie. Are you nuts?"

"No, but…I'm having a contraction…wait…."She breathes, willing the tightness to pass, until it does. Dara looks alarmed.

"Are you sure you're okay?"

"I'm fine. If he pulls right up to the door, and they bring her out in a wheelchair, with blankets, and two of those big orderlies lift her up into the SUV. They could even put her in the back seat, so she can lie down—"

"That's insane," Dara interrupts. "It's too cold. It's nasty out there, and raining, and she's so frail, Maggie. For heaven's sake—honey, think about it from her point of view."

"Don't say that—she's not so frail. Besides, I am thinking about it from her point of view. I'm in labor. She needs to come. She'd want to be here."

"You mean *you* want her here."

This distinction confuses Maggie for a second, but she plows ahead. "Of course I do. I need her, Dara." She looks at her sister, hoping she will understand and not force her to say it all.

Dara, hands on hips, chews on her upper lip. "Fine. I'll talk to him as soon as I get a chance. I'll let you know."

"Thanks, Dara. See, Sam? I told you she'd help."

Sam grunts; Maggie sees the look that passes between Sam and Dara.

"It is too going to work. You two are just pessimists."

"We'll see." Dara moves toward the door. "I have to go, but I'll come back as soon as I can. And, um, Mother will be by after work. She's got wall-to-wall meetings today. She can't get away till late. She said to send you her best."

"Are you serious? I'm in labor, and that's the message she sends? When did you talk to her?"

Behind Dara, Sam frowns, listening to their conversation.

Dara hedges for a second. "I called her on my way over here. She said she had gotten a voicemail from Ellen, but hadn't had a chance to call. Oh, don't get all wound up about it, Maggie," Dara rushes on, seeing Maggie's eyes darken. "You're always jumping to conclusions. She'll be here this evening! She's every bit as excited about the baby as the rest of us are. It's just taking her a little while to get used to the idea."

Maggie hears Ellen mutter something about nine months, but she's too distressed to appreciate her mother-in-law's loyalty, as begrudging as it often is.

"Did you ask her about the house?" Maggie asks, not looking up.

"What? Oh, that note? No." Dara shrugs. "I'm not worried about it." She glances at her watch. "Whatever it is, today's not the day to deal with it." She lets out a little squeal and hugs Maggie again, before she bustles out of the room. "We're having a baby! A real live baby!"

Maggie listens to Dara's quick footsteps receding down the hall. She can't fully appreciate her sister's excitement. Sam and his mother are quiet in the corner, giving her space. She feels sorry for herself, and sniffs a bit after Dara has gone. The moment doesn't last; before she has even wiped her eyes, Sam's sister Melissa shows up with the children in tow.

For a brief but intense five minutes, her niece and nephew fill the tiny room with uninhibited chaos, descending on the food, playing with the bed controls, examining every cabinet, slamming the heavy bathroom door. They pelt Maggie with questions, crawling onto the bed, trailing crumbs and discarding pieces of damp clothing. They are old enough to be able to disrobe whenever they please, but not old enough to be embarrassed by any state of dishabille. Maggie has always found their tendency to strew their clothing about a room disorderly and vaguely disconcerting. Now, with damp socks and icy-cold jackets piled on her feet, it's downright annoying.

Anna, who is three, looks perplexed. "Where's the baby? Mom, where's the baby? I want to see the baby." Her voice tends toward a whine at the best of times, and Maggie tries to tune it out. Michael, who is six and missing two teeth and insatiably curious, spews cracker crumbs. "Where does it hurt, Aunt Maggie? What's that bracelet on your arm? Is that your nightgown? Are you going to sleep here? When will the baby come? Can I see it come out of your vagina?" Maggie stares at the child, then turns pointedly to his mother. Melissa created him—she can deal with him.

Mercifully, their visit is brief. Bored with Maggie, they turn to their grandmother, pestering her for treats and gifts. And she indulges. Maggie wonders how, today of all days, she came to be surrounded by Sam's family and not her own. As if to emphasize the disparity, Melissa sits down in the chair by Maggie's head, hovering sympathetically, wanting to bond over their sisterhood of labor pains. Her voice is full of dramatic agony when she tells Maggie that two centimeters is nothing, she still has *ages* to go. "Oh, honey. Things don't even get going till you're at least seven. Eight is when it really starts to hurt."

Maggie feels trapped, immobilized, with no idea where to hide. The tale of horror is interrupted when Michael begins clicking on Sam's computer, earning his uncle's reproof and prompting his mother into a frenzy of apology and self-defense. They leave in a flurry of boots and hoods and assorted paraphernalia.

Maggie sniffs some more. She feels a little bruised by the parade of people through her room. She is accustomed to gingerly negotiating the complicated relations with her own family and with Sam's, but today it all seems too difficult. She knows she should work harder for Ellen's approval, she should humor Melissa more patiently, she should, she should—but today she can't carry anyone else. Their emotions press against her, battering against the fragile wall that is keeping her own panic in check.

The phone next to her head shrills again, and Maggie grabs it reflexively, heart pounding unreasonably.

"Hello?"

"Hi baby. It's Daddy. Ellen called—I gather she called everyone she could think of—so it looks like it is going to be today after all?"

"Apparently. I wish you were here. I'm not having any fun yet."

"I know. I miss you, too. Tell me what's happening."

"Well, at the doctor's office I was at two centimeters. I really hope it's further along now, though; the pains are still about five minutes apart, but they're starting to hurt. I'm tired." She knows she's whining, but she can't help it. She has always leaned on her father, and now he's too far away. *Everyone* is too far away; she is once again struck by the sensation that her family is spinning away from her, and she is standing at the center, trying to hold them all together, fighting a losing battle with the centrifugal force that is driving them apart.

"I know, Maggie. Nobody ever said having a baby was a walk in the park. Nothing ever is. Except, you know—walking in the park. But you can do this."

"Hah. Do I have a choice?" She can barely catch her breath.

"Not really. So how's the food?" Ben's voice is far away, gravelly over the distance, but Maggie can hear the laughter behind the question. This is their private language, the way they assess of any place or activity or experience—yes, but how was the food? Her smile is wistful and blurry, but she forces her voice to convey her complicity in the joke. "Kind of sucks. How about bringing me something edible?"

Her father pauses for a second. Maggie has traveled for years, to jobs and dig sites, but she's never been the one left at home. She has no idea how to trade roles with her father. "I wish I could, baby. Can't Sam get you something?"

"Nah. It's fine, actually. Well—I don't think the hospital is going to feed me anything—they don't want me eating. But Ellen's here, and she smuggled in some soup. I won't starve."

"How was your lunch with Yaya?"

"I didn't make it. I hope she's not upset."

"Good heavens. You're in labor. You don't need to be worrying about Yaya. Your mother will go out there if there's a problem."

"Maybe." Maggie is doubtful. "She hasn't come to see me yet. Ellen's here, and Melissa and Dara have been, and Rachel called…"

"Do you *want* your mother there? I could call her, if you want me to. She might not realize …."

"No," Maggie interrupts. "Don't call her. I'll cope. She'll get here eventually." She imagines Katharine showing up under duress from Ben, and shudders.

"Of course she will, sweetheart. She loves you. She just has a hard time showing it."

"Yeah. I know. I'm just hormonal and wacky." She forces her voice to sound more cheerful than she feels. "I probably ought to go now, Daddy—I think I'm supposed to be having a baby or something."

Maggie hangs up the phone, feeling somewhat comforted, and ponders her mother for a moment. A random memory pops into her head, of a rare moment when her mother's orbit was exactly the right place for her to be. She knows now that it was a gift, however inadvertent, because when it comes right down to it, she has her mother to thank for her introduction to archaeology. It had been on the same family trip when they'd gone to Stonehenge, but by contrast, it had been a moment of perfection that stood out in contrast to the days of misery.

§§§

A late February sun was gathering strength as the fog blew away on a breeze that smelled of earth and animals and promise. The air was still brisk, but spirits lifted as the gloom dissipated. The next stop on Katharine's detailed itinerary was a small archaeological site, a dig in progress. She had read an article in *National Geographic Magazine* about a huge Viking hoard that had been discovered in the southeastern corner of England, and she was determined to see important work while it was being done.

With no particular interest in ancient Anglo-Saxon history, she was a bit disappointed to arrive at Sutton Hoo and see nothing spectacular happening. A large field had been stripped of vegetation and was now awash in black, rich mud. One small area had been marked off with a grid of stakes and strings, and several college students were wandering around in Wellington boots, washing gravel in a trough, jotting notes on clipboards, and eyeing the sky pessimistically.

The Lamberts were told they might have a look, and to let someone know if they had questions. The girls' boots squelched gloriously with every step. Ben quickly took Dara back to the parking lot in search of drier ground. A Quonset hut had been set up to shelter the scientists cataloging the find, and when Maggie followed her mother into the long, grubby room, she found herself entering another world.

Katharine was less than impressed; she understood the obvious historical importance of the artifacts laid out on tables, but her interest was clinical. Her only concession to the mysticism of the place was a murmured comment, perhaps not meant for Maggie's ears, about how much *her* mother would love it. Maggie felt a piercing ache of loneliness; Yaya would love it, indeed. She would do her best to memorize everything, so she could describe it to her when they got home.

Maggie wandered the length of the room, her eye caught by a dull metal armband, still crusted with mud, then by a small pile of coins, oddly misshapen to her twentieth-century eye. She ran one finger timidly along the edge of the long table, then finally reached out to graze a huge goblet that looked as if it had once been quite glorious. Instantly, a tale started spinning in her head—she had heard enough Viking mythology to be able to visualize a tall, Nordic man with braids and horned helmet, raising the goblet in a loud, bloodthirsty battle cry. Katharine snapped her out of her reverie with a hissed warning against touching, but something had settled into place in Maggie's mind. It was the touch that mattered.

She loved this room. Each artifact had a tag with a number on it; some had lengthier descriptions on slips of paper. They were in various stages of rehabilitation, each item in its own clearly delineated square of table top. She felt secure, yet the orderly table of objects fairly pulsed with untold stories. It was as if her mother's *National Geographic* articles had come to life, and they were even better than she had imagined. When she looked back on that day as an adult, she would realize that she was, and always would be, absolutely fascinated by the interplay between fastidious attention to clinical detail and the wildly romantic capacity to imagine worlds long gone, and to speculate about lives long since lived. Her imagination had met up with science, and found itself a home.

§§§

Now, twenty years later, she thinks about her father's conviction that everything is fine—will always be fine—and isn't so sure. She wishes her mother would think to go get Yaya and bring her for a visit, but that's not going to happen, and there's nothing she can do about it right now. She still yearns for Ben's presence, but perhaps she's feeling a bit more ready to tackle the job at hand. Something tickles the edge of her memory, another conversation she meant to have, but the thought stays out of reach. She closes her eyes and doubles the thin pillow under her head. The phone call has opened some emotional conduit for her; her feelings, so tangled a few minutes earlier, have smoothed into distinct threads. The colors are separate and distinct now, and she is soothed by the sense of order and containment. Perhaps it's the sudden reconnection she feels to herself as the little girl whom Ben had so often comforted. More likely, it is the simple memory that she does indeed have a life outside of this hospital, this bed, this pregnancy.

Archaeology is Maggie's lens on the world. It helps her order herself, make sense of her life and surroundings. Her career has taught her how to categorize emotions, compartmentalizing, labeling, and tucking away the uncomfortable ones, like artifacts. She can examine a messy feeling with a clinical eye. Turn it over, look at it from all angles, take its measure, document its aspects. She can even theorize its history, its genesis. Archaeology has given her the tools to do this objectively. Then she puts it away, tightly packed, protected against the harsh light of day, never to be seen again. Preserved, unchanged, permanently removed from the flow of life that might absorb and absolve it. Over time, she has become increasingly weighted down by these little boxes of unexperienced emotion. Neat and tidy, but burdensome. And entirely unacknowledged. Without even realizing it, she adds another box to the pile now.

The messy feelings swirling around this birthing room threaten to overwhelm her, and she muses on the beauty and simplicity of archaeology. She has missed it ever since her maternity leave began—when she began to feel very hormonal and confused. Now, with the slow but undeniable progress of her labor, Maggie can feel her tentative emotional control slipping. She is suddenly aware of all the neatly packed boxes in her psyche. She walks carefully through the windowless rooms in her mind, cautiously tiptoeing past doors she mustn't open. She's too busy right now—she hasn't any extra emotional energy available for healing old wounds. She casts about for a distraction.

Sam and Ellen have stepped out; she wonders where they are. For the first time since she got to the hospital, she takes a deep breath and consciously tries to relax. She's still wearing the birth amulet—she rubs it between her fingers, half-smiling at the memory of how she stole it. No one, not even Alex, had ever noticed that it was gone. At least, no one had ever commented on its disappearance. Good old Alex—truly a man of few words. She thinks briefly, but gratefully, of this other man in her life, her steadfast companion in dirt and dust and jungle muck. Partners in crime. She reminds herself that Alex is still a real person, in the real world, who is even now in his real office, working on their grant proposal. She isn't sure how she's going to juggle the baby and a three-month stint in Belize, but they'll figure something out. The whole scenario is too vague still to be particularly worrisome, and it gives her a real concept outside of herself to focus on for a few minutes. She rubs the tiny fat woman, trying to visualize herself with a baby, until she begins to feel more settled.

Chapter 11

The books say it's best to stay on top of the pain; she's trying to control her feelings, but the effort is making her peevish. She glances up at the clock on the wall; it's almost five. The afternoon has gotten away from her, like everything else. Sam and Ellen come back with cups of coffee. The smell bothers Maggie a bit, and their chatter is irksome

"Did you bring me anything? I *am* the one in labor," she points out.

Her husband and his mother look at each other guiltily. "Oops. We forgot," Sam says.

Maggie is well aware that they forgot, and is considerably less amused than they are by the fact. She waits for their laughter to subside, then announces, with only a little sarcasm, that she would like some hot chocolate. Maggie looks pointedly at Sam.

"Mom—would you go get Maggie a hot chocolate, please? I saw it on the menu in the coffee shop. I'll stay here in case the doctor comes." Ellen looks ruffled, but having no graceful way out of the errand, she leaves.

Sam looks around the room as if he owns it; satisfied that things are moving right along according to plan, he sits down at his computer and settles in to get some work done. He frowns at the screen, scrubs at his head, and looks blankly around the room. Maggie, irritated by his nonchalance, feels a contraction coming on; it's not a particularly difficult one, but she breathes noisily through it nonetheless, consciously striking a martyred pose of sacrifice and hard work. The ritualized breathing patterns she learned in birth class seem useless to her at this point. She finds it easier to go inside herself, focusing on breathing evenly and calmly. Sam glances up at her, back down at his computer. The contraction passes. She is comfortable enough in between pains; it's only when she's in the throes of them that doubt creeps in. She doesn't hear herself sigh. Sam looks up.

"What's wrong?"

"Have you heard from Dara?"

"No—she was just here. Why?"

"I mean about her friend, the guy with the SUV. I was just wondering."

"I don't know. I wouldn't count on it."

"You don't understand. I should've been there for lunch. I told her I would be."

"Sweetheart, you need to let it go. She's already forgotten about lunch. And being hauled over here in some stranger's car would make her cold and tired and miserable."

Maggie stares at the rain streaking down the window and shivers.

"Are you okay?"

Out of nowhere, tears well up in her eyes, and she blinks them back. "I'm fine. No, I'm not fine. I don't know. I'm scared."

Sam reaches over and rubs Maggie's foot through the blanket.

"You're doing great."

"What does that mean exactly? I'm not doing anything. I'm just sitting here, like a big fat sitting duck, waiting for something horrible to happen."

"What are you talking about? This is how it works—this is how babies come out. I think they covered the details in class."

Maggie's lip pokes out, of its own accord. She feels like a petulant child. "I don't like being scared. I feel sick."

"What can I do? Do you want something else to drink? Or a book? What can I get you?"

"I don't know. Nothing, I suppose. I just want it over."

Sam chuckles. "Me, too. Hurry up and wait."

Maggie's emotional pendulum swings again. "So sorry. You could at least engage a little more."

"Umm—okay. In what exactly?"

Maggie rolls her eyes. "The birth of your child."

"Ah. Well, I'm trying. I'm not sure what you need, really. Can you tell me?" Sam speaks slowly, like he's talking to a small child.

"Wait. I have to breathe now."

"I'm right here. Let me know when you're done." He looks back down at his computer.

In a minute or two, the pain subsides, but Maggie's dread lingers. She shivers again, and picks up the thread of their conversation, craving the security of Sam's attention. "*That* is what I'm talking about. I can't do these contractions by myself. I told you—I'm getting really scared. This *hurts*." Her throat tightens, and she swallows.

Sam looks up from the computer at her for a moment, two vertical lines creasing his brow. "Oh! Wait! All that stuff we did in class—I forgot. I'm sorry—it didn't look to me like you needed anything—nothing seems to be going on. Let me find my notes...." He clicks away on the keyboard.

Maggie is flabbergasted. "What, do you seriously have all that Lamaze stuff on your computer?"

"Well, yeah. I figured there was no way I'd remember it all, so I scanned the notes so I'd have them. And here they are!" Sam beams at her.

"God, you're so anal. Sweet, but anal."

"What do you want me to do?"

"Well, next contraction, help me breathe through it."

Sam looks dubious, but nods his agreement. Then he sits watching her. After another minute or so, the contraction begins. Maggie closes her eyes, prepared to focus on the rhythm of air flowing in and out of her lungs. She is startled out of herself.

"Okay Maggie. It's time to breathe now. Let's go. In." Sam takes a deep, aerobic breath, standing over Maggie like a yoga instructor gone badly astray. "Now out."

He exhales loudly, and Maggie finds that she can't hear her own breathing over his noise. The contraction is getting stronger, and she's having trouble staying ahead of it. Sam is distracting her, loudly breathing in and out again and again. With her eyes closed, she imagines that he is throwing his arms up in the air with each breath. She realizes the absurdity of the moment, but can do nothing to acknowledge it—the contraction is peaking. She can feel this one more clearly than the previous ones. It hurts inside, and down through her groin into her inner thighs. She feels trapped, pinned against the pillows, unable to move or even think, until the ache begins to ebb.

She glares at Sam, middle finger in the air.

"What? I was helping you breathe. If there's one thing I've mastered in life, it's breathing. I actually do some every day."

Maggie rolls her eyes. "Not in the mood. Not today."

She watches him, and knows from the softening of his shoulders, the relaxing of his spine, that he is mentally packing up his funny-man act. She wants to appreciate it, wants to be drawn into his light and cajoled into laughing. But laughter requires buoyancy, and she is all weight and heft. He feels so far away.

He presses a kiss onto her forehead and drops into the chair beside her. She reaches for his hand, and curls her fingers into his. At the same moment, there is a tap on the door. Dr. Morgan blows in immediately, without waiting for a response.

"Maggie! How're you feeling? Making any progress?"

Sam sits up, but Maggie hangs on to his hand, keeping him with her, not wanting to give up his attention. She makes an irritable sound in her throat, but ignores the question. Red hair corkscrews out from under Dr. Morgan's green scrub cap. She is already at the sink, scrubbing her hands, talking nonstop.

Sam squeezes Maggie's fingers, not letting go, but directs his words at the doctor. "She's kind of cranky, but I guess she's doing fine. I don't really have anything to compare it to, you know?"

Dr. Morgan chuckles, drying her hands and tugging on gloves. "Let's check and see how far along you are."

Maggie is half-sitting, half-lying on her right side, and has to roll uncomfortably toward her back for the doctor to be able to slip her fingers into her vagina. She is much more sensitive than she was four hours ago, at the office, and the pressure of fingers palpating her tender cervix sends small, almost electrical shocks through her belly. She frowns, holding her breath, pushing back nausea until Dr. Morgan drops the sheet back down over Maggie's feet and pats her on the knee.

"Well, things are slow, but definitely making progress. She's somewhere between five and six centimeters. It'll be a while yet."

"Hello! I'm over here." Impatience leaks out of Maggie's voice at being referred to in the third person. She can't believe the number of people today who seem to be forgetting that she's still a cognizant human being, even if she is in labor. "Sam doesn't care. He's not even paying attention."

Dr. Morgan looks from Maggie to Sam with questioning eyebrows.

Sam, in the chair by Maggie's head now, rolls his eyes. "Like I said, someone's getting a bit cranky."

Dr. Morgan considers them both, then nods. "Maybe things are moving faster than I thought. We'll see. Try not to bite his head off, okay?"

Maggie pouts, trying hard to regain her dignity.

The doctor takes a doptone from her pocket, presses the microphone against Maggie's stomach, and turns up the volume on the transmitter so they can both hear their baby's heartbeat. That odd, electronic sound mesmerizes Maggie. The first time she heard it, she found herself instantly in the baby's world—dark, muted, oceanic. The heartbeat sounds always as if it were coming to them through miles of water, so her real-time visions of the baby are always floating, immersed, liquid. This rapid, watery thumping is the audible conduit between her and her child, and when she hears it, *every* time she hears it, her soul feels the touch of this other life. She moves beyond her irritability, soothed by that reminder of the baby's presence.

"Baby sounds good. Nice strong heartbeat. So what's it going to be named?"

No one answers for a second; Maggie watches Sam in the sudden quiet, waiting to see what he'll say. He has said he's fine with dropping the patronymic—he's a fourth, after all, so she'd expected it to be an issue—but Maggie's been wondering if he might change his mind at the last minute.

"We haven't quite decided yet," he says.

"Aren't you cutting it kind of close?"

Sam looks surprised, as if this has never occurred to him. Maggie knows it has; this is one of many details they've talked about, but haven't quite worked out yet. The birth has seemed so theoretical. Now, suddenly, the baby is definitely coming. He stretches his neck and scrubs at his head again, causing his sandy hair to poke up every which way.

"Oh, we'll figure it out. Have to wait and see who comes out. Besides, we don't even know if it's a boy or a girl yet." Sam is laughing at Dr. Morgan. Maggie had thought he was silly for insisting that she not tell them the baby's gender, but he had been adamant. The multiple ultrasounds, given Maggie's history, were detailed enough that every technician who had seen them knew whether their baby was a boy or a girl. But Sam refused to know—Maggie thought his sentimentality about wanting this particular surprise was a bit extreme, but she also knew that if Dr. Morgan told her, and not Sam, the truth would slip at some point. So she has reached this point not knowing a fact widely-known by others, and she's desperately curious. Her hunch, from the first confirmation that a heart was really beating inside of her, was that she was hearing a daughter's heart.

Dr. Morgan strikes a pose of dramatic innocence, and throws his teasing back at him with a smile. "I'm not committing to anything. You'll just have to wait and see. Just to taunt you, here's another issue: if it's a boy, do you want him circumcised? The nursery will need to know."

"Oh, the forms! I forgot! They're in my bag—there, by the window." Maggie blushes a bit. The last few weeks have felt so messy. She has a to-do list somewhere that never got done, and the thought of all those loose ends makes her itch.

Sam looks at Maggie like he's not quite sure who she is, then rummages through the bag and pulls out the forms. He flips through the pages, then hands them to Dr. Morgan.

"We filled those out weeks ago. I thought you were going to turn them in."

"I was. I forgot." Maggie feels her color rising even more.

She had brought home a pile of forms from her eight-month tummy check. One of them asked a variety of questions about how their baby was to be treated during their hospital stay. Maggie had read the form out loud, pencil in hand, between bites of scrambled egg one Saturday morning. They had stared at each other, shell-shocked, as the reality of parenthood began to dawn on them. No, they wouldn't circumcise (she couldn't think of any good reason to), they would breast feed (she couldn't think of any good reason not to), and yes, they had a car seat. Actually, they had gone out the next day and bought one, Sam ranting the whole way to the baby superstore.

"They can't make us buy a car seat."

"Yes, they can. They won't release the baby if we don't have one."

"They can't. That's illegal. It's OUR baby."

"Yes, but we still need a car seat. It's the law."

"To have a car seat, yes. But we can choose to break the law, if we want."

"But we don't want."

"That's not the point."

"Can we just buy the car seat?"

"Isn't that what we're doing?"

"Why are we having this conversation?" Maggie had wiggled in the passenger seat, already bursting to pee. As soon as they got to the store, she had made a beeline for the bathroom. By the time she got out, Sam was already in line at the cashier, holding the most expensive car seat in the store.

Sam now squeezes Maggie's fingers, still curled in his.

Dr. Morgan laughs. "You two sound like the dog ate your homework. Don't worry about it. These are just for back-up, anyway, and to get you to think about things before you get here."

"In that case we needn't have bothered. This is all anyone's thought about at our house for a while now. I'm just glad to be getting on with it." Sam grins at Maggie, like a little boy clamoring for a surprise.

"Easy for you to say," Maggie grumbles. Her belly begins to tighten, and she is trapped in the grip of the contraction. Dr. Morgan looks at her pager and moves toward the door.

"You're doing great. Keep breathing, and I'll check back in on you in a while. Sam, help her stay on top of it, okay?"

Sam nods, looking at Maggie. The door closes behind her with a thunk so deep and solid that it's more of a sensation than a sound. Even as the breath is being squeezed out of her, Maggie registers the fact that she and Sam are alone in the room. She feels a small, cold sliver of fear in the pit of her stomach, underneath the strength of the contraction. She doesn't know how to do this—she needs help. She hears an odd noise, and realizes that her breathing sounds more like whimpering. She can't control it. Sam comes into view, and she sees the concern in his eyes. He's right up in her face now, holding her eyes with his.

"Maggie. It's okay. Breathe."

"I am. I can't." She can feel the contraction deep *inside*, and she is helpless in its grip. Her eyes well up with tears. "I can't do this. I'm too scared." It comes out as a whisper.

Sam is inches from her face. He's so close she can see the gold flecks around his pupils, the pores on his nose. His gaze is strong.

"Shh. It's okay. We're in the hospital. Everything is fine. You're doing great. The baby is safe. It's all going to be fine."

Maggie wants to believe him; she tries. His eyes hold her, keeping her here, now, as the contraction subsides. The cold pit in her stomach deepens. "That's just it. We should've stayed home. I don't want to be here."

"Oh, pumpkin." Recognition dawns in Sam's eyes. "No. Don't go there. It's different this time—the baby is *fine*. You're fine. That's all in the past."

Chapter 12

There. The memory is there, on the table, but Maggie still refuses to look directly at it. If she doesn't think about that day, it can't hurt her any more. She touches her belly with the tips of her fingers, tracing small circles. She cups one palm over the baby's bottom, realizing that it's lower now than it was a little while earlier.

It's big, this baby—Dr. Morgan, at her last regular visit, pressed and poked all over her huge belly and guessed seven and a half pounds. Maggie was dubious; she thinks it's at least eight, if not more. Sam had snorted when she reported this at dinner a few days before Christmas.

"Of course she told you seven and a half. How would you feel if she said it was as big as a Thanksgiving turkey, and oh, by the way, you'll need to push it out next week? She probably tells all the first-timers something small, so they don't all die of fear."

Maggie had blanched slightly at this pronouncement, while Sam attacked a plate of Blue Point oysters with gusto. In the ten days since then, her suspicions regarding her baby's size have grown—as, presumably, has the baby. She has come to terms with the idea, convincing herself that its size is a result of unusual height, not of some freakishly large head that will get hung up on her bones and tear her open from the inside out. But yes, compared to last time....

The memory of the miscarriage strikes like a rattlesnake—she had a warning, she knew the memory was lurking, it always is—but even so, she reels from the blow. A contraction grips her, and suddenly she's there, in the Tidal Basin, bleeding and scared and hurting so much, and losing a baby. For almost two years now she has shut this memory away, locked it up behind a tightly closed door. The door flies open now, and it all comes pouring out, rushing past her wide-open eyes, all the sights and sounds and smells.

§§§

They were at a party. Every spring, Sam's firm held a huge fundraiser for the Leukemia & Lymphoma Society. The firm's founder had survived childhood leukemia and was religious in his zeal to give back to the community that had played such a role in his formative years. This was the big annual event. It lasted a week every April, beginning with a marathon that attracted more runners every year, and ending with a gala art auction and cocktail party under the blooming cherry trees around the Tidal Basin.

White tents lined the banks of the river, and violins could be heard all the way to the Lincoln Memorial.

Maggie had been accompanying Sam to this grand soiree since her first year out of college. She had grown from feeling awkward and unsure of etiquette and protocol to relishing a few hours of pretending to glamour and wealth and elegance. Year before last, the evening had started off promising to be a Memorable Occasion. Maggie had been four months pregnant and was still surprised by her new mantra: "I'm pregnant." The words sounded oddly grown-up and official, and she had only recently started saying them out loud.

When they did the pregnancy test, watching television during the three-minute wait with studious nonchalance, neither she nor Sam knew what to feel or say. When they looked at the stick, and saw the pink line, clear as day, Sam burst out laughing, startling Maggie. That sentiment had marked the intervening weeks—a wild swinging between trepidation and euphoria, with a bizarre undercurrent of relief (as Sam had pointed out, at least they knew for sure now that all systems were functional). Maggie had promptly concluded that positive confirmation of their own virility did odd things to the male psyche: Sam was suddenly consumed by a quest to acquire as much life insurance as possible. At the same time, he seemed bored by the pregnancy itself, whereas Maggie could think of nothing else.

They followed the conventional wisdom from all the books, resolving not to tell anyone until the first trimester was over. Maggie found this a bit frustrating; the theory was presumably that if you didn't tell anyone you were pregnant, then you wouldn't have to tell anyone you were no longer pregnant if, heaven forbid, you had a miscarriage. This seemed illogical to Maggie—wouldn't she want to tell *someone*? she had argued endlessly to Sam. He had glanced up from his computer and said she could tell whomever she wanted; he would wait. Then he turned back to his analysis of the relative merits of term versus whole life insurance.

So she let hints slip out, making it abundantly clear to her father that no, she couldn't possibly have even a tiny glass of wine with dinner, dramatizing her nauseated nibbling of saltine crackers instead of seafood quiche at lunch with Dara—even allowing herself to fall asleep on Yaya's couch one evening. She wore increasingly baggy clothes to work, convinced that her waistline was expanding almost immediately; she could see Alex speculating, but he graciously refrained from comment. As a result, when, on the morning of the first day of week thirteen of the pregnancy, when Maggie began telling everyone she interacted with, "Oh, and guess what? I'm pregnant," fully half of her friends and relations rolled their eyes, confirming that her expectant condition had been totally obvious for weeks.

By the time the gala rolled around, she was over the hump of first-trimester misery. She had stopped throwing up every morning and was able, even happy, to eat food beyond crackers and plain baked potatoes. Her appetite had returned with a vengeance, and with it energy and enthusiasm. She could stay awake past 8:30 p.m. (for two months, she had been passing out right after dinner, and dragging during the day). She went back to the gym at school and swam laps, no longer feeling like she might collapse from exhaustion. She felt like she finally had that radiant, pregnant glow that she'd read about in novels.

Melissa had insisted on a girls' shopping afternoon, highlighting all of her favorite maternity stores. They found a perfect little dress, a sumptuously soft, thick black knit, with a shocking fuchsia chiffon overlay that draped and fluttered and swung just enough to be flirtatious instead of voluminous. With sleek black heels and a manicure—a true rarity in Maggie's life, but a weekly necessity in Melissa's—Maggie was certain that she looked almost as glamorous as she had in years past, slightly poochy tummy notwithstanding. She had piled her thick, dark hair high on her head (Melissa—every girlfriend Maggie had ever had, actually—was desperately jealous of such amazing and well-behaved hair) and put on simple diamond earrings. With a black velvet wrap and her omnipresent bottled water, she and Sam headed into the city for an evening of elegant food and witty repartee.

It was cool, but not unusually so for April. Daylight Saving Time had begun the weekend before, and the evening descended on springtime perfection: a luminous sunset lingered, reflecting off the glassy water of the river and bathing the froth of cherry blossoms and the gala setting in a rosy-apricot glow. Maggie wandered under the trees, smiling and chatting and nibbling here and there. Silent waiters in evening dress floated through the gathering with silver trays piled with exquisite morsels—velvety pâtés, twists of pastry stuffed with earthy mushrooms, slivers of pink smoked salmon flecked with dill and rolled around crème fraîche.

Maggie placed in her mouth a tiny, heavy nugget of chocolate that exploded with the dark essence of cocoa, causing her to close her eyes in pleasure. She declined the delicate flutes of champagne, choosing the bubbles of a European water instead. She knew enough of the upper echelons of the firm, and their spouses, to feel comfortable making her way between the high, snow-white tents glowing with candlelight and warmed by good food and generous drink. Sam was in his element; she could see him holding court at the far end of one of the tents.

She watched him for a moment, with a frisson of pleasure that such a physically beautiful man would be taking her home tonight. The candlelight flickered and glowed, making him look romantically patrician. He was at ease in his tuxedo; unlike many men, he had worn one regularly all his life, and he took great pride in his snowy white pleated shirt and glossy black studs and cufflinks. His thick, honey-dark hair had the tiniest hint of curl, just enough to make him human, Maggie had always thought. He ran a hand through it now, laughing at something a senior partner had said, and glanced up. He saw Maggie and flashed her a smile and a barely perceptible tilt of his head. She smiled back, and began to wend her way through the tables in his direction.

She paused to pay a compliment here, to accept one there. She was conscious of Sam's presence in an almost physical way. Even with her back to him, she could feel her skin tingling, as if he were giving off heat, or exerting some sort of magnetic pull on her. She deliberately slowed her progress across the tent, reveling in the almost sensual anticipation, as if she was being slowly, inexorably drawn toward him. Moments like this had not happened as much of late, and she knew he was feeling the chemistry as much as she was. She could feel his eyes on the nape of her neck, where a lock of hair had slipped loose.

When she reached Sam and his companions, the men shifted slightly to make room for her at his side. She slipped her right arm into the crook of his elbow, and glowed in the smile that lit his eyes.

"So did I tell you that Maggie's pregnant?" he asked, putting one proprietary hand on Maggie's stomach.

This particular group of men apparently didn't know enough about women's fashion to have figured out that Maggie was wearing a maternity dress, and they lifted a small cheer. She blushed. Someone raised a glass, and she found herself being toasted and congratulated.

She smiled and nodded, leaning into Sam slightly. She was overwhelmed by the kindness of these people; she knew that she was sometimes less than generous in her feelings toward Sam's colleagues. Perhaps she had been too harsh. These four men were clearly genuine in their respect for Sam, and their joy in sharing the news of the baby. She looked around, smiling beneficence on her admirers. She felt, at this moment, that she was the luckiest person in the world. As a matter of fact, she felt that she was the center of the world—that this moment, this spot, these people, were what it all boiled down to.

The world radiated out from her belly, where an actual little baby was forming, all those cells, constantly splitting and growing, tiny little fingernails and eyeballs—eyeballs!—suddenly manifesting, right here, inside her very own body. The thought nearly brought her to tears. Everyone here under this glowing white tent had formed inside a mother's womb.

Every person she could see, every person in the world, actually, represented some woman, like her, who had worried and fretted and dreamed over a growing belly, while little eyes grew inside. She couldn't get over this—eyeballs seemed so incongruous. Skin wasn't such a leap of faith—all she had to do was look at her own hands, and it seemed remotely possible, somehow. But no matter how much she looked at herself, she couldn't see her own eyes (looking in the mirror wasn't the same, somehow). The rest of a baby seemed plausible, because knees and fingers and tummy weren't that different from what she saw when she looked at her own hands. But eyeballs....

She looked up from this reverie, blinking a bit, to see Seth, Sam's assistant, joining the group. She felt benevolent even toward him. Usually she found him obsequious. Unfairly, perhaps. Maybe she had even felt jealous? She was having an unusual moment of clarity. All the feelings in her head had lined up neatly, labeled, laid out for her to examine as if they didn't even belong to her. The flickering light, the bubbles in her water, the warmth inside her body contrasted with the cool night air on her flushed skin. She was definitely feeling a bit odd. It wasn't so much clarity, after all, as transparency. It was as if her body was dissolving, but expanding somehow at the same time, to encompass all these lovely, happy, laughing people. She was crystal clear, filled with brittle light. She felt as if she had slipped beyond the limits of her body, and was spreading through the room. She turned slightly, to nod to Seth, and felt as if her body lagged behind. When she dipped her head in greeting, it moved in slow motion. A small ripple of nausea followed it.

She gripped Sam's arm slightly, and carefully turned to him. He seemed to shimmer faintly in the candlelight.

"I think I need to go to the ladies room. Where do you suppose it is?"

"At the far end of this tent. In that white trailer down there."

"Thanks."

She slipped around to the outer edge of the crowd, and walked carefully toward the bathrooms, a few feet beyond the glow of the tent. The cool dark touched her warm face, and came between her and the people at the party. She fell back into herself, once again filling up the normal space of a normal human. The physical sensation of re-inhabiting her body was nearly overwhelming; she stumbled up the trailer steps and fell into the first door, hoping it was the right one.

She pulled the stall door closed behind her, and immediately threw up into the toilet. Shaking, she leaned back against the wall and wiped her face with toilet paper. She felt clammy and confused. She had a feeling that vomit might have splashed onto her dress, but felt too bad to care. As she stood there with her eyes closed, waiting for the shaking to subside, she realized that there were no other sounds in the bathroom—she was alone. Good. No one had to hear her horrible retching sounds. Faint strands of music burrowed into her awareness, and she realized that everyone must have headed down to the lake shore. There was to be a small orchestra, playing from a boat anchored in the tidal basin. She would just rest here for a minute till she felt a little steadier on her feet.

Her stomach settled down slowly, but she still felt shaky and woozy. She leaned against the flimsy wall of the stall, abandoning usual aversion to bathroom germs. She couldn't figure out what was going on; had she let her blood sugar get too low? Was this hunger, hitting her all of a sudden? The morning sickness had virtually disappeared in the last couple of weeks; surely it wasn't coming back. She groaned quietly. She was so tired of feeling sick. She hadn't even gained any weight yet—she had been too busy throwing everything up. Was this ever going to end? Her stomach lurched again, and she bent over the toilet, bracing herself against the wall of the stall.

She managed to flush the toilet and wobble out to a sink. As she splashed her face with water, she felt dampness spreading between her legs. How odd, she thought, with that slow-motion clarity again. She couldn't possibly have splashed water all the way down her dress. She turned back into the stall she had just come out of, thinking maybe she had somehow wet herself. She had heard that pregnancy could cause you to leak urine—this seemed a bit early, so it would certainly be ugly by the end—but this evening, it wouldn't surprise her. She hiked up the swirly, floaty dress and pulled down pantyhose and underwear in one movement.

As she sat down, she saw the blood. Her white panties were soaked in bright red blood. Too much. This was way beyond spotting. She could see a red smear down the inside of each thigh. She looked between them, into the toilet, and could see small, dark globules floating in the pink-stained water. Her head swam, and she whimpered. Something bad was happening. The stall tipped slightly, and she closed her eyes to try and still the spinning. She whimpered again. She didn't know what to do. No one could hear her. She didn't know how to get Sam, she couldn't go out there, the blood was going to drip down her legs. Someone might see.

But she couldn't stay in here. She needed help. Terror came bubbling up in her chest, and she could hear herself making odd, strangled mewling noises. She couldn't catch her breath. She was trying not to cry, but she couldn't figure out what else to do. Somehow, without a clear plan, she tugged her hose up and stood up. She couldn't turn the knob to open the stall door. Her fingers kept slipping; she was shaking too much. Everything kept tipping, and she was cold. The door finally opened. She found the door to the bathroom and pushed it open; it seemed to take her whole body weight. She was sobbing now, panic tearing at her throat.

She lurched down the steps of the trailer, stumbling, catching herself on the rail, twisting her ankle. She could see the candles, the bright circles of wavering light surrounded by darkness. She felt like her insides might be coming out. Pain was ripping through her now. Something truly horrible was happening. She might be dying. She couldn't figure out which direction to go, where Sam was. Everything looked blurry, like she was swimming. She was running out of air; she couldn't keep holding her breath like this. Her ears were ringing, and everything was going dark. Even the stars were fading. She was sinking, losing control. She hit something, hard, and the darkness closed over her head.

"Maggie!"

The sound of her name broke through the darkness, sliced open her cocoon. She fought it, tried to stay burrowed down in the dark.

"Maggie! Wake up! Help! Somebody help!"

This time she had to wake up. She opened her eyes, and sensation came rushing back. She closed them again. Her body was splitting open. Something was tearing her to shreds. There was a blinding pain in her head. She tried to focus on the voice. She turned her head toward the sound.

"Maggie! What's wrong? Are you awake? Talk to me. What's wrong? Are you hurt? Aw, shit! Don't close your eyes!"

Her voice wouldn't work. She couldn't get her eyes to focus. Everything hurt so much. Her stomach started to heave, and she gagged and coughed.

"Shit! Help!"

She threw up, managing to fling herself onto her side as it came roiling up from deep inside her. She curled into a ball and moaned, not caring anymore. Hands rolled her over, tried to pull her up. She couldn't help, but she did get her eyes to open a bit. A blurry head swam into focus.

"Seth?" she whispered.

"Yes! Oh, thank God. Yes, it's me. What's wrong, Maggie? Can you get up? Let's go find Sam."

"No." She didn't seem to have enough breath to talk. "Can't move. Bleeding." The words came out in breathy bursts. She swayed, and something inside her burst, sending waves of sharp-edged pain rippling out from her center. She moaned again, and collapsed back onto her side. She could feel dampness spreading between her legs.

"Come on, Maggie. Don't pass out again, please. Stay awake. What happened? Can you tell me what happened?"

She could hear Seth's questions, but couldn't figure out why he was asking. Couldn't he tell? Wasn't she lying in a pool of blood? Why didn't Seth know? He was mumbling something about a tree now. She squinted up at him.

"What?" she asked weakly.

"The lump on your head. Did you run into the tree?"

She put one hand up to her head, realizing as she did so that her head was throbbing. She hadn't noticed; it was only one of many miserable sensations. She tried to push up on one elbow.

"Seth," she croaked. "I'm bleeding. Help me."

He squatted down and peered at her head.

"It's a big lump, but I don't think it's bleeding." He sounded mystified.

She pushed herself up a bit further.

"No. Not my head." The darkness was beginning to encroach on her vision again. "The baby. Need help. Please." She slumped back onto the ground, breathing shallowly, trying to slow her heartbeats.

"Oh, shit. Oh, my God. Okay. Hospital. I'll take you—my car's here in the service lot. Can you walk? Shit, do you have your phone? Maggie?"

She could hear him talking, but couldn't make her voice answer. It was too hard to open her eyes. She could just manage lying still and breathing.

The next time she woke up, she was lying across the back seat of an unfamiliar car. It screeched to a halt, nearly throwing her to the floor, then sped up again. She coughed and gagged a bit, and Seth called her name. She mumbled something, then closed her eyes again. She could hear him talking to someone on the phone. At least they were moving. She could stop trying to hold on now and let go, let her body take over.

She woke up again when Seth slammed on the brakes at the emergency room entrance. She could hear him shouting for a doctor, for a stretcher, for help. When someone asked her how far along her pregnancy was, she whispered, "Fourteen weeks." An intern looked at her for a long moment, and she couldn't understand what she saw in his eyes. Once again, she allowed the unconsciousness to close over her head.

She had lost the baby. It was a painful and protracted miscarriage, ending ultimately in a lot of blood loss, a D&C, and a great deal of vague anxiety in the Franklin household. Dr. Morgan seemed to think it was an aberration, unlikely to happen again. She convinced Maggie, who was terrified of reliving the experience, that there was no inherent flaw in her body, and that another pregnancy would most likely be blissfully uneventful.

§§§

CHAPTER 13

Maggie doesn't know when it will be okay to let down her guard. Even at full term, this second pregnancy has never felt quite safe enough. That nightmarish memory is always hovering at the edge of her consciousness. When the contraction ends and she catches her breath, Sam is still there, right in her face, dragging her back into the present.

He nods as she comes back into herself, but still holds her eyes with his. She can see the three little horizontal lines up high on his forehead that always make him look confused when really he's worried. He's not frowning so much as questioning.

"Thanks. This is getting scary. And hard. I'm not having fun anymore. Could you hand me a tissue, please?"

Sam breaks the gaze, and reaches for the tissue box. "It's all going to be fine. Really. You have to trust your body. Dr. Morgan knows what she's doing."

Maggie looks at him for a long moment, trying to feel the security he's offering, but hearing the disconnect in those words. That small, cold knot of fear won't unclench.

"I'm trying. But it hurts. I want to leave."

Sam chuckles and sits back in the chair. "Pumpkin, you can't very well leave now. Where the hell would you go? If you walked into a coffee shop looking like that, people would run screaming into the street."

Maggie sniffs. "I know." Her voice is very small. "I just want to go home." She sniffs again, and swabs at her nose. "I want Yaya." She pauses. "No. I want Mother."

Sam watches her, thinking. "I'll get her over here if you really want her."

"She won't come."

Sam looks Maggie in the eye, and says it again, emphatically. "I *will* get her over here if you want me to. Unlike Yaya, she's perfectly able. But…are you sure that'll help?"

"I don't know," she whispers. "I thought it would. I really did." She closes her eyes. What she wants is to hide from this fear. She wants her grandmother, or her mother—*someone*—to take it all away, make it all better.

"Maggie. She loves you, but she's too freaked out by this baby stuff. I don't know—maybe she never dealt with her memories, or maybe she doesn't want to be old enough to be a grandmother. Or maybe she's just so absorbed in her own stuff she doesn't realize—I don't know—how to be any different than she is. It doesn't matter right now. We can't do anything about it anyway. If she wants to be difficult, that's her problem. We're busy right now."

"But…it does matter!" This is the worry that has been hovering at the edge of her consciousness all day. Her mother's roses. "The roses. They're piled up on the deck, in the cold. What am I going to do with them? That note…. Sam? Do you really think she's going to sell the house?" Maggie feels hot tears on her face.

Sam looks down at his thumb, rubbing across the back of her knuckles. "Sweetheart, I'm surprised she didn't sell it a long time ago."

"What? You too? God, you sound just like Daddy. Why can't you people see how much this upsets me?"

"Oh, I see it. I just …." he shrugs. "Honestly, I think you're overreacting. Wait, hear me out." She tries to pull her hand away, but he holds on. "Think about it. You're smack in the middle of a giant life change. You're understandably nervous: that's normal. I'm nervous too. Having a baby is more complicated than they tell you, I think. And yes, dumping that on you in a note, today, was colossally bad timing, bad form, bad everything. But the house is just a thing, isn't it? Just a place. You haven't lived there in years. You're not even all that comfortable when we go over there. So why don't you just make up your mind not to let this bother you?"

"How would you feel if it were your house?"

"You mean my parents' house? Because you and I have a house—that's my home. What my parents do with their house …." He shrugs again.

She glares at him. "Fine. Point taken. It's not my house. That doesn't mean I have to like it."

"Of course not. But I don't see how being mad at your mother helps anything. You need to just let it go."

Maggie grimaces as another contraction begins. "I can't…I *need* her."

"No, sweetheart. You don't. That's just it. You always do fine, whether your mom is totally engaged or not. You can do this, too. *We* can." Sam is inches from Maggie's face, holding her eyes; his gaze pins her in place, here and now. When the contraction ends, her mind is wrung-out, empty.

The next few contractions are a little less intense. She squeezes Sam's hand and breathes up and over the top of the wave. Desultory chitchat fills up the spaces in between. Sam updates her on the whereabouts and travel plans of all their respective family members. Maggie asks where Sam's dad is; she's forgotten—he's at a bowl game in Atlanta. It crosses her mind, with a pang of guilt, that this is New Year's Eve. She thinks that various members of the unlikely group slowly converging on this little room in the birthing center might have had plans for the evening, but there's nothing she can do about that. Maybe they won't be too annoyed with her, when they meet the baby. Maybe.

The nursing shift has apparently changed. A new nurse comes in and introduces herself: Tracy is angular and looks strong. She enters the room with authority, and collects Maggie's vital statistics efficiently. Maggie ventures that she has a birth plan, if Tracy would like to see it. Tracy looks amused, and not likely to be impressed. She humors Maggie by glancing at the neatly formatted pages, then drops them back into the file. She informs Maggie that each labor is highly individual, and she doesn't like to be bound by the idealistic notions of a plan written by someone who hasn't actually been through a labor yet. Sam twitches, suppressing a snicker. He has been openly amused by Maggie's mental preparations for childbirth, and has very specifically questioned the need for a plan for a process that he believes is going to hinge largely on medical competence, not Maggie's visions of ancient rituals or female empowerment or beatific perfection. She tries to glare at him, but another contraction begins, and she has to pay attention to stay on top of it. Tracy watches her, but makes no effort to get involved.

When it ends, Tracy continues with her work, checking the baby's heartbeat, jotting notes, tidying the counters that line one wall. She pulls on a pair of gloves and checks Maggie's cervix—apparently a tiny bit of progress, but nothing remarkable. Maggie is beginning to tire of this poking and prodding. She has read books with an academician's thoroughness, and thinks ruefully that she must have been wrong when she thought she had anticipated all the indignities of labor. She knew she would cease to be modest, that she might lose control of her bowels or bladder, that there would be blood and sweat and tears. She had come to terms, she thought, with the profoundly *physical* nature of giving birth. But the touching is a surprise. She is weary of spreading her legs, of clenching her teeth against the intrusion, of the slow, wet suck of fingers withdrawing from her hypersensitive body.

When she first thought, early this morning, that she might be in labor, she had had a brief sense of euphoria thinking of sharing this primal experience with all the women who've gone before. She touches the birth amulet now, trying to remind herself of that feeling of connection, of essential femininity. This is it. She is doing what her body knows how to do, has evolved to do. She will tap that well of historical perspective that informs her academic work, and gain strength from the women whose lives she has imagined, documented, resurrected. She will become one of the motherline.

But it isn't working. There's nothing primal about this experience. It's clinical, modern, medicalized. She can feel a slow, damp leak from her vagina, making her fidget uncomfortably on the rough bed sheet. The heparin lock in the back of her hand (hospital policy for first-timers; she couldn't talk her way out of it) is beginning to itch. The intercom speaker built into the bedrail emits startling squawks, transporting disembodied voices into the quiet of Maggie's focus. A contraction subsides, and for a moment, she feels clear-headed and calm; wrung-out, but focused. It occurs to her that she can use this moment: she can't do much about the contractions, but perhaps she can get a grip on her mind, and get back on top of the waves of pain. She doesn't like this scattered feeling; when a contraction starts, she feels panic rise in her chest. Fear and pain make it hard to breathe. She'll never get through it if she can't calm down. The books all said to ride the contractions, to breathe and focus and relax into the intensity. Her brain is refusing to cooperate, though. It keeps spinning when it should be relaxing.

Her belly tightens again, painfully rigid. But as the wave crashes over her, Sam is there, talking her through it. He's telling her to breathe, and she latches on to the sound of his voice. She breathes on Sam's cue—the patterned, artificial-sounding "hee, hee, hee, hoo" of that months-ago childbirth class. It had seemed utterly ridiculous at the time. Sam had made fun of it all, balking during the practice sessions and mimicking Laura, their instructor, relentlessly on the drive home after each class. Maggie had laughed in spite of herself. He was absolutely dead-on in his imitation of Laura's sincerity. Her demonstrations of labor breathing were a little too realistic, and the pushing breathing—well, that was too graphic for words. Maggie had gotten fairly comfortable with words like *cervix*, *perineum*, and *vagina*, but even she was discomfited by Laura's deep concentration when she pretended to push—she moaned, she grunted, she turned red in the face, her legs sprawled open, knees pulled up to her chest. Then she expected them to breathe like she did, while she moved them into uncomfortably vulnerable positions—to "open up that birth canal." She had touched Maggie, invaded her space, manipulated her limbs, had prodded her discomfort with her intense gaze….

But the breathing. That's working now. Sam is right next to her, breathing out the pattern. The words and images and sentences fade into the back of her mind, and she hears only the strong exhalation, the quick intake, the repetition. The contraction is subsiding. She opens her eyes and manages a small smile. This passes for gratitude, and she can see the reciprocal concern in Sam's face.

"Better?"

"Tremendously. I can't believe you remembered all that."

Sam draws back in mock injury. "Who, me? Are you implying that I didn't memorize every pearl of wisdom that fell from Laura's lips? That I didn't practice every day, like I was supposed to? I'm here—I'm ready— let's do some breathing!" His jocularity, his sarcasm, are a bit large for the moment, and his voice is loud in the small space. Maggie rolls her eyes, then remembers Tracy, leaning up against the counter on the other side of the room. She can feel her ears turning pink.

"Apparently you were paying more attention than I realized. That helps a lot. Thank you. I feel calmer now."

Sam settles a bit, and watches her. She squirms; she is wearing two hospital gowns, one over the other, the top one opening in the front, the other opening in the back. Somehow they are bunching up, restricting her movement. She finds the opening in the top gown and pulls the right side open, reaches behind her back to find the edge of the back, under-gown opening, and wrenches it free of her weight, so that she can move her arm and leg freely without tangling in the pink cotton. She is begin-ning to breathe heavily from the effort. She begins to work on the left side of the gown, next to Sam, but he stops her with a hand on her arm. His cool fingers untie the top gown, which is bound with a single bow at her collarbone.

"That's all. Just take it off. You don't need it in here anyway."

Maggie feels looser and cooler without the gown tangled around her, and is able to shift her weight a bit toward her left side. Tracy stands up from her stool by the door.

"Since you're stripping down already, why don't you get up and try to use the bathroom? You need to keep your bladder as empty as you can, and it's better if you keep moving around a little."

Maggie blinks at the nurse for a moment. She can feel another contraction beginning to grip at her insides, and she is afraid to move too much. She shakes her head a fraction—"No," she whispers. "Not now." She closes her eyes; it's hard to get the breathing going, hard to remember the pattern. She's losing track, but then Sam is there. She catches his rhythm, and finds herself relaxing into it. As long as she can follow that sound, she can ride the wave without being pulled under. With her eyes closed, in the quiet room, she can lose herself completely in the in and out of Sam's breath. Nothing else matters, until the contraction begins to release her. As it subsides, Maggie opens her eyes to see Tracy watching intently.

"Nice teamwork. You actually look better than you did before that one," she says, unhooking and lowering the complicated rail that guards the left side of the bed. "Potty time."

Maggie rolls all the way on to her left side, and pushes herself up with her hands. Her feet swing over the edge of the bed, and she sits, shaking, for a second.

"All right?" Tracy asks. She and Sam are standing back, watching Maggie move at her own slow speed. She nods once, looking down at her feet as the blood in her head settles into this new vertical position.

"Okay. I'm ready." Maggie pushes herself forward, off the edge of the bed, and stands unsteadily. She waits, again, until her body seems to adjust, then shuffles toward the bathroom. She's aware that she's not standing up quite straight, that there's a draft across her back and butt, that the colorless floor is cold under her feet. She wonders irrelevantly where her slippers are; she knows she packed some. And she remembers her special labor nightgown too—hah! She can't even be bothered to think about what her plans were for how to do this. She has to focus completely on walking. She takes tiny, careful steps, afraid any movement at all will trigger another contraction. She keeps her feet close to the ground, and her legs close together.

Something wet is seeping out of her, making her thighs rub stickily against each other. It dawns on her that her back is aching more loudly than the other parts at the moment. She reaches the bathroom door, and turns her bulk around to back onto the toilet. She realizes, with huge relief, that those two stainless steels rails sloping on either side of the toilet were actually put there for her. She grabs hold with both hands and lowers herself slowly, not bothering to move the gown out of the way. As she bends forward, it simply falls away from her body anyway. As the backs of her legs make cold contact with the seat, she takes a breath and looks up to see Tracy standing in the doorway watching. She nods slightly that she's okay, closes her eyes, and tries to pee. Nothing happens. She slips her hands under her belly to give her bladder a little space, and instantly regrets it. A contraction starts.

"Uh oh," she moans.

Sam steps into the bathroom and squats down in front of her. He starts the patterned breathing, but Maggie doesn't fall into the rhythm. It hurts much worse in this position. Her crotch is open, exposed, this huge weight inside of her pushing down with nothing to hold it up. She whimpers.

"Maggie. Listen to me. Can you hear me? Maggie. Open your eyes. Look at me," Sam demands.

She shakes her head no, whimpers again. Panic is taking over.

"Maggie," Sam says, more loudly now. "Breathe. In," he inhales exaggeratedly, then "Out." The second time, Maggie manages to grab onto the rhythm, and hangs on for dear life. This time, the internal pain has a sharper edge to it, and threatens to engulf her. She can feel Sam's exhalations on her face, but can't open her eyes to look at him. All she can do is breathe.

As the pain releases her, her head sags forward and tears well up in her eyes. She looks up at Sam miserably.

"It hurts," she whispers.

Before he can respond, Tracy's voice cuts in over Sam's shoulder.

"All right Maggie. You need to pee now, between contractions. Scoot out of the way Sam, and let me help her for a minute."

Sam heads back toward his chair, and Tracy comes into the bathroom. Maggie is trying again, but nothing's coming out. She looks up at Tracy and shakes her head. Tracy turns on the hot water tap in the sink. She takes a white plastic cup from the stack on the shelf, and tests the water on her hand. She fills the cup, leaving the water running, then turns to Maggie and bundles up the folds of the gown and drapes it over Maggie's left shoulder.

"I need you to spread your legs for me Maggie; I'm going to pour this over your crotch. Sometimes warm water helps the muscles relax. It's not too hot—it should feel good."

Maggie sits back on the toilet and spreads her legs as well as she can. This is intrusive and embarrassing. She's been poked and prodded and invaded all day, but never while vertical, looking the invader in the face. This is a whole new level of intimacy. Tracy leans over Maggie, directing the stream of water right into her pubic hair. Maggie has a perfect view of Tracy's left earring, a tiny little gold hoop. One creamy white pearl floats under the hoop, attached by a single, delicate thread of gold. The pearl rolls along the curve of the hoop, dancing with every move of Tracy's head. Her hair is cut efficiently short, neatly clipped above the outline of her ear. Maggie focuses on that little pearl, bobbing about inches from her nose. She can smell Tracy's shampoo, something clean but faintly flower-sweet. She has the sudden impulse to lean her head on Tracy's shoulder, but can't quite let herself do that.

The bathroom is so tiny that Tracy doesn't even stand up to refill the cup. Maggie tries to relax with the flow of warmth over her swollen labia. She takes a breath and thinks very hard about softening all her muscles, letting everything go. Finally, she feels the thin, hot stream of urine mingle with the warm water. It ends too quickly; the relief in her bladder is only partial. But better than nothing.

"Better?" Tracy asks.

Maggie nods. She grabs a wad of toilet paper and dabs herself halfway dry; she pulls herself up to standing, and is immediately caught by another contraction. Her hands grip the steel bars on the wall. She leans her head on the tile wall; it's cool on her sweaty forehead. Her hair is damp and sticky on her face, but her feet still feel chilly on the cold floor. These warring sensations are just part of the turmoil that is engulfing her body.

Sam comes back into the bathroom, at Tracy's summons, and begins the breathing. This time he stoops down, seeking eye contact. Maggie is withdrawing into herself, trying to escape sensation, but Sam catches her before she goes too far. With an effort, she forces her breathing into his pattern, and feels herself slip into the narrow track that holds her in place, keeps her from spinning off into an oblivion of panic and pain. She is vaguely aware that Sam is rubbing her back, but as the contraction begins to subside, it is her legs that command her attention. The backs of her thighs tremble, her knees threaten to buckle. The dull, hard ache that seems chronic now in her pelvis seems to be spreading, pressing misery through her back and down through her hamstrings. Her legs are done with holding her up. As the contraction releases its grip, she clutches Sam's arm.

"I need to lie back down now."

"Okay. Take it easy. Slowly to the bed."

Maggie shuffles out of the bathroom, stooped over, hunching along like an ancient crone, the weight of years pressing her toward the ground. Her body is folding in on itself; she knows instinctively that standing up straight would cause her aching stomach muscles to clamp down even harder. She leans as heavily as she can on Sam.

"Here, put your arm around my neck," he offers, as he stoops to carry more of her weight on his shoulder.

"No!"

He looks at her, surprised. "It's okay. Whatever you want."

She hears the bewilderment in his voice. "No. I just… I have to keep my body close together."

Sam looks at her as if she makes no sense, but she keeps her arms tucked in close to her sides, dragging Sam's arm down with her own. She can't help it. Any stretching, any sort of loose, expansive movement—well, it won't work, that's all. Her body has become this central ball of push-ing, aching muscles. Limbs are irrelevant, peripheral. Her overwhelming instinct at this point is to lie down and curl in on herself. She makes it to the bed, slowly, and crawls right up.

Tracy has lowered the bed and raised the back so that it's fully upright, but the gown catches under her knees, falling all the way open. She feels cool air touch the entire back side of her body, all the way down to the bottoms of her feet. She doesn't care. What she does realize is that her hair is becoming a problem. It's matted and damp, sticking to her forehead and neck, prickling and itching. She hovers for a moment, on all fours across the bed, unsure of how to right herself, but panicking, knowing the next contraction has to come soon. The covers are turned back, but Sam, seeing her teetering, unsure, pulls them all the way to the foot of the bed.

"Maneuvering room. Can you do it?"

"Yeah. Wait." She breathes shallowly, almost panting. Carefully, she eases back onto her haunches, pushing first her right leg, then her left, out in front of her. She leans back against the bed, sitting upright, and Sam pulls the stiff white sheet up over her feet. Almost immediately another contraction begins to build.

"Down." She fumbles at the control panel on the right-hand railing of the bed, but can't figure out how to drop the top half of the bed. She needs to roll on her side; she can't get through a contraction sitting here with her legs all sprawled out like this. "Down!" More urgent now; whimpers are beginning in her throat. Sam is just looking at her; why doesn't he fix this damned bed?

"She wants to lie down." Tracy, bless her, understands. The bed rumbles down to a bit of an angle, and Maggie, moaning now, manages to roll slightly onto her left side. Enough to close her body in around her belly. Just enough.

"Maggie. Breathe now. Listen to me." Sam is in her face again, laying down the rhythm for her, helping her slide her breaths into the pattern. It helps. If she follows the rise and fall of his breathing, she can stay on the path that leads to the other side. It's like following a light that keeps her from getting lost. They breathe together.

As the contraction eases, Tracy, standing at the bottom of the bed, pats Maggie's foot.

"Good job. They're getting pretty strong now, but you're doing great. Stay on top. That's great teamwork."

CHAPTER 14

There's a tap on the door, and Ellen peers into the room.

"I'm back, darlings. Hot chocolate delivery!"

She tiptoes into the room. Maggie opens her eyes halfway, registers her mother-in-law's oblivious, beaming smile, and lets her eyelids drift down again, hiding tired eyes. For a second, Ellen hesitates when no one answers her, but she recovers and focuses her attention on Sam.

"Sam? How is it going? Is she awake? I brought the hot chocolate she wanted," Ellen stage-whispers. She gestures toward Maggie, who grunts a bit in lieu of a greeting. "Oh. You are awake. How are you dear? Here's your drink." She sets the paper cup down on the tray-table that Sam has pushed up against the wall behind his chair.

"She's doing great, Mom. She's resting between the contractions. Have a seat. We're trying to stay kind of quiet." Maggie is relieved when Sam answers for her; she manages to open her eyes all the way now, but can't be bothered with extraneous speech. Ellen drops into a chair opposite Sam, at Maggie's head.

"So." She beams around the room, at Sam, at Tracy. "Sorry I took so long. I had a little cup of coffee myself. Well, no, actually it was coffee-flavored water. Horrible hospital stuff, but the weather's too dreadful to go out in. The roads are all nasty by now. Have you heard from your father, Sam? Shouldn't he have landed by now?"

"Not quite. The plane's not due in till four, and it's only 3:30 now. But it's New Year's Eve. Who knows how backed up they might be. Either way, he's definitely in the air still. He'll call when the plane lands."

Maggie looks up in surprise. "I thought he was in Atlanta. Is he coming back?"

"Of course, darling! He couldn't possibly miss the birth of a grandbaby, could he? I called him this morning and told him to get on the first plane headed this way. But now with this ice…."

"He'll be fine, Mom. They'll salt the runways and nobody will even notice there's an ice storm."

Ellen fidgets in the pink plastic chair. Maggie mulls over the idea of her father-in-law rearranging his plans to come home for this. She's touched, but surprised. As far as she can tell, Samuel has barely even registered the pregnancy—come to think of it, she's only seen him a handful of times since her belly began to swell. Even less than she's seen her mother, who can't be bothered to drive across town, never mind rebook a plane ticket. She wonders who went to Atlanta with him, and if he's coming back alone, or if her labor has ruined everyone's trip. As she begins to feel utterly sorry for herself, another contraction begins, and Samuel and his football game slip from her mind altogether.

When this one ends, she pushes at the top sheet with her feet; she's hot and prickly. Her hair is sticking to the edges of her face, and she shoves it back with one hand. She can hear Ellen behind her, rummaging in the bag that she deposited in the corner earlier in the day, but Maggie is preoccupied—the room seems uncomfortably overheated. Suddenly, Ellen is leaning over her.

"Here, dear. You look miserable. Your hair is getting all tangled. Let me get it tidied up a bit for you." She pulls Maggie's hair away from her face, and begins brushing it back.

"No, wait! Ellen. I don't really need…." Ellen is her usual self, a steamroller, fixed on a forward path, undeniable. Maggie's hair is being brushed whether she wants it or not. She has rarely been able to stand up to her mother-in-law, and has never told her no to her face. At the moment civility seems impossible, but it's a deeply ingrained habit. A flash of hot irritability wells up nonetheless, and she is suddenly, surprisingly, furious.

Unwanted tears spring to her eyes. Her head flinches under Ellen's hand even as the sharp words die on her tongue. She can feel her mother-in-law gentling out the knots, protecting her scalp from the bristles of the brush. She doesn't remember anyone ever brushing her hair except her stylist—it seems like an indulgence.

Maggie feels cool air on her sweaty neck as Ellen smoothes the long hair into a ponytail. Her touch is intimate; Maggie can't remember anything more than perfunctory hugs and air-kisses from Ellen in the past, and she's not sure how to respond.

"Thank you," she finally says. That seems inadequate. There's a lump in her throat. She can't see Ellen's face, but the older woman's hand rests for a moment on the crown of her head.

"Of course, darling." Ellen's voice is husky. "Do you need anything else?"

"No. That feels better. I'm so hot."

Ellen fusses with the sheets, then asks, "When is Katharine coming?" Maggie sees the warning look Sam flashes at his mother, but her vision blurs as the pain begins again, deep inside her, almost choking out the pain in her heart. She closes her eyes, and tears leak down her cheeks. For a moment, the room is silent, until she whimpers, once, and Sam comes to draw her attention out of herself, back into the room, into his eyes.

Once again, her mind is wiped clean, drawn in on her body, filled up with the effort of riding above the surface of the pain. Sam breathes her through it, and when she is able to drag her eyes away from his face, she realizes that Ellen is holding her hand. She gives it a small squeeze. Ellen returns the pressure, staying right where she is.

Tracy comes into view, doptone in hand.

"Let's check on the baby, okay Maggie? I'm going to listen for a minute here between contractions. You tell me if it starts again, and I'll stop, I promise."

Maggie nods assent, still hanging on to Ellen's hand, and flinches when Tracy mashes the cool black plastic end of the doptone against her rigid belly. It's not like she has any choice in the matter, anyway. It seems the notion of being left alone to labor in peace is a fiction, something she read about in a book. Nothing about this day is going the way she thought it would. She waits, listening, until the liquid pulsing of the fetal heartbeat fills the room, and Maggie listens to the sound, familiar from all those visits to the obstetrician.

She has always held her breath slightly, fighting off dread, while Dr. Morgan maneuvered the receiver, searching for the spot that would give them a strong, clear signal. Maggie was always struck by the amazing juxtaposition between the oldest, most primal sound on earth—the human heartbeat—and the sophisticated, modern, manmade technology that made it audible. It was amazing to think that this sound was coming from her own body, and would continue even when she stopped listening, all day, all night, without hesitation, strong and steady, a part of her that was nonetheless completely independent. And without that little machine, she would never be able to hear the inconceivable sound of a heartbeat within a heartbeat. She has pondered this for months now, the role of the technology in her relationship with her pregnancy, with each visit feeling the stab of panic in that moment before she could hear the proof of her baby's life (and later, when she could feel the swooping and kicking and stretching), then the warm flood of relief when the steady rhythm filled the tiny exam room.

Now, though, she's having trouble remembering why she's here—her deep philosophical musings on the anthropological significance of the childbirth experience have given way to the experience itself. Her ears hear the sound of her baby's heartbeat, but the only image her tired mind can conjure is of an outboard motor, trying to start cold, hiccupping, unable to turn over that final spark and roar into action.

The thumping engine sound fades away, and the cramp of pressure on her belly subsides when Tracy steps away from the bed, turning off the doptone and reaching for the call button.

"Could you get Dr. Morgan to come down to 3-C, please?"

"I'll call her. She's still in 2-C. When do you need her?"

"I'd like her to come listen to the doptone. In the next few minutes."

A stab of alarm penetrates Maggie's fatigue; she feels Sam stiffen in the chair by her head. Ellen's grip on Maggie's hand tightens.

"What's wrong?" The question comes out in unison, the same concern in both their voices. Ellen smoothes Maggie's hair back with her free hand. For a second, the room is silent and tense. Maggie is watching Tracy, and Sam turns to look at the nurse as well.

"The heartbeat sounds a bit different to me, that's all. I'd like Dr. Morgan to hear it." Maggie stares at Tracy, trying to read the meaning in her voice. She meets Maggie's gaze directly, and Maggie can see nothing lurking behind her open face.

Sam is sharp, though. "How is it different? What's wrong?"

"I really don't think anything's wrong. I think Maggie's getting a bit tired, that's all. The baby's strong and fine—you heard it. I just think it's time for Dr. Morgan to have a listen. Don't worry, she'll be right here." Tracy looks back at Maggie, who decides to be reassured by her calm gaze. Apparently, Ellen has chosen likewise. She lifts one small shoulder in a delicate shrug, and takes Sam's seat at the head of the bed. Maggie closes her eyes, and hangs on to Ellen's hand for dear life. On some level, she knows there's something new here, something she wants to think about and sort through, but she knows, too, that Ellen's presence is making her feel better. It's all so complicated. Maybe Ellen will straighten everything out.

A few seconds later, Dr. Morgan strides into the room. She's wearing scrubs now, her wild hair contained by a blue surgical cap, her loud fuchsia sweater hidden by the monochromatic uniform of a doctor at work. Maggie has seen her like this at the office a couple of times, and is always surprised by the contrast. Dr. Morgan in street clothes always looks a bit of a character—her color combinations are unpredictably flamboyant and her scraggly red hair curls of its own accord in odd directions. But on the few occasions that Maggie has seen her come straight from a delivery, she has inhabited a different personality altogether. Now she exudes calm authority, and Maggie relaxes the tiniest bit as Dr. Morgan listens intently to the baby's heartbeat. Ellen withdraws to the other side of the room as the doctor drapes her stethoscope around her neck and gazes at Maggie for a moment.

"Where's your drink?"

Maggie is surprised; this is not what she was expecting. She glances around the room and shrugs. "Um, I had a hot chocolate a little while ago, but I don't know where it got to." Something tells her this is the wrong answer.

Dr. Morgan frowns, encircles Maggie's wrist with her fingers, and checks her pulse. "I think you're getting too dehydrated; I want to give you some fluids. We won't need to start a new line. We can use this one that's already in your hand."

"Oh. Oh, no, can't I drink something? I can drink a lot. I will, I promise. Sam, could you get me some water please? See—I'll drink right now, I will." She'll drink whatever she has to—she's determined to do this without medication, and all the natural childbirth books say that the IV is the first step onto that slippery slope. Besides, the whole idea of an IV frightens Maggie; she knows she's already got the needle in her hand, but somehow the idea of a tube dripping strange fluids directly into her veins is so much more alarming. She takes the pink plastic cup of water that Sam hands her and sucks it down, eyeing Dr. Morgan over the top of the cup.

"That's not going to do it, Maggie. Your body needs more than just water. The baby's heart rate is dropping—it's not a problem yet, it's only a little, but it's enough that we need to get some electrolytes and glucose in there."

"Wait! I brought Gatorade! How about Gatorade? Sam, it's in my bag—I brought the whole eight-pack. I'll drink it right now—won't that help?"

Dr. Morgan crosses her arms over her chest and leans back against the cabinet by the sink. She watches silently as Maggie fumbles the tiny little straw into a box of Gatorade, and sucks it down as quickly as she can swallow it. When the box is empty, she relents. "Okay. Drink some more of that; Gatorade might do the trick. I'll come back in about fifteen minutes and see if the baby has perked up any." She pulls a tiny voice recorder from her pocket and speaks into it. Maggie catches the words fetal distress, and pouts guiltily. Tracy hands her another box of Gatorade, straw already inserted and bent. Maggie sips obediently. Dr. Morgan nods, and heads out the door, pocketing the recorder. Tracy follows her, saying she'll check back in a bit, as well.

Maggie sets the drink down on the bedside table, grimacing. "Yuck. I hate that stuff."

"Drink it anyway," Sam says. He looks concerned. Maggie reaches for the box, then thinks better of it.

"In a minute." She curls in on her stomach, taking the first deep breath to begin the pattern that will take her up over the peak of the contraction.

When it ends, Sam hands her the Gatorade. "I don't care what that birth plan says, Maggie. If Dr. Morgan thinks the baby's having a problem, we're going to do what she says. So if you don't want an IV, you'd better drink up now. She'll be back in ten minutes."

Ellen hovers by the sink. She has a fistful of brown paper towels, and is wiping and re-wiping, nervous energy radiating from her small body.

"What about the hot chocolate? Or a cup of coffee? I can go get whatever you want."

Maggie makes a face. "No. I feel sick."

"Oh, but sweetheart, you heard the doctor. Think of the baby."

Maggie can't think of the baby. She can't think at all. "I don't care. I just want to be left alone." She feels, rather than sees, a look pass between Sam and his mother, and it grates. Ellen stops wiping for a moment.

"You know, Maggie, an IV is not the end of the world. You might feel better, and maybe the baby would come faster, too."

"No. Fine," she says. "I'll drink the damned Gatorade." She sips the sweet, tepid drink. Ellen and Sam exchange looks again, but this time Maggie catches them.

"Would you two stop? I'm drinking!"

Ellen pats her foot through the sheet, kisses the top of her head, then shoulders her purse.

"We know, dear. We just want what's best for both you and the baby, that's all." She turns toward the door. "I'm going to go make some calls. Samuel is probably on the ground by now, and I'm sure Katharine is dying to hear from us."

"No, she's not," Maggie says as the door closes. "Sam, tell her not to call my mother. If she gave a damn, she'd be here. Just don't bother."

Irritability wells up inside her.

"You know what? I don't really give a damn, either. I hate Gatorade, and I don't care. I'm sick of this stupid bed." She kicks out against the bed sheet.

"Maggie, settle down."

"Don't tell me to settle down! You can settle your own damn self! I'm not a child!" Anger bubbles in her chest.

"Nobody said you were! What the hell is your problem? Why are you screaming at me?"

"I'm not screaming! Because I'm mad, that's why! You could at least help me!"

"Help you what, pumpkin? I'm here. I'm with you. You're totally over-reacting—calm down!"

"You shut the fuck up! I am not overreacting! I have every right to be mad if I want to—I don't…I can't…I don't even want to be here! This is a terrible idea!" Maggie is seething now, fury burning in her veins. She wants to throw something at Sam, to hit him hard, to hurt him. Devastation is written on his face.

"Oh, God. I can't believe I said that. I didn't mean it. Not like that."

Sam is quiet, watching her.

"Don't look at me like that. You know I didn't mean it. This just hurts. I didn't know it was going to be like this."

"It'll be over soon."

"It doesn't feel like it will."

"But you know it's not ruining your life, right? Just changing it."

"I'm such a horrible person. What if—what if that's who I really am?"

Sam is still quiet and she wants to disappear into the floor.

"I didn't mean it like that. I only meant…shit. Why does everything have to be so screwed up? I just wanted to have a baby, and have a nice, normal family that would show up and be excited for me."

Her voice breaks, and Sam hands her a tissue and sits in the chair, coming down to her eye level. She sniffles and scrubs at her nose. He leans in very close, and pushes her hair back from her face. He holds the Gatorade box up for her to sip, and she finishes it off. He blinks at her for a moment.

"Are you better now?"

"Yes," she says in a small voice.

"All right then." He nods, and watches her. "Apparently labor makes women insane—I never knew that before."

Maggie manages half a grin. She is horrified by the rage she felt a moment ago; now she is wrung out and empty. She's not sure what she was so furious about, which bothers her as much as the fury itself—and that look on Sam's face.

"Thank you."

He nods.

She slides off the edge of the bed, stands, holding the edge of the mattress for a second.

"Where are you going?"

She looks at Sam and ponders. "I wanted to move around for a minute."

His eyes are dark with worry, and the little lines between his eyebrows look deeper. He hovers next to her, as if she's going to collapse under her own weight.

"I'm okay."

He sinks back into the chair, still watching her.

"Well, keep drinking." He picks up the *Wall Street Journal* from a pile of papers under his chair, but doesn't open it right away. Maggie looks around the room. She doesn't think she could pee; that was too difficult. She fusses with the growing pile of stuff on the bedside table, extracting two empty cups, half a pack of vending machine peanut butter crackers, and the take-out menu from the deli that lunch came from. She shuffles over to a garbage can and deposits the stuff. She leans up against the wall, breathing, waiting for a slightly smaller contraction to pass. Then she putters around the room some more, soothed by the sound of rain pattering against the window, the rustling of Sam's newspaper, and the muted murmur of activity beyond the room's heavy door. She feels cocooned here in this quiet room, sheltered from the rest of the world. She surveys the space, trying to imprint this moment of calm on her frazzled brain.

Chapter 15

Before another contraction can start, she moves carefully over to the windowsill and peers out at the late afternoon, savoring the moment of peace. She's surprised to discover that she got a room with a real view. Beyond the three rows of cars in this arm of the parking lot, she can see the wet, bare trees of Potomac Park. A trail curves up close to the tall iron fence, and she can tell from here on the fifth floor that the park is damp and chilly and empty. She presses her forehead against the cool window. She can see movement in the parking lot. One figure, with a bag over his shoulder, looks familiar, hunched in on himself against the grey cold.

She tears her gaze away from the darkening parking lot and looks for a chair. There is a rocker tucked between the bed and the wall, where Ellen was sitting. She backs into it, leaning heavily on the smooth wooden arms. It's not cushioned, just a plain, blonde institutional rocker. A nod toward cozy, like the pink wallpaper, and the botanical prints. She finds that there's enough room in this back corner to rock the chair a bit. As she rocks, the contraction begins, and she manages this one without Sam, the rocking carrying her up and over, instead of the patterned breathing. Apparently rhythm is the key. She blows out her breaths anyway, just in case. The pain subsides.

She rocks gently, pushing off from the floor with her toes. She likes this enclosed space right now. That earlier flash of anger has left her rattled, and she needs to feel safe and contained, in case the anger comes back. She tugs a white cotton blanket off the bed, and drapes it over her lap and legs. She wonders if she'll have to pee again, since she drank all that Gatorade. Probably. Tracy will have to help. It's odd, but Maggie doesn't want Sam involved in that, paying that much attention to her basic functions, pouring water over her crotch, watching her huge body release all kinds of alarming fluids into the toilet. Somehow, Tracy feels safer, more… intimate? Maggie thinks about this. She barely knows Tracy. But she's seen this before, probably hundreds of times. She obviously knows exactly what Maggie is feeling, and she knows exactly what she needs.

This whole birth process is far more physical than Maggie anticipated, and her body feels vulnerable. She has an instinctive urge to curl in on her belly, to shield and protect it. But she recognizes dimly that she is incapable of protecting herself. She wants to hand herself over to Tracy, to offer up her body, her belly—her most intimate parts—to Tracy's safe-keeping. Because she's a nurse? Maggie's not sure; maybe it's because Tracy is another woman, and is therefore connected to the process automatically, by default, in a way that Sam can never be. He doesn't have labia. His perineum will never ache with the weight of a head bearing down. She has a fleeting image of her mother, and Yaya, and *her* mother before, a whole line of mothers stretching back in time, but doesn't see herself in the line—not yet.

There's a knock at the door. Maggie ignores it, not wanting to give up this peaceful moment, rubbing her hands slowly over her belly. Sam looks interrupted—"Yes?" The door is flung wide, and Seth strides in. Maggie looks at the young man, stunned by the audacity of his presence. He has no business here, she thinks, and he knows it. This is the worst part—he knows it. But here he is, with that brown leather satchel he always has slung over his right shoulder. He doesn't even need to put it down to remove whatever unwelcome stack of papers he's bringing for Sam's urgent attention. He blows into the room—this room, any room—always energetic, always eager. Always unwelcome, in Maggie's mind. She can't help but be bothered by his appearance. Sam has reminded her that Seth *did* save her life, but her gratitude is canceled out by the horror of the memory she associates his presence with. His timing is dreadful.

"Hi all," Seth announces to the room at large. He goes directly to the chair next to Sam, on the far side of the room from Maggie. Then he looks around. "Hey, Maggie. How's it going?"

"Fine, thanks, Seth." Maggie deliberately shuts out his gregarious good cheer. There is a voice screaming in her head, *NO! Not here! He can't be here now!*

She will not give him an inch. If she can shut him out entirely, he will not be in this room; she won't have to think about him or feel the panic that swirled through her chest when he opened the door. She consciously shifts her weight to turn slightly toward the window, and takes a small sip from the Gatorade box on the sill. She will not deal with this intrusion. Another contraction begins, and she closes her eyes and rocks in time with her breathing. When she comes back to her awareness of the room, she can hear Seth yammering to Sam about a meeting, a client, an agreement that needs to be signed "day-before-yesterday, if not sooner." She opens her eyes a slit and sneaks a peek; Sam is watching her. She looks back out the window and continues to rock, determined to maintain her calm.

Sam shuffles papers, blessing them with his attention, his signature. Seth keeps it all organized, rearranging deft piles for delivery to a multitude of recipients. They confer over one last folder; Sam puts it in his briefcase, then, with a thoughtful glance in Maggie's direction, pulls it back out and hands it to Seth.

"I don't think I'm going to get to this today. Probably not tomorrow either. I'll let you know when I do. Leave it on my desk in the meantime, in case anyone else needs it."

Maggie doesn't look for Seth's reaction, but she's sure he disapproves. He has a way about him—he seems to live for work, for Sam, even. Whenever she's around the two of them together, she gets this little lurking feeling that he disapproves of her entire existence. He makes her feel too female, too not-of-the-firm, as if she has no right to make demands on Sam's attention. She squirms a bit in the rocking chair, wishing he would leave. Silence settles over the room. A contraction begins, and for a few minutes, Maggie forgets about Seth. When it ends, she slowly realizes that they're both watching her, and she forces a tight smile. Sam looks concerned.

Seth, of course, is unfazed. "Wow. That looks intense. Does it hurt?"

"Yes."

"Wow."

For a moment, Maggie's rocking chair fills the silence. Then Seth speaks again. "I'm glad everything's fine this time. I mean, you know, compared to last time, when I had to take you to the hospital. It was this same hospital, wasn't it? Wow. Seems like a long time ago."

"All right, Seth. Time for you to get that agreement delivered. I'll walk you down to the lobby." Sam is already halfway to the door, herding Seth out in front of him. He glances back at Maggie. She shrugs and rocks, and turns back to the window, but is suddenly struck by a thought.

"Wait—Seth."

"Yes?"

Sam, one hand already on the door, frowns at Maggie; she ignores him. "What do you drive?"

"Pardon?"

"What do you drive? What kind of car?"

Seth looks mildly uncomfortable, but he comes to the window and points. "An old Celica. See, next to that red emergency box in the back of the parking lot?"

Maggie peers, and deflates slightly when she realizes that the battered car won't work at all for transporting Yaya.

"Why do you ask?"

"Oh, never mind. I had an idea, but it won't work. I need an SUV."

There's a pause, while Seth absorbs this, then he shrugs and turns back toward the door. "Well, sorry I can't help with that. Good luck with the baby, though." He's gone before Maggie can respond. Another contraction begins, and she sets the chair in motion, rocking through the intensity.

When she looks up, Sam has pulled his chair up next to hers, and is leaning in close, peering at her. She looks at him. "I'm alive," she says, dryly. "Why are you staring at me?"

"I'm wondering why you're still fussing about getting Yaya over here right now."

"I'm not fussing. It's just, I want to see her, that's all. Plus, even if she can't get here today, she has to come tomorrow. She'll want to see…us. You know that." Maggie can't quite bring herself to say *the baby*, not right now. She needs Yaya for herself, for her own sake, not anyone else's.

Sam is silent for a heartbeat. Maggie meets his gaze.

"I realize you want to see her, but …."

She cuts him off. "No. You don't realize. I *need* to see her. I feel like I can't do this. There's too much on my plate. I feel like I'm holding them all together."

"Who? All who?"

"All of my family!" The words burst out. "I feel like my whole stupid family is falling apart, and I can't stop it." She fights back tears.

"Okay. I understand. I get that you're feeling that. But even if it's true, which I don't know that it is," he raises one hand to stop her objection, "what in the world do you think Yaya's going to do about it? You talked to her on the phone a couple of hours ago, sweetie, and she had trouble following the conversation, remember? She can't fix everything, not anymore."

Maggie looks out the window, rocking steadily, ignoring Sam. She finally reaches over and squeezes his hand, without meeting his eyes. He squeezes back, then gets up and heads into the bathroom.

His words have struck a chord. Maggie remembers hearing Yaya say almost the very same thing.

§§§

It was the day Yaya was moving to Glenlake, the assisted living facility. She was giving up her little bungalow in Arlington, Virginia, a few miles from the house Maggie had grown up in. At ninety, Yaya was still getting around fairly well on her own, and Maggie hadn't wanted her to give up her independence. But Katharine had insisted that the whole family show up to help with the move. While Ben and Dara drove back and forth to Goodwill, gradually dismantling the house Maggie had counted on for refuge during her rocky adolescence, she followed Yaya around, trying to understand.

"I'm not giving anything up. I'm just getting what I need—company, and help if I need it. Don't act like it's some kind of awful thing—I'm happy about it. You should be too."

"But you don't need help. You have us."

"Oh, stop, Maggie. You're all busy—and that's how it should be. I don't like having to drag you all away from your lives every time I have a little problem. I'd rather be somewhere that makes it easy for me. I'm starting to slow down, whether you like it or not."

"Well, I don't like it at all."

"I know. But this is what's right for *me*. Now go do something useful."

Maggie wandered into the guest bedroom, still untouched by the whirlwind of Katharine's packing frenzy. She poked around in the top of the closet and pulled out several shoeboxes stuffed with photographs. She stacked them on the bed then sank down next to them, and took the lid off the top box. When she was little, she'd spend hours poring over the snapshots in Yaya's photo box, making up stories about the mysterious-looking strangers in the quaint clothes. Men in vests and skinny little ties; women in bathing suits that looked more like granny-panties. Hats, and cigarettes, and lots of pearls. Taken together, the pictures implied a long, glamorous party that ended before she was born. But she had no idea who any of the people were. She could pick out Mother and Yaya, of course, but all those other laughing, dancing, posing people were strangers.

Sometimes Yaya would sit with her on the couch, pointing out aunts and uncles and cousins who looked completely different when she met them at family reunions, all old and wrinkly, with thin, cottony hair and thick glasses, or wearing jeans and beards and baseball caps. She told

Maggie all about her own mother, Granny Florence, who died right after Katharine was born. The world didn't look the same anymore; she would stare and stare at the photos, memorizing the details, until Dara dragged her out to climb a tree or hunt for tadpoles.

Katharine stuck her head in the door. "Maggie! What are you doing just sitting there? Get out here and help pack up the china. You may have time to lounge around with old pictures, but the rest of us don't."

Stung by her mother's words, Maggie fitted the lid back on the box, but as soon as she heard Katharine's steps receding down the stairs, she opened the second box, and found the snapshots from her own childhood.

There were photos of her own early years, of course. Some she remembered vividly, moments that someone—Mother, Daddy, Yaya—chose to freeze in time with the old Polaroid. Others were more intriguing. She recognized the players: Dara and Jamie and herself, caught in the normal sibling pile-ups of childhood, all smiles and stringy hair and scabby knees, or posing with friends and classmates and the backyard posse. Here was the original of the photo on her nightstand—the one of her holding the newborn Jamie. The next one in the pile, though, she didn't remember: it was the same pose, but Dara was sitting beside her on the couch, and Katharine was on the other side, encircling all three children in her arms, beaming at the camera. It must have been the day they brought him home from the hospital. When she peered at the photo, she could see that her mother was still wearing the hospital ID bracelet. She pondered the photo, trying to remember what it must have felt like for everyone to be smiling, but came up with a blank. All she could recall was how perfect and tiny Jamie was, and how it felt to hold a sleeping baby.

She dug some more pictures out of the pile. There were more of her than of either Dara or Jamie—the curse of being the oldest, with every milestone documented, every new experience, every missing tooth. The pictures of Jamie ended abruptly; her mind glossed over this fact, turning again to the older photos, wondering about their stories.

As she reached for the next box, Yaya appeared in the doorway, hands on hips. "Didn't you hear your mother? Come help me with the china."

She looked around at the guest room, then saw the shoeboxes piled up on the bed. "Ah. I wondered what you were up to." She sat down next to Maggie, and took a photo from her hands, chuckling. "I remember that. You were being a real pill."

It was a posed shot of Maggie's twelfth birthday dinner, right before Ben had moved out for good. Katharine was serving cake, a grin lighting up her face; Ben and Dara were sitting at the table, laughing at something, but from this remove, his face looked tired and drawn. Maggie was nowhere to be seen.

"No, I wasn't. Mother was. She always was." She couldn't remember what the problem had been, but she would never forget how she had felt: like an outsider in her own family, chronically misunderstood.

"That's not how I remember it at all. If I recall correctly, she had gone to a lot of trouble to get you the exact cake you wanted. What was on it—those blue creatures?"

"Oh! Smurfs. Now I remember."

"That's right. Smurfs. You had said you wanted a Smurf birthday. Then when Dara started teasing you about watching a kids' program …."

"Okay. I remember. I was a pill. But Dara was being a brat little sister."

"Dara was being a *normal* little sister. But it wasn't Dara you were mad at."

Maggie closed her eyes, remembering. She'd been so mad. But what she remembered was being mad at her mother, not her sister. "Not really. I was mad at Mother."

"That's right. You were mad at your mother. For no reason—because Dara had teased you."

"Not for no reason. Look at Daddy. Look how tired he was."

Yaya gazed at the photo; her thin shoulders drooping under the weight of her own memories. "I tried. I did. But I just didn't know what to do. Some things, even a mother can't fix."

Maggie shrugged, uncomfortable. She was beginning to feel like she had as a child, when a look from Yaya could make her stomach churn. The pain in her grandmother's eyes, so visible now, so naked, was just as bad. Maggie looked away. She felt slightly ill.

"She tried. We all did. But you were always mad at her, Maggie. You still are. And you need to let it go."

"No, I'm not," Maggie protested, bewildered. "I'm not always mad. I can't help it if she's…" Her voice trailed off. Manners kicked in, and she couldn't bring herself to say *a bitch* out loud. Yaya gave her that gimlet eye again.

"You, my dear, have been carrying a grudge against your mother ever since Jamie died. For no reason. Your mother loves you, and you've been pushing her away for years."

Maggie blinked back tears, stunned. No one had ever said such a thing to her before. She jumped up from the bed and ran into the tiny bathroom, turning on the faucet in the sink. She looked around wildly for a glass—she needed a glass of water.

"You can't avoid it, Maggie." Yaya came to stand in the door of the bathroom. "We've been needing to have this conversation for a long time. You can't keep acting like your mother's the bad guy. She's not. You have no idea what she went through when Jamie died."

"I needed her!" The words burst out, and Maggie clapped a hand over her mouth, as if she could snatch them back. Tears were streaming down her face.

Yaya wrapped her thin arms around Maggie, and held her while she cried. "I know," she murmured soothingly. "But I can't always fix everything. I'm not always going to be here to run interference between you two. You have to meet her halfway, Maggie."

Maggie broke from her grandmother's arms and ran down the stairs and straight out the front door. By the time she got to her office on campus, she had brushed her hair and shoved the conversation to the back of her brain.

§§§

As another contraction starts, she replays the morning's expedition to her mother's house, and wonders what Yaya would tell her to do if she were here, whether Yaya will be well enough to help her figure out this mothering business. She wants—needs—an ally. She wonders if Katharine is ever going to show up, and cringes. This contraction is stronger, squeezing like iron bands around her belly, and pure pain inside, driving the memories out of her head.

Sam squats down in front of the rocker and begins to breathe audibly. He reaches out one hand to rub Maggie's belly, but she smacks it. "Don't… touch," she forces out between breaths. By the end of the contraction, she is whimpering.

"I can't." As it ends, a tear leaks out of each eye. She's so tired, and it hurts so much. She wants to collapse on the floor and never get up. She knows she needs to lie down; her strength is dwindling, and sitting upright is sapping her energy at this point. "Bed."

"Okay. I'll help. Tell me when."

"Now. Quick."

Sam helps her stand up, and backs her straight onto the bed. As she falls toward the pillows, he swings her feet up, and she rolls onto her side as the next contraction starts.

Tracy walks in during this one, and watches until it ends. Maggie wants to cry. She looks at Tracy when it ends.

"I can't do this anymore. I need help."

"Are you still drinking?"

"Some. Probably not enough." Sam answers for her, handing her the Gatorade box.

Tracy ponders Maggie for a second. "What about your birth plan?"

"I don't care," Maggie whispers. "I can't. It hurts too much." She's aware of Sam's look, but hasn't the strength to meet it.

"Okay. If you're sure. I'll go get Dr. Morgan to come check you. Are you sure?"

Maggie nods miserably as another contraction draws her into a ball.

After what seems an interminable time—three contractions worth—
Dr. Morgan bustles in. This time, Maggie lies limply on her side. She'd help
if she could, but she can't. Dr. Morgan pulls the sheet up to Maggie's waist,
and slides two gloved fingers into her vagina. Maggie can barely breathe
through the pain.

"You're getting there! You're seven centimeters. How're you feeling?"
Dr. Morgan sits down in the chair by Maggie's head and peers at her, as the
next contraction begins.

Maggie can hear Tracy saying something, but can't concentrate. She
manages to get out the word *drugs*, but that's it. She's not even sure if Dr.
Morgan heard her.

When Maggie's breathing has returned to normal, the doctor pulls out
a stethoscope and listens to the baby's heart. Maggie misses the doptone,
wondering what those little tubes of rubber and metal are reporting. Tracy
jots notes in a thick folder. Dr. Morgan pulls out the earpieces, and drapes
the stethoscope around her neck.

"The Gatorade helped. You need to keep drinking." She motions Sam
back into the crucial chair in Maggie's line of sight. "You're so close. You're
doing great. This is the worst part. I don't want to give you anything right
now, because I really think the baby's going to be born soon."

Maggie closes her eyes. The decision has been taken from her. Panic
and relief and fear and pain swirl together in the pit of her stomach. There
is nothing left to do but survive.

CHAPTER 16

Maggie looks at the door as it swings shut behind Dr. Morgan's cheerful back. She looks around for Sam, wanting explanation and reassurance. The wheels in her head are turning very slowly, and she can't quite figure out why Sam looks so alarmed. Something to do with the doctor…

She sniffles into the pillow and tries to remember how she's supposed to breathe. It's losing its effectiveness; she's beginning to feel like the waves of pain are crashing over her now, instead of swelling underneath and buoying her along. This one makes her want to cry. All that comes out is a whimper. She can hear her own mewling noises and somewhere in the back of her head she realizes that she sounds pathetic, but she can't help it. She can't help anything. She can't even lift her head. It's all she can do to keep breathing. Someone steps into her line of sight and bends down to her face.

"Maggie? Listen to my breathing. Come on, follow my pattern," Tracy urges.

She tries. It's hard. Her body is so loud. The pain seems to have a sound, a voice of its own. It's screaming at her, shouting its triumph as it possesses her body and rips it apart. She can't hear Tracy breathing. She can see her lips pursed, inches from Maggie's own mouth. Her lips won't come together like that, in that little round bow shape. They're peeled back over her teeth, permanently plastered in a death-grimace. The muscles that control her mouth seem to have locked; they aren't obeying her will. She manages a ragged breath, and feels it whistling out through her clenched teeth. Another breath, like inhaling against gravity. Her mouth still resists; it's so hard to get the air in.

"Doing great, Maggie. That's it. Keep breathing. In," Tracy breathes. "Out."

Maggie feels air on her face.

She can hear Tracy now, remembers the sequence. Inhale, exhale. Again. The pain rolls past, and she is depleted, limp against the pillow. Sam is hovering at the end of the bed, and she can see the creases between his eyebrows. He shouldn't frown, she thinks irrelevantly. He'll wrinkle.

But what comes out is a whisper. "I can't do this. I need help."

"Maggie, listen to me. Your baby's going to be born soon. Dr. Morgan doesn't want to give you anything now because you're going to start pushing soon, and we want you to really help your baby come out. But you've got to focus on the baby. You're doing great. Just think about meeting your baby—it won't be too much longer now." Maggie tries to process Tracy's words.

"No. I can't. I'm finished. I want to go home now." Tears threaten to spill over. Her voice feels quavery. "You don't understand. It hurts too much. I'm quitting."

She struggles to launch herself out of the bed. She'll just leave, that's all. It's only since they got to the hospital that she's been so miserable—clearly, this is the problem. She has no business here. She'll go home, and then she won't need help from anyone. Everything will be normal. Other women can do this baby stuff. Not her. She touches the amulet, still hanging from the cord around her neck, and hesitates. She looks down at it, at the soft curve of huge belly, the mouth stretched wide, the deep squat. For a second, she half-remembers the spark of connection that first flashed out at her from the amulet. But it's gone. The magic has left her. She's alone in this misery, and she can't even clearly remember why. She pushes all the way up to sitting, but the pain of another contraction pins her back to the pillow again. When it ends, she is really crying.

Sam is here now, in her face, making an annoying rattling sound. It's too loud. She tries to turn away but he catches her gaze, holding her there.

"Open up, Maggie. I've got ice. It'll cool you off. Come on, just a little bit."

She opens her mouth automatically. The ice is cold. She didn't expect that. It packs into her teeth, jarring her ears, chilling her eyes. The harsh splintering sound reverberates through the bones of her face. It's all too loud. She winces, and quickly swallows what's left.

"No more. Too cold. I need to leave now."

"Honey." Sam's voice is gentle and quiet. She can hear him if he's not too loud. She can see him, too. He's right there in front of her. "We can't leave. The baby's coming. It's almost here. You're doing great. Just a little while longer. You can hang in."

"I can't." She's crying again. "It hurts so much. Please make it stop. I want to go home." Now Sam's face is replaced by Tracy's. She, too, is holding a paper cup. It doesn't rattle.

"I've got some Gatorade for you Maggie. I'm going to raise the bed up a bit more so you can drink a little bit. I think your blood sugar is dropping again and that's why you're feeling so bad all of a sudden."

The top half of the bed slowly rises, causing Maggie's torso to pinch sideways. Another contraction leaves her gasping. She struggles to get comfortable, dizzy in this new upright position. Tracy holds a straw to her mouth, so she sips on it, like a child being helped by her mother. With her eyes closed, the reality of the hospital room begins to recede, and her little-girl self is home in bed, feverish, sipping at the drink held up to her lips. The details of the memory are fuzzy—hands, no face, a vague, miserable illness—but the warm sense of home is real. She gulps greedily at the sweetness, and can feel the track of the cool liquid down her throat. Something is annoying her feet, though, and she snatches them away from Sam's rubbing hands. She sucks on the straw until it gurgles dry. Irritability floods her, hot and prickly. She pushes away from the cup, rolling onto her right side, searching for a cool patch of sheet. It's all so damp and tangly. She pushes at the sticky strands of hair that are stuck to her face and neck. The ponytail has come loose and is in her way; she wishes someone would tie it back.

"Hair."

Sam comes around to the far side of the bed, bends to look at her face. "What did you say?"

She forms the word carefully. "Hair." Sam looks at her, and touches the top of her head. He doesn't seem to be understanding, so she tries again. Slowly, with great concentration, she says, "My hair is hot. Ponytail, please."

"Oh! Sure! One second." She's not sure why he's grinning, but he disappears from view. After a few seconds, she feels him pulling her hair back, away from her face. She lifts her head a tiny bit to help. Her neck is a bit cooler; this helps tremendously. When Sam puts the Gatorade straw to her lips again, she dutifully drinks again, but after the first few sips, it begins to cloy. She pushes the straw out of her mouth.

"Water, please."

Sam frowns at the half-full cup. "Drink the Gatorade, Maggie. It'll help you feel better."

Tracy chimes in. "It's already helping. You did much better on that last one. Water won't give you any calories or sugar. We need to get a steady stream going in so that you'll have some energy for pushing. It won't be long now. That Gatorade will help you meet your baby sooner."

Maggie shakes her head doubtfully, but takes one more sip from the proffered straw. It's too much. A wave of heat rolls over her and she can feel her face flush. Her stomach roils and objects. She pushes the cup away. It's too much—she wants to die. This is more misery than she can handle. The insides of her eyelids are black; her normal senses have shut down. She is awash in this dark void of pain and sick and misery. She's burning up, drenched with sweat, dragged back, again, into a childhood illness, remembering the agony of waiting to be sick. Her stomach lurches and heaves. Instinctively, she leans up on one elbow. A threatening belch rolls out of her throat, and spit gathers in her mouth. She cracks open one eye, moaning, "Help." Somewhere, in the back of her mind, her six-year-old self is waiting for her Mommy to help her get to the toilet, waiting for Katharine to rub her back and make everything better.

Relief washes over her when a small pink bowl appears on the bed in front of her, and the relief releases the floodgates. A contraction grips her, and her stomach rejects the Gatorade entirely. The hot, acrid liquid spews into the bowl, splashing onto Maggie's chest, dripping down her chin, spotting the tumbled sheets. She sees it, but doesn't comprehend. It's all she can do to keep from flopping her head down into the bowl. She needs someone to hold her up, to smooth her hair back and mop her brow. She wants to lean into her mother and be taken care of. Tears mingle with snot and sweat as she heaves again, and again. Her now-empty stomach retches. She eases slowly back down onto the bed, and the pink bowl is whisked away. Someone dabs at her with a damp cloth; it's cold. A chill wracks her body, and she shakes. It passes, leaving her with that strange, empty clarity that often follows necessary vomiting.

"Oh, my God."

"You're fine. It happens." Tracy's voice, here and now, is suddenly the greatest comfort Maggie has ever heard. Tracy pats her forehead with the cool cloth again, and lifts up the ponytail to rub the back of her neck.

"No more Gatorade, please."

Tracy laughs. "No. It doesn't seem to agree with you. Maybe we'll stick with ice chips. They shouldn't cause any problems. But you let me know if you need that basin again."

"Where's Sam?" Maggie is still facing the window, and cranes her head to see the room behind her shoulder.

"Here I am." He sounds odd, but moves into view at the end of the bed. "Are you all right?"

"No," Maggie responds immediately.

Tracy laughs again. "Neither's Sam. He was looking a little green there for a minute. I thought I was going to have to clean both of you up."

"I wasn't counting on that bit. Nobody told me she might throw up."

It doesn't occur to Maggie to look amused. "Me, either."

Sam rubs her foot ruefully. She meets his gaze, but her eyes are flat and empty. She closes them in defense against the next wave of pain. When she opens them, moaning again, certain that she is trapped in an infinite loop of agony, Tracy is still there in front of her.

"Maggie, we're going to roll you over so you can get up on all fours. That'll help the baby drop down a little more."

"I can't." Maggie's protest is as weak as she is. The idea of supporting herself on her arms and legs is preposterous. But she can't fight Sam and Tracy as they flatten the bed and push her over onto her stomach. Her legs won't hold her up, so she rests on her heels, folded forward over her belly. She can see the humor in this, but she can't express it. Yoga, she thinks faintly, and collapses forward, ungainly, naked, covered with God-only-knows-what bodily fluids. She feels like she's balancing on a gigantic beach ball. Oddly, there is some sort of relief in this position. Her back relaxes—she hadn't realized how much it hurt.

The next contraction begins differently, down low in the very front of her belly, above her pubic bone. But, like the others, it moves rapidly down and down and further inside her. She can't breathe like this. She feels her own exhalations in her face, bouncing off the mattress. She grinds her forehead into the bed, trying to escape. This one is so much more intense. Breath-taking. It leaves her gasping. "Can't…breathe."

Tracy bends down to peer at Maggie's face.

"What's wrong? Why can't you breathe?"

Maggie heaves her chest upward to make space for her lungs. "I'm too stuck down here like this. There's no room. The bed's in my face."

Tracy frowns at her. Maggie's not sure if she's made herself clear.

"I need more space."

"Hmm, I have an idea. Sam, you handle the next one. I'll be back in a minute." She rushes out the door before they can stop her.

Sam comes around to the head of the bed and stoops down to look at Maggie. She can see the concern on his face. She's not sure if it's for her, or for himself, responsible now. He smoothes the hair back from her forehead. "Shall I pull the sheet up over you? Your ass is kind of hanging out."

Maggie smiles a bit. She manages a whisper, "Whoop-de-doo." They work together through several contractions, Maggie feeling as if she's hanging on by a thread. By the third one, though, Sam has regained his earlier confidence, and his help buoys her up just enough. She rides over several more before Tracy bursts into the room, preceded by a huge purple rubber ball. Maggie and Sam both look dubiously at it. Maggie starts a question but is interrupted by a contraction. It ends, leaving her once again feeling oxygen-deprived.

"It'll help open up her chest. She'll have more room to breathe, and gravity will help the baby drop faster. All we have to do is get her up onto it."

She hears Sam snort. He leans down and looks at her. "Did you hear that Maggie? We're going to pull you up and let you flop over the ball. That might feel better."

Maggie's neck is contorted on the bed so that she is lying on her left ear, unable to move her head. Sam is standing by the top of her head, and she has to roll her eyes up to look at him over raised eyebrows. Not exactly the glare she intends. She tries very hard to make her eyes look daggers, but suspects that she looks merely deranged.

"All right Maggie. I'm going to lift you up, and Sam's going to slide the ball under you. Just lean into it and let your whole weight rest on it."

Tracy slides her hands under Maggie's armpits and levers her up onto her knees. Sam puts the ball onto the bed in front of her, and she relaxes onto it, amazed at the relief. Her spine stretches long again, and she breathes deeply, resting for a brief, blissful moment. She can feel the ball sticking to her breasts, but she doesn't care. She rests her face against it, smelling the rubbery gymnasium smell. This next contraction once again shifts the locus of intensity. It's all inside now. She has lost all awareness of the irrelevant muscles she once thought of as her abdominals. Her stomach no longer has anything to do with this.

Sam is kneeling on the bed, facing her. He breathes her through this one, holding both of her hands, locking her in his gaze. She can't escape, but as long as she stays there, the pain can't completely engulf her. As long as Sam holds her in that gaze, she is still Maggie. And as long as she can hang on to her self, she can remain separate from the pain. It is trying to overwhelm her defenses, to consume her, but Sam won't let it.

He feeds her ice chips, one at a time, between contractions. Some she sucks on, letting them melt into cool puddles under her tongue. Others she crunches, feeling her teeth squeak on the hard ice as it yields, disintegrating, changing in an instant from a hard, frigid lump to a few drops of water trickling down her hot throat. She is managing, now. Sam is there with her, anchoring her in time and space, keeping her from falling into the whirlpool of pain. They work together; he follows her body's rhythm, she follows the sound of his voice. He coaxes her through each wave: "All right. It's starting again. Look at me, Maggie. Listen to my voice. You're doing great. Keep breathing. Good job. That's right. Breathe like this. In… and…out. That's my girl. Hang in. It's about to peak. There you go. That's the worst of it. I'm so proud of you. You're doing a fantastic job. Keep breathing. Good work. It's coming down now. Not much longer. Hang in—this one's almost done. You're doing great. There you go—it's over." And at the end of each contraction, as she lies panting, draped over the ball, she opens glazed and exhausted eyes, and he tells her, "I love you." The patter keeps her going. Her energy is waning, but Sam's voice buoys her, holds her up, carries her along.

She gives herself over into Sam's safekeeping, knowing that she can't even survive this, let alone carry it off gracefully, by herself. She struggles against it. She has never been in the habit of abdicating control but now she finds she has to let go of herself in a way that she hasn't since she was a child. Sometimes, when she was very young, her mother could make her feel cared for and safe, as if she could roll over and sleep without a care or concern in the world. She wishes she were here now, but she's not. Nor is Yaya. Vigilance is too hard to maintain by herself, but she has Sam. He is, after all, the father of the child. This thought flits through her tired brain during a short moment of respite, and she tries to grin at Sam. He's mopping her face with a damp cloth.

"What?" He pauses mid-wipe.

"I was… I just thought about it. This is your baby too."

She's not sure if the look on his face is horror or hilarity. He snorts. "Well, I should hope so. This is a fine time to tell me if it's not!" He laughs.

Tracy, who has been writing in Maggie's chart, looks up. "I read a statistic somewhere that something like 85 percent of American men wonder at some point during the pregnancy if they might actually not be the father," she says.

Maggie manages to look aghast at this pronouncement. Sam chuckles.

"Well, it is kind of questionable, you know," he says.

Maggie quirks her eyebrows at him; facial expressions are beginning to stand in for articulation at this point.

"The whole scenario. It puts men in an untenable position. We have no real way of proving whether the baby is our own, or some interloper's. Unacceptable, really."

Maggie and Tracy both turn appalled looks on him. Then everything stops—chatting, trains of thought, time itself, while Sam breathes his wife, the mother of his child, through another contraction. It ends, and Tracy glances at the clock on the wall, jots the time on the chart.

"It's a matter of faith," Tracy points out, picking up the conversation where it left off. "You really ought to trust the person you're married to, or the person you're having a child with."

"Ought to, but who really does?"

Maggie glares at him. "Cynic," she whispers.

He chuckles, and wipes her face again. "No news there."

"You didn't really wonder, did you?" she asks.

He looks at her for two beats. "No. Not in any real way. I guess maybe it's normal to have the thought cross your mind for a second, but no. Theoretical possibility and real potential are two completely different things." He reaches over, behind the ball, to the curve of her belly. He touches the taut skin, grazes it with his fingertips. He stretches out his hand, pressing the palm flat against his child, still sheltered in her body. Maggie looks at him, and sees that his smile is coming from somewhere back behind his eyes. His face looks as if it is lit from within. She could rest and be safe in that smile.

"That's what I meant," she says.

The next contraction breaks the moment. By the end, Maggie is feeling sick again. Her head droops on the ball. "Basin," she whispers. Sam looks at her, then at Tracy. They're puzzled. Maggie wobbles upright, and looks around for the small pink plastic basin she used earlier. She spots it on the tray table, and points. Words are too risky. Tracy grabs it and holds it out in the nick of time. Now there's absolutely nothing left in Maggie's stomach. She heaves, sagging over the ball. Somewhere in the back of her brain she registers the fact that Sam is no longer sitting on the end of the bed, but she looks no further. Her world has narrowed suddenly to that basin under her nose.

The storm passes, leaving her trembling. She pushes the ball out from under her, and lies heavily on the bed. Relief washes down the backs of her thighs; she hadn't realized how tired her legs were.

"Oh, God. Here it comes again," she pants. "I can't…get a break." Her body clenches involuntarily over her belly as the pain of the contraction ripples outward from her center. This one is harder. She's alone, lost in the middle of it. The vomiting has knocked her off balance, and now the pain pounces on her, catching her vulnerable. No steady build of intensity this time; the pain crashes over her all at once. She grinds her teeth and strains her neck, trying to burrow into the bed itself to escape. She can't breathe. She's suffocating. She whimpers. This one doesn't feel right–there's no flow, no rhythm. Her breath comes in jerks and gasps. She can feel her eyes rolling around in her head, but sees only black. There is nothing left. The world has disappeared, leaving her alone in this hell.

When the pain finally recedes, Tracy is there, in front of her, calling her back.

"Maggie."

She opens her eyes, and nods that she hears and understands.

"After the next one, in the next break, I want you to try and empty your bladder one more time. You want to keep it empty so it doesn't block your baby's head."

Maggie tries to wrap her mind around this. She looks uncomprehending at Tracy.

"I don't…I…no. I can't." Her voice fades out.

"Yes you can." Tracy is firm. "Sam and I will help you. I have a bedpan for you and we'll get you up onto it."

"Sam?"

"I'm right here, sweetheart."

Tracy snickers. "He's fine until you throw up. He's not so good with that."

"It hurts too much. I don't want it any more. It's not worth it. Nothing is worth this." Everything Maggie has ever thought or felt or believed is summed up in that feeble whisper. It all boils down to this moment, this truth. She can't go on.

"I know honey. You're doing great, though."

She looks at Sam. She's sure it's all there in her eyes. But he has missed the point entirely, she realizes. She closes them.

When the next one ends, they haul her upright and Tracy slips a pink plastic basin under her, this one shaped like a toilet seat. Sam fiddles with the buttons on the side of the bed until the top half rises up to support her back. The phrase "perched on her throne" wanders through her mind. She would smile at the irony, but she's too miserable. The hard plastic of the basin is difficult to sit on, even though it's designed for precisely this purpose. The act of balancing on this improvised toilet seat snatches at her muscles in an uncomfortable way. She strains to force out some urine, but her bladder is trapped behind the baby's head, and she can't find release.

She wobbles, and clutches at the bedrails for support. Her lungs have trouble finding room to expand when she's hunched over like this. She can see a dark smear on the inside of her left thigh and she wonders hazily what it is. For a brief second she wonders what she must look like: stark naked, legs akimbo, gigantic belly rising up over the humiliating bedpan. The thought passes as she sways through the next contraction, trapped upright. Her whole body yearns downward. She can barely hold herself up. Her head droops lower and lower, dangling at the end of her neck as she curls in on herself against the battering. Her chin is hard against her chest. Her arms have been drained of their strength.

It ends, and she lifts her head to take a deeper breath. She realizes that Sam and Tracy are holding her shoulders, keeping her from toppling forward. With eyes still closed, panting slightly, she leans back against the bed, and tries to lift her belly up off of her bladder one last time. No luck. The baby squirms at the pressure, and she grimaces.

"Whoa! That was bizarre! Did you see that?" Sam asks. He looks both fascinated and horrified by the visible undulations of Maggie's abdomen. She glares sideways at him.

Tracy peers between Maggie's legs into the basin. "Wow. That's pretty cool. Most babies don't really move much this far along in labor. This one must not like being wiggled. Nothing?"

Maggie shakes her head. "No. I need to get down."

Sam struggles to lift under her armpits, while Tracy pulls the pan out from under her, the plastic dragging friction across tender skin. She may not have peed, but she can tell that she is leaking fluids. The sheets are uncomfortably damp, but the thought of what might be flowing out of her is too frightening to contemplate, so she sinks back into her haze of misery. The top of the bed slowly rumbles back down to its horizontal position, and she curls up with relief into a fetal ball on her side.

Chapter 17

A few minutes later, someone knocks on the door, startling Maggie. Sam, who has once again been pacing her breathing, looks perplexed. As Tracy goes to open the door, Maggie is relieved when he pulls the sheet up over her exposed body. Now she feels like one of those beached whales she has seen on the news, a giant, inert bulk covered with a tarp as crowds of people struggle to push it back out to sea.

A delivery woman billows in, her loud voice a shock in the dim quiet of the room. Her face peers out from a mass of flowers. Maggie has never seen so many shades of pink in one arrangement. They are the decadent stargazers that she loves and their exotic scent fills the room immediately. And roses—innocent pink sweetheart buds, alongside some blowsy cabbage roses. They're all so extravagant! With another of those roller-coaster emotional swings, she smiles with contentment. Sam is the center of her universe. She looks at him—so many? But he looks as surprised as she feels. The screen of flowers parts, and the young woman appears, beaming through her lush load.

"Aren't they gorgeous? This whole hospital smells like lilies now. You have some dedicated admirers."

Maggie puzzles over this then realizes that there are two distinct vases of flowers—one is lilies, the other a multitude of pink roses. But when the next contraction releases her, the young woman has disappeared, and she has forgotten the mystery. Tracy is chuckling.

"Well, you've convinced that one to use birth control. She's new. I've never seen her on this floor before. She's probably going to refuse to come back. She looked horrified when you started moaning. Couldn't get out of here fast enough."

One corner of Maggie's mouth lifts slightly, as much of a smile as she can manage.

"Who are they from?"

Sam harrumphs. "One is from me, the other is from Ben. I've been upstaged by your father."

"Oh! I can't believe he did that." Maggie is touched. She squeezes back the tears that suddenly blur her vision, and sniffs a little. She has avoided thinking of her father all afternoon—it would only make her miss him more—but now her emotions do another disconcerting nosedive. She would feel so much better, so much *safer*, if he were here, down the hall in the comfortable family waiting room, or maybe sitting in the hall, right outside the door, in one of those plastic chairs she saw stacked up in an alcove when she came in. He could check on her every now and again, pop his head in, make sure she's doing all right. That would help so much. The tears leak out a little, and she sniffs harder, trying to stop them. Someone hands her a tissue; she looks up. Sam is looking at her. She can see a struggle going on behind his eyes. He rubs her hand.

"Do you want to call him? I might be able to make my calling card work here in the room."

"No, I don't suppose so. What time is it there?"

"Umm—three a.m., I think. On second thought, maybe you shouldn't call right now."

"Hah. I guess not. Besides, I'd just cry. Not very useful." She imagines what that would be like: Ben bolting awake at the shrill of the telephone— he's a light sleeper; when she was a small child, her parents always came running together when she called out in the night, frightened by a bad dream—then picking up the receiver, but hearing only her snorty, wet, crying sounds. No good for anyone.

It's not till the next contraction passes that she realizes her gaffe.

"Oh! Sweetheart—I forgot to say thank you."

Sam's smile is comfortable. "That's okay. I would've chosen to have mine come first, but all together, they're pretty impressive, aren't they?"

"They're beautiful. I love that smell so much."

"Well, I'm about to asphyxiate over here," Tracy says from across the room.

Sam ignores her. Maggie can see that he's working hard to say this, and it comes out a little rushed. "I know. I figure there'll be plenty more after the baby comes, so I wanted some that were just for you…. That's why the lilies."

This statement throws Maggie for a second. Her husband loves her, and has sent her a vase of her favorite flowers. It seems so ordinary, but at the same time like a scene from a life she might have lived, once upon a time, but barely remembers now. She looks at the hothouse stargazers. Pale pink petals, edged with pristine white, curve outward, away from the deep pink throat of each bloom. The pistil and stamens stand delicate and erect, but shorn—the anthers, with their rust-stained pollen, have been fastidiously snipped. The opulent fragrance fills the room.

Maggie inhales deeply, half-remembering a warm summer night, a cool breeze playing across her bare skin, the luxury of long, slow, midnight lovemaking. Stargazer lilies smell like sex, or maybe passion, which is different, perhaps, she thinks. But the thought vanishes as quickly as it appeared, and all she can do is squeeze Sam's hand before she has to focus again on riding the wave of the next contraction.

He is there with her, whispering in her ear, reminding her to breathe, but she is so overwhelmed by her body's out-of-control misery that she has lost sight of the end goal—the baby. She spent so much of the pregnancy trying to visualize the actual person inside her, but the tenuous bond she felt seems to have dissolved. She tries to summon up that sense of human connection, starting with the simple visual image of a baby curled inside her. She has done this often in the last nine months. It has become a ritual. But now it isn't working.

She tries to see the details in her mind's eye—tiny fingernails, eyebrows, the slope of small shoulders, the curve of fragile skull under soft, thin skin. No luck. When she looks at her belly, trying to conjure the images, all she sees is the rigid peak of fundus as the contraction rolls over her. When it ends, the impulse to reach out to her child has passed. She has lost her bearings, can't remember what shore she's supposed to be heading for. It doesn't matter anyway.

The door opens again and, as if summoned by Maggie's fleeting thought of childhood, Dara is peering into the room.

"Dara!" Maggie plucks at the sheet, aware of her nakedness, but unable to really care. As if catching her feeble thought, Sam reaches over her and pulls the sheet up to cover her swollen breasts. Maggie sees shock flit across Dara's face before she can force herself to smile.

"How're you doing, big sis?" Her voice is gentle, concerned. She glances behind her, then comes to the edge of the bed. "Can I do anything? What do you need?"

"To go home."

Dara looks up at Sam, eyes wide. Something in her face is not quite right.

"Maggie's doing great. She was at seven centimeters last time Dr. Morgan was here. She's getting there."

As if to disprove Sam's point, Maggie moans, calling Sam's attention back to the task at hand. When it ends, Dara edges back to the door, looking strained.

"Wait—did you bring Yaya?"

"Not exactly. I brought Mom."

Maggie looks toward the door, speechless. Her mother is hovering there, not stepping fully into the room. No one moves; for a split second Maggie feels like she can't breathe. Her field of vision has narrowed to the edges of the bed, so she hadn't registered her mother's presence. Time is beginning to blur, too, and Dara's earlier visit now seems like another lifetime ago. She is coming unmoored.

"Hello, Mother," Maggie finally says, unable to bear the awkwardness.

"Hello, Maggie. Sam." Katharine comes to the edge of the bed and surveys Maggie, a frown wrinkling her forehead. Dara, wary and pale, pulls a hard plastic chair in from the hallway and sits down by the door.

"No baby yet, obviously. How are you feeling?"

"Oh," Maggie tries to force some energy into her voice. "I'm getting tired. But I think it's moving along."

Katharine sniffs, then turns slowly, taking in every detail of the disheveled room. Maggie watches her mother's back, looking for some clue to Katharine's mood, finding none in the trim, straight back, the confident set of her head. Her suit looks fresh and clean; Maggie notes that it isn't even particularly wrinkled in the back, and is suddenly conscious of her own nakedness, of the mess in the room. Her suitcase in the corner, contents spilling out where Sam was rummaging for her hair band, newspapers piled on the nightstand, half-empty cups littering every available surface. Katharine turns to look at her, one eyebrow cocked inquisitively.

"Nice room. Planning on staying a while?"

Ah. The sarcastic mood. Maggie knows better than to be bothered by this one. She can ignore the barbs if they get too sharp. Katharine is generally harmless when she's like this—it's what passes for jovial in the Lambert world. At least she's not feeling martyred, Maggie thinks. Sam steps into the breach.

"What? Don't you like what I've done with the place?"

Katharine shrugs at him and drops her purse to the floor next to the door. Maggie wonders if she's already planning her escape. The silence in the room careens from comfortable to tense.

Maggie has to ask; she can't help it. "Did you go over there, Dara? Did you try?"

Katharine looks Maggie directly in the eyes for the first time since she had entered the room. Maggie tries to read her mother's face. Like Dara, she doesn't look quite right, as if she's off-balance somehow.

"Mother wasn't up to it. I'm here."

"Thank you." But before she can catch herself, the words slip out. "But I wish you'd brought Yaya too."

Maggie, between contractions, has a brief, bizarre sense of visual clarity—details in the room jump out at her. The glove one of Melissa's children left under the chair, the large box of sanitary pads on the counter next to the bathroom door, the clear plastic stake Sam left poking up out of the flowers when he handed her the card from her father. But she has to strain to catch Sam's and Katharine's words. She hears them as if coming to her through ocean water—far away, but startlingly clear.

"… Of course."

"Do you want me to try …"

"No, she'll be fine—"

Something feels wrong. The silence is suffocating. Dara and Sam are looking at her, expectant. Katharine has moved over to the window. Maggie looks from Sam to Dara.

"What? What's wrong?"

Dara looks uncomfortable. "Nothing, honey. Nothing's wrong." She widens her eyes, and looks pointedly at Katharine's stiff back. Maggie frowns, perplexed.

"What? I don't understand."

The next contraction slams into her. It builds, tightening first across her abdomen, then settling deep inside, pulling and stretching her insides beyond their limits. Even as the pain drives out all conscious thought, her heart settles on that image, of her mother's narrow shoulders, still and tense at the edge of the room.

The contraction subsides, leaving her gasping and flattened. She can't remember what was gnawing at her. Dara is standing by the bed, smoothing damp strands of hair back from her forehead. She nods again in Katharine's direction. Maggie frowns.

"Did you make her come?"

"No! Of course not!"

"I know you two are whispering," their mother says, without looking around. Maggie blushes.

Dara mouths words at her—"Yaya really wasn't up to it; maybe tomorrow. But Mom really did want to come, I promise."

Maggie wants to ask something else, but the next contraction drives the thought from her mind. When it ends, Sam has moved back into his chair at the head of the bed. Dara is gone. Maggie can hear water running in the bathroom. Katharine is still standing by the door, but appears to have aged ten years in the last five minutes. Her shoulders droop, and her face is pale under makeup that needs a touch-up.

"If it makes you feel any better, I went to see your grandmother before I came over here. I wanted to make sure she understood. That you're in labor. I thought—well, I knew she'd want to know."

"How is she?" Maggie whispers, not trusting her voice.

"Feeble, to tell you the truth."

"Was she…what did she say?"

Katharine comes to stand at the end of the bed. Sadness is etched on her face, deepening the lines that Maggie realizes have been there all along. She gives her head a tiny shake. "Not much, really. She had just woken up from her nap. That's never a great time to try and talk to her."

"Oh. I knew that."

"Of course you do." Katharine dabs at her eyes with a shred of tissue, until Sam grabs the box from the nightstand. He doles out handfuls to each of them, then takes one for himself. Maggie is confused, not sure why they all seem teary.

"I don't understand. I just talked to her a little while ago. She was fine."

"Maggie, honey," Sam interrupts. "You know that's not true. She was totally out of it."

"No! She wanted to be here. She wanted to come meet the baby. She did—I know she did." Maggie trails off, weeping.

Katharine fusses with her handful of tissues, finally laying them out in a tidy stack on the end of the bed, and folding them over and over until she has a small square. She looks around the room, eyes blank, and stuffs the square in her pocket. She sways slightly; Sam grabs her arm and backs her into a chair. She seems to deflate into it. Maggie hears the puff of her exhale in the silent room. Maggie looks at her mother, crumpled, dimin-ished, and the world seems to tip on its axis. She swallows back another wave of nausea. The pain begins again, and she can't remember what it's for, why she's here. It doesn't matter. There's no point. She surrenders to it, whimpering. The churning, angry surge grabs her, flings her to the bottom, and holds her there, trapped and drowning.

As she comes back to awareness, she realizes she's moaning, and catches a breath to stop the sound. Dara edges out of the bathroom, her cheeks damp, and scans their faces, stopping at Maggie's. She shrugs, helpless.

"Are you positive I can't do anything? You just look so … trashed."

Maggie shakes her head quickly, unable to speak. Dara comes over and kisses the top of her head.

Sam steps in.

"There's nothing, Dara, but thanks. Maggie's doing great. The nurse'll probably be back in a few minutes to check on her."

"Well, in that case—I don't really need to be here for that, do I?" She looks worried.

"Definitely not." Maggie tries to smile, but her chin wobbles. Dara turns toward the door.

"Then I'm going to go wait in the hall. Sam, you holler if I can help at all. Mom, don't you want to come sit with me?"

Katharine moves as if to push up from her chair, then stops and looks at Maggie. The world tips a little more. The barriers are gone. There's nothing between them now, no buffer, and there's nothing—no one—beyond Katharine. She's the end of the line.

"No," Katharine says in a strained voice. She is perched on the edge of the chair now, as if she might bolt at any moment. "I think I'll stay."

Dara nods slowly, then slips out the door.

Chapter 18

Maggie, wary, watches her mother, now standing by the door. Katharine's eyes roam the room; she looks poised for flight, in spite of what she said to Dara. The air is heavy with tension. She doesn't know what to say, how to bridge the divide. She's not even sure she wants to.

She inhales sharply as another contraction begins. Sam sits back down in the chair next to her head, easing her through the pain, guiding her to the back side of the contraction. When it ends, Katharine is standing at the end of the bed again. Maggie plucks at the sheet, pulling it over her arms, trying to shield herself from her mother's sharp eyes. That old, familiar desperation twists through her: she has no idea what her mother wants from her. She grips Sam's hand, anchoring herself here and now.

Katharine reaches out one hand and touches Maggie's foot. Maggie snatches her foot away instinctively. Her mother, almost as if she expected the reaction, reaches out again, tracing the outline of her toes through the sheet.

Maggie can't meet her eyes, but she nods, and feels the pressure increase. When the next contraction begins, Katharine stops rubbing, waiting for the pain to pass. When it does, she begins to massage the foot in earnest, beginning at the heel, working up through the arches, pausing to push the top sheet up past Maggie's ankle, again to let a contraction pass, although this time she doesn't take her hand away, but holds Maggie's foot, still and firm. Maggie's mind has ground to a halt—this is unprecedented. Conflicting instincts battle in her body. She wants to let go, to relax into her mother's touch, but she can't. She has to hold herself back, maintain control, because that's what she does. That's what she has always done.

Katharine doesn't often touch her daughters. Maggie knows that this is an effort for her mother. No one speaks. The only sound is breathing, controlled, focused during the contractions, ragged panting in between. Katharine and Sam are both breathing with her, carrying her over the waves with a unified rhythm. A line from Whitman flits through her brain, the bit about "out of the cradle, endlessly rocking." That's what she feels like—she has entered a state of eternal damnation, consisting of peaks of pain punctuated by valleys of slightly less pain.

But even on the peaks, Katharine holds on to her foot, never letting go. Maggie is conscious of the connection, of her mother's touch, even through the dark heat of the pain that seems to remove her from her thinking self altogether. And in the moments of respite, when the pain recedes, the massage is exquisite. Relief flows up her calves, all the way up to her thighs.

"Thank you," Maggie whispers.

Katharine merely nods. She perches on the end of the bed, lifting one foot into her lap. Maggie relaxes into her mother, letting go of the full weight of her leg.

Her mind is beginning to turn strange circles around itself. She tries to get back to that snippet of poetry; she likes its rhythm. But it nags at her, running around and around in her brain, like a song that gets stuck. It's frustrating when she can't breathe. She wants to rock, to feel the momentum of her body swaying back and forth, like a pendulum, moving effortlessly of its own accord, but doesn't seem to be able to. The thought fills her mind. She hangs onto the image—not even an image, really, more of an inarticulate concept banging around in her head. It moves of its own accord, powered from within, without volition. Somewhere in the back of her mind, she knows her leg is splayed across her mother. She can feel it rubbing against the smooth wool of Katharine's pants, jabbing her soft stomach, but she can't help it. This is where she is, and it's where Katharine is, and she can't change anything.

Maggie's forehead pushes forward, grinding her face into the pillow. And again. And again. She can't breathe, she can't stop. The tendons in her neck strain and twist. A noise escapes her throat as she begins to fall down the back side of the pain. Not a grunt, not a whimper. Just sound in its rawest form.

When Maggie opens her eyes, Katharine resumes the deep, steady, methodical massage, this time on the other foot. Maggie blinks to clear her vision, and the empty plastic baby holder across the room jumps out at her. It looks hard and clinical. It is made of clear plastic, on wheels with a small cabinet built underneath the waist-high tray lined with tiny white cotton blankets. It is trim and neat and medicinal. The word *cradle* doesn't seem applicable.

"What is that called?" She waits for Sam's answer, but he looks utterly perplexed, peering into her face.

"Pardon?"

She uncurls one finger from the fist clenched against her breast, and points. He twists to look, and still seems confused.

"Which, sweetie?" Sam is trying to understand. Katharine keeps rubbing, never breaking the pattern.

"That. The cart."

He looks again. "The cart for the baby? I'm not sure. Does it matter?"

"I can't remember…." She trails off, frustrated. Definitely not cradle, but what could it be? "Endlessly rocking." Her voice is small, wandering.

Sam looks confused again. She's not sure which of her thoughts are coming out of her mouth, and which are staying in her brain, flying around in repetitive circles, tormenting her. It's too hard to figure out. She can't see why Sam looks so puzzled. It's wrong if it won't rock. Why is that? Something about that cradle….

When the next contraction backs off, Tracy is there.

"Maggie, Dr. Morgan called. She wants me to check and see how far along you are." She is kneeling by the head of the bed, speaking slowly, peering into Maggie's face. "I'm going to check on the baby, as well."

This is too many thoughts all at once. Maggie can't process them. The word *baby* catches her attention, so she grabs at it as it floats by. She's back to where she was earlier, trying to see the baby in her mind's eye. Tracy puts the doptone against her stomach, and the steady, murky sound of the baby's heart beats into the room. They all listen for a moment, while Tracy looks at her watch, counting, Maggie supposes.

"I want …." she begins, in a whisper, but the impulse dies. She sees an image of Yaya, impossibly brittle, being helped into her bed at the nursing home. She swallows against the lump in her throat, but it still hurts. Her heart feels ragged in her chest; it's hard to breathe. A tiny bright pinprick of sadness is beginning to crystallize deep inside her, and she boxes it, then walls it off out of sight.

Tracy looks up from her watch. "What did she say?"

"Nothing." Sam jumps in, glancing at Maggie. "Is everything okay?"

Tracy nods, looking satisfied, and pockets the little handheld monitor, the miracle machine that can hear the not-yet.

"Sounds good. I was worried you might be dehydrating again, given the vomiting."

Maggie's stomach lurches a bit at this memory.

"Were you vomiting?" There is a hint of something in Katharine's voice; Maggie's sure it's not amusement. How could nausea possibly be amusing?

"A bit," Sam confirms. "The baby's heartbeat was a little slow earlier, so she drank some Gatorade, to be sure she wasn't getting dehydrated, and it all came right back up again. So we switched to ice chips, and that seems to be working fine."

As if to prove it, he fishes the last chip out of the cup and puts it in Maggie's mouth. It melts almost immediately. Sam dumps the water out of the cup and goes to the door, looking for Dara.

"Would you mind refilling this? You can go to the nurse's station and ask."

Dara sticks her head in the room but Sam has already turned, distracted. Maggie can see her sister hesitating by the door; she seems very far away. She wants to reach out, to ask her to stay, to stand with her in their old habit of defense against Katharine, but the words seem flat before she can speak them. She settles in, trying not to panic, as another contraction takes over both her body and her mind.

Tracy takes advantage of the next pause between contractions to check Maggie's cervix. Maggie knows she is trying to be gentle, but even between contractions she is in pain. Tracy's fingers invade and prod. Katharine has moved to the head of the bed, standing by Sam. Maggie is aware of the silence in the room. She hears herself grunt, involuntarily, then the sharp intake of her breath as Tracy finds her cervix, gauging how wide it has stretched.

She burrows into the pillow, hiding from the web of emotions that she can see in her mother's eyes. She would like to be somewhere else, anywhere else, away from those eyes. She doesn't know how to interpret what she sees there—pity, fear, embarrassment, horror—what else? Nothing makes much sense at this point; better to ignore it all. She is surprised to find herself still so bothered by the indignity of the exam. She had thought she was beyond modesty this late in the game. She hears the snap and rustle of latex as Tracy pulls off her gloves and throws them away.

"You're not quite there yet, but you're getting really close. I know it's intense. Hang in. You're going to make it."

All of these statements strike Maggie as unhelpful. It's not as if she has a choice at this point. If she thought she could quit, she'd have done so several hours ago. And where exactly is the *there* that she's getting close to? Tracy makes it sound as if she's on some sort of a quest. An image of maternity armor pops into her head and strikes her as funny. She would laugh, but that would take energy that she no longer has. The urge dissipates.

Tracy is still talking, but Maggie has stopped listening. The pain closes over her head, taking her down with it, but no one notices. She can't stay on top, so she lets it roll right over her. Her eyes are closed, but there is no dancing screen of images playing in her head. All is black. She sees nothing, hears nothing. The murmur of voices and the hum of computerized equipment in the room fade away. Maggie is somewhere else; she has gone inside. She cannot escape, so she has gone to meet the demon head-on, let it take her and devour her.

Sam's voice drags her back into her senses. "Maggie? Come on, you can breathe through it. Listen to me."

She peeks out at him, opening her eyes only enough to avoid having to speak. The breathing seems sort of pointless at this moment, as the contraction wanes. As she comes back to herself a bit, she realizes that Katharine is back at her feet. Someone has mercifully pulled the sheet over the middle part of her body, but her feet jut out at the end of the bed, where her mother is once again kneading and pulling. Tracy is standing next to Sam, hands on her hips, watching.

"Maggie. You're doing great. Your baby's doing great. When I checked you, I could feel the top of the head. It won't be too much longer. But I know it's intense now. You need to let Sam help you. Try and stay with him."

Maggie looks at Tracy, forcing her eyes to focus. When they do, she stares hard at the nurse. She heard all those words, but they didn't make much sense. She can't get her brain to process all that. She knows she should; the best she can do is memorize Tracy's frank brown eyes. They're wide, naked, ringed with thick, dark lashes. She has a freckle just past the corner of her left eye, toward the temple. It's tiny, but it animates her face, wiggling and dancing when a smile crinkles the lines around the edges of her eyes. Right now she looks earnest, and a bit cloudy. She is peering into Maggie's face, pulling her back into her body.

"I can't." It comes out as a whisper. It's the most she can manage.

"Yes, you can. You are. All you have to do is let your cervix open up so your baby can come out. That's all you're doing—making room for the baby to come out."

"Baby." This word jumps out at Maggie again, lodges in her mind.

"Yes. That's it. Your baby. Think about your baby coming out. Think about holding it. Here," she takes Maggie's hand and puts it on her belly, down low, right above her pubic bone. "The head is down here. It's so close to coming out. Keep that picture in your mind's eye. Here. Right here you can feel its bottom. Soon you'll be putting diapers on that bottom. But we have to get it out first."

Tracy pushes Maggie's hand firmly into the rigid hump of her distended abdomen. The pressure triggers another contraction. Tracy gets down in her face, breathing her through it, talking her through it, dragging her along ahead of the crest, while the pain pulls at her, trying to drag her back down. It is an entity now. It has a life and a mind and a will of its own. Tracy has gone into battle against it, but Maggie doesn't think she'll win. Where is her mother? She can feel the pressure on her foot, but it's not helping any more. They're all helpless. She tries to do what Tracy is telling her. She tries to think about her cervix stretching wide open—it feels more like her entire body is ripping open. She tries to think of the baby moving down, tries to visualize its head pushing its way out through her vagina. It's hard to tell where the real pain ends and the fear of pain begins. Tracy keeps talking about little fingers and toes. Maggie can't see them. She's whimpering again.

When it abates this time, she cries, sniffling into the tissue that Sam holds up to her nose.

"I can't." She hears her own voice, small and whiny and desperate.

"Yes, you can, sweetheart. You're doing great. This is the hard part. Remember when you kept telling me about the stages, when you thought I wasn't listening? This is transition. I was listening. This means you're almost to the pushing part, but you've got to hang in through this last little tough bit. You're doing great. They're just starting to be really close together. Hang in a little longer. We're here. You're doing great." Sam's voice sounds odd; she's not sure what that edge is. But she is the tiniest bit comforted by it. She nods a little. He wipes her nose. "Blow." She does as she's told.

Katharine stops rubbing Maggie's foot and squeezes it hard enough to get her attention. She squints down the bed at her mother. Katharine looks at her, unblinking, her eyes boring into Maggie's. Maggie can feel the intensity radiating out from Katharine; she feels it almost viscerally. She's caught in those eyes. She doesn't know what they mean, or what Katharine wants from her. Whatever it is, she can't have it. Maggie has nothing left to give anyone. She's just trying to survive. Katharine keeps looking at her. She is standing perfectly still now, clearly trying to convey some great meaning that is beyond Maggie, gripping Maggie's foot. Maggie tries to pull her foot away. The weight of her mother's gaze is almost too much to bear. But Katharine holds on harder.

"What?" Maggie mouths, unable to raise her voice above a whisper.

Katharine doesn't answer immediately. But then she swallows, and says "You can do this." She pauses, visibly forcing out each sentence. "I did it. I did it with you, and with Dara, and with Jamie, and…I know it hurts like hell. And it doesn't get any better. But you can do it. This is what mothers do."

The silence in the room is heavy with the weight of Katharine's words. Maggie is neither comforted nor encouraged. Something is wrong, but she can't pinpoint what the problem is. It's like she's forgotten to do something important, but can't remember what it is, or her pantyhose are twisted, and she can't get them straight, or there's a car alarm going off in the distance, far enough that it doesn't consciously register but near enough to grate in a low-level, below-the-radar sort of way. She looks past the end of the bed at her mother, trying to read her. Katharine is tall, imposing from this angle. Even so, she is no match for the pain that is rolling over Maggie again.

"No! I can't!" But it sounds more like a sob.

"Maggie! Listen to me!" Katharine speaks sharply now, almost urgently. "You need to stay on top of this. The baby is depending on you. You can't just disappear into your own head like that."

Maggie gasps—even through the haze of pain and exhaustion, she hears the echo in her mother's words. She can't escape—all these years later, no matter what, those words still ring in her ears: "I'm depending on you."

She is aware of Sam rousing himself. "All right, Katharine. That's enough. This isn't helping. Maggie needs to focus. You go get a cup of coffee and I'll call your cell if the baby comes."

Katharine ignores him. Maggie can barely see her, still at the end of the bed, staring hard as the contraction drags Maggie back into herself. She flounders in that gaze. As she closes her eyes, she is still aware of Katharine's look. She's trying, really she is. She wants to be good, to help, but Katharine won't tell her how. She hears voices murmuring through the darkness.

CHAPTER 19

A door thunks closed. She wants desperately, more than anything, to go out that door, run away from this agony. She floats down the corridor, skimming over the tiles, barely moving, flying away from them all. She's floating down an empty hallway, narrow but luminous—it seems to glow. She can't tell where the light is coming from. It's white all around, the ceiling, the glossy floor, the smooth walls. All is quiet—the only sound she can hear is the air rushing in her ears.

Right in front of her, a door flies open, forcing her to veer suddenly. There's no time to slow down and see what's inside. She didn't even realize there was a door in this seamless wall. There, another one. The door makes no sound—just pops out in her face. She glances to her right as she glides past. She sees a jumble of people, but can't sort them out—must keep moving. Another, and another—they're flying open all around her, ahead of her, right and left like dominoes. She's dodging to avoid being hit. Doors pop open and noises pour from them, and light—a swirl of images, sounds, even smells and tastes seem to tumble out—a cacophony, getting louder and more insistent. The doors are flying open, and their contents are pouring out, pulling at her. She is forced to slow down, to peer in as she passes.

In this one is her piano teacher from elementary school, holding a sheet of paper over Maggie's hands, while her fingers trip over the keys, clumsy without her eyes to guide them.

In the next door is her junior high softball coach—she hated that man. He's yelling at the team, at her, chastising them for missing a ball, for running like girls, for letting in too many hits, for missing practice.

Now she sees herself, towering over Dara, screaming at her in a rage, throwing shoes at her.

There's a high school boyfriend, driving too fast, tearing around corners, burning rubber, scaring her half to death, but she doesn't know how to tell him to slow down without pissing him off. All she can do is grip the edges of her seat, waiting for it to be over, one way or another.

Here's her eternal graduate school nightmare—she has to teach a class, but has forgotten to read the assignment herself. Her students are laughing. Here's the other one—they've found her out. She never finished high school, and now she has to go back, Ph.D. and all, and finish typing class.

There's the dog that chased her on her way to school all through the fifth grade. She had to cross over and walk on the opposite side of the street to avoid the caramel-colored Jack Russell. He never crossed, but he ran up and down in front of his house, snarling and growling. She has never gotten over it—the sound of a dog growling still pushes her heart up into her throat. She pushes at the door, trying to close the dog back into whatever hellish box in her past he's popped out of. It won't close.

She turns back, to push her other dreams back behind closed doors, and they're right there, out in the hall, pressing up against her now, propelling her forward. She can't go back—a wall of fears blocks her completely. She has no choice but to move forward.

She can't see the end of the hall; it stretches on in front of her, glowing bright, doors flying open even as she looks. Perspective plays tricks on her; the hall seems to shrink down to a Lilliputian passageway as she strains to see past the doors in front of her. She runs again, trying to escape, the doors flying open as she rushes past. Noises assault her; she can't cover her ears. Then suddenly, out of the chaos of sounds and words, she hears the one that stops her in her tracks.

§§§

"Maggie! Help me! Please—quickly!" It's Mommy. She's hurt, she's crying and bleeding and muddy, and Jamie is…something's really wrong.

He's bent all strangely. She's carrying him in her arms, even though she's not supposed to carry heavy things because of her pregnant tummy, but his head wobbles, and his eyes are closed. There's blood on his face, and on Mommy too. She stumbles, tripping over the long metal poles in the bottom of the ditch. Maggie doesn't know what to do, how to help. She can't move.

"What happened? What's wrong with Jamie?" Her voice quavers with fear. Mommy looks horrible. Her face is twisted and crumpled, and her eyes look wild. Maggie backs away, terrified.

"He fell—help me…." Mommy grunts as she pushes Jamie up onto the bank of the ditch, then hauls herself up after him. She crouches there on the edge, clutching at her big belly, making a scary noise. Maggie is frozen. When Mommy stands up, tears are streaming down her face. They well up in Maggie's eyes, too. Her whole body has gone so cold she is shaking.

"Maggie." Mommy's voice is deep and raggedy. "Go. You can do it— I'm depending on you. Get help. We need an ambulance. Now. Run!" She sinks down on her hands and knees next to Jamie, curls up around his body. He doesn't move. Neither does Maggie. She is stuck there. Her feet won't run. She lifts her head up, looks around, and remembers where she is. The car is to the right, at the front of the construction site. But it's a long way off. They're way back in the back, far away from Mommy's trailer and the gas station across the street. Mommy was showing Jamie where the loading dock would go on her new building. Maggie stayed here, playing by the ditch. Now she doesn't know what to do.

"Maggie! Go, dammit! You need to hurry! Find someone—bring help!" Maggie shrinks back, paralyzed.

"What's wrong with Jamie?" she whispers.

"Just go! Hurry—run! Help me!" Her mother is screaming now, howling. She sounds more like an animal than Mommy. The words reach something in Maggie's mind, and set her feet in motion. Mommy needs her. She runs away from this hideous, writhing creature, away from the nightmare. She runs past piles of huge metal beams, a giant cement mixer, cables and scaffolding and huge, dirt-encrusted machines whose functions she can't imagine. She trips over ropes and ladders and piles of earth. She winds through a labyrinth of construction debris and portable potties and the trailers that her mother and the building staff use as offices. There's the station wagon, and beyond, through the chain link fence they left ajar, the busy corner in Arlington where the new shopping mall, Mommy's new shopping mall, is already changing traffic patterns.

She doesn't know what to do now. The road stops her short on the curb, and she has to throw her arms out to stop herself from teetering into oncoming cars. A horn blows; she backs up a foot or two. She looks quickly right and left. No buildings yet on this side of the street, all the way up and down the block. A Shell station across the street. She can see the attendant inside and two cars in the parking lot. No one is at the pumps. She looks back over her shoulder, not sure what to do. At ten, she has never crossed a street this wide alone before. She counts. There are seven lanes, all together. She looks for a hole, a chance to dart across between cars. At the same moment, she realizes it's impossible.

Tears well up in her eyes. Mommy needs her help. Jamie needs her. She pants, trying to catch her breath and calm down. She hears a beeping sound to her left and she follows it to find the source. In a burst, she knows what to do. The beeping is the crosswalk sign—what Daddy calls the "walkie-guy."

When they're in the city, they are supposed to cross only at the corners. Daddy says crossing in the middle is jaywalking. She's not sure why it's called that, but she knows not to do it if there are cars coming, or if there's a police car parked on the block. They always push the big button on the pole at the corner; she and Dara usually race to see who can get to it first. She's racing toward the corner now, but it doesn't feel the same as racing with Dara. She wishes Dara were there, or better yet, Daddy. She wishes they had gone into the city today like they usually do on Sunday mornings. Mommy doesn't go with them; she likes to work on Sunday mornings. She says that's the only time construction sites are quiet. But Daddy takes the children to do wonderful things in Washington. Maggie hopes Jamie is okay now; he was so still. She wonders how he fell.

Now she's at the corner. She pushes the button and waits, out of breath, pushing the button over and over again, trying to will the walkie guy to pop up on the screen across the street.

Daddy always has to call out to Dara and her: "Walkie guy! Look sharp, ladies!" She and Dara are big girls, big enough to cross without holding a grown-up's hand. But Jamie's only little; Daddy knows he has to hold onto Jamie to keep him safe. He drags Jamie across, gripping his little hand in his big one, and watches the girls, to make sure they're moving along, paying attention to traffic, dodging puddles and grown-ups.

The little white outline of a man pops up; Maggie looks both ways, then scurries across. She's made it to the far side and she races down to the gas station, through the parking lot, and in through the door. She throws herself at the counter, gasping. The man sitting at the cash register is smoking. He looks a bit surprised, but that's okay. She's tall enough now to see over the counter.

"What can I do for you, young lady?" His hair is kind of long and messy looking, but his voice is kind.

"My Mommy," she gasps. "She's hurt. So is my baby brother. Please help me!"

He is paying attention. Good. Grown-ups don't always listen. "What's wrong with your mom?"

"I don't know. She fell down. I think she's bleeding. But something's really wrong with Jamie. He's… he looks bad. He's not moving."

The man looks worried now. She hops up and down on one foot. "Please! Come with me! They need help!"

"Hold on. Where are they?"

She points straight across the street. "Over there. That's our car. They're way in the back. That's my Mommy's building." She stands up tall. She always loves saying that, at all the different buildings Mommy has worked on.

The gas-station man looks doubtful for a second, then looks up over Maggie's head. She realizes that another man and woman have come up to the front of the store. They're standing behind her now. He has a Coke in one hand, and a Snickers in the other. She has a bag of potato chips. They are staring at her. The woman squats down and looks at Maggie; now Maggie is a lot taller than she is. She looks nice, like she could be somebody's mama. She has on little tiny glasses, and her hair is curly all over, longer than Mommy's. It's pulled back in a ponytail, and she's wearing sneakers and a blue tracksuit. She has nice eyes, with little lines around the edges as she looks into Maggie's face.

"Does your mommy know you're here, sweetie?"

"She told me to get help. She…she was crying." Maggie hesitates. "She was all bloody." Maggie starts to cry now, her lip and chin quivering first, while she tries to make them hurry. "She's lying on the ground. Please help me!"

The nice lady's husband looks at the man behind the counter. "You'd better call an ambulance. I'll go over there and see what's going on. Anna, you keep her here. Buy her a Coke or something." He puts his things down on the counter and jogs out the door. Maggie notices that he's dressed like the lady named Anna. She's crying all out now, sobbing and shaking and scared. The nice lady puts one arm around her shoulders, and leads her to a table in the corner. She hands her a pile of napkins, and comes back in a minute with a paper cone full of very cold water.

"Here you go sweetheart. Take a sip. Can you tell me your name?"

"Margaret Dale Lambert." She hiccups. "But my nickname is Maggie."

"Maggie Lambert. That's a pretty name. Do you live here in Arlington, Maggie?"

She sniffles, and mops at her face with the napkins. "No. We live in Silver Spring. Mommy works in lots of different places. She's an engineer." Pride creeps into Maggie's voice. "Daddy's an architect. They both work on buildings, but not usually the same buildings."

"Where's your daddy now, Maggie? Do you think we should call him?"

"Oh! I didn't think of that. Yes, please." Her eyes fill up with tears again. "I want Daddy!" she wails.

"Oh, dear. Okay. Let's get this nice young man at the front to call for us. Come on dear, you'll have to tell him your phone number."

The woman goes up to the counter and asks the man with the long hair, who is smoking again, to call Silver Spring for Maggie. He looks doubtful, but she glares at him. He says okay. He pushes the phone toward Maggie and she dials, but when Daddy answers the phone, she bursts into tears again. The nice lady quickly takes the receiver and speaks into the phone. Maggie tries to stop crying while the lady is explaining in a very fast voice that Daddy needs to come right away. She gets the address from the cash-register man, then hangs up.

"He'll be here in a jiffy, Maggie." Just then, they both hear a siren, and an orange and white ambulance bumps over the curb, rushes through the gate, and disappears into the construction site. Maggie looks wildly around, ready to bolt for the door. The woman puts one hand on her arm.

"Why don't we stay here and wait for Daddy, okay? I told him to come here, so he's probably on his way. When he gets here we'll tell him the ambulance came, and he'll probably take you right over there to check on your mommy. Okay?"

Maggie doesn't know what else to say, so she nods slowly, still watching the dust kicked up by the ambulance.

"Would you like a candy bar? Or some potato chips, or something?"

Maggie looks around helplessly. "I don't have any money," she whispers.

The woman half-chuckles. "Oh, that's all right. My treat. What can I get you?"

Maggie's mind moves slowly, bogged down in confusion. The stern warning from a school assembly rings in her ears: *Never take candy from strangers.* Does this count? She doesn't want to be rude and she really does love M&Ms. But what about Mommy and Jamie? She looks toward the window, hoping Daddy will be pulling up. She isn't sure how long the drive is from Silver Spring, but it seems like he might be a while. She twists her left foot against the floor. The sole of her summer deck shoes is coming loose. She drags the dirty rubber across the dirty floor, prying it even further away from the sole of the grubby shoe. The nice lady is still looking at her, waiting. Maggie's voice comes out very small.

"Could I have some M&Ms, please?"

"Of course. Plain or peanut?"

"Plain, please."

They sit side by side on the curb in front of the gas station. Maggie watches for Daddy's green car, eating her M&Ms one by one. She tells the woman that she likes to suck the coating off the brown ones, feeling the slightly grainy shell dissolve into silky smoothness, then slowly melt away to nothing, leaving a round of solid chocolate. The yellow ones she likes to crunch, feeling the candy shatter into sharp, tiny shards of sugar mingled with soft-but-not-melted chocolate, sticking for a second in her big back teeth. She looks sideways at the lady. Maybe she should be quiet, but it feels safer to keep talking.

She finally runs out of things to say and sits looking across the street, at Mommy's station wagon. Anna sips a cup of coffee. She pats Maggie on the knee. "I'm sure everything will be fine, Maggie. Your Daddy will be here soon."

Maggie crumples up her M&M wrapper, then smoothes it back out again. She carefully separates the seam down one side and across the bottom, so that the bag opens up into one piece. "Mommy said Jamie was hurt bad. She's going to have another baby."

The woman looks down at her and nods a little bit. "Try not to worry too much. Can I get you something else to eat?"

"No thanks. I feel kind of sick. Mommy said… she said…."

The woman frowns a little, waiting for Maggie to finish her sentence. But she never does. Daddy's green Volvo tears into the parking lot, and soon they're careening toward the hospital, screeching around corners and barely slowing down for traffic lights. Later, Maggie falls asleep on a couch in a waiting room, curled around Dara. When they wake up, Jamie is dead, and so is Mommy's new baby. She wasn't fast enough, and everything has started falling apart.

§§§

Maggie hasn't thought about the nice gas-station lady, or her husband, in many years. Now, with Katharine standing at the end of the bed bringing all of her own desperate experiences of childbirth into the room with her, Maggie can't keep the doors in her mind shut. It floods in, all of it, mingling hospital smells and primal sounds and over all a sheen of fear, brittle and sharp and unforgiving. She sobs as the contraction ends, and the room comes back into focus. She's crying now, great wracking grief tearing at her throat. A cloth dabs at her face. She opens her eyes and sees Sam. She comes slowly to herself. She's here, she's a grown-up, she's having her own baby. Jamie—oh, God—Jamie. It was so long ago. She still misses him so much. Sam calls her back from the memories. Katharine is no longer standing at the end of the bed. Maggie doesn't recall seeing her leave.

"Maggie, honey." He sounds panicked. "What's wrong? What can I do?"

She can barely catch her breath. "It was my fault. I couldn't help."

"What? I don't know what you're talking about, but it's okay. It's almost over."

"No—wait! Where's Mother? I need…something. To tell her."

"She'll be back, honey. It's okay. You're almost ready to push. Hang in there. The baby will be here soon."

Baby. Her own baby. And this one is fine. She can't do anything else—she can't make everything okay again. She closes her eyes against the onslaught.

She just wants this misery to end. She forgets, for whole moments at a time, that this is pain with a purpose. It becomes her reality—she has ceased to exist beyond the moment. She forgets that she is in labor. For that matter, she forgets that there are words for this. Language slips beyond her grasp. She loses her senses, slipping ever deeper into her body. The world outside her closed eyelids ceases to exist. The rise and swell of the contractions merges into one long agony of intensity. She thrashes, twisting her head into the pillow, trying to escape, unable to stay on top, overwhelmed, finally, slipping under, drowning in panic.

If she had to name the pain, pinpoint where it hurt, she'd be at a complete loss for words. There is no describing the opening of a cervix—it is a sensation unknown to humanity outside of the context of childbirth. It's not a toe that gets stepped on sometimes, or an elbow that bumps into the doorframe accidentally. It's tucked away deep inside, protected, sheltered, hidden from the jarring exposure that desensitizes the rest of the body. So when it suddenly develops a life of its own, growing from a tight little knot of an opening to a gaping hole large enough for a baby's head to squeeze through, all in a matter of hours, some great force has clearly been brought to bear.

All day, all week, for nine months now, even, she's been picturing it in her mind, seeing this round nose of flesh, with a tiny hole in the middle. She has visualized the muscles connected to this ring of firm tissue, seeing the muscles contract and pull on the flesh to open it up. She could see it in her mind's eye, the slow, gradual pulling outward and upward of that tight little collar her baby would need to slip through. But now, instead of visualizing her cervix, she has become her cervix. All the other parts—arms, knees, shoulder blades, earlobes—have dropped away, and she's falling into the endless pain, no longer able to look at it from a distance.

Her brain catches a word from the room around her—*precipitous*—and it lodges itself in the pain with her, and she can't get it out. It rolls with her through the contraction, chasing itself in circles in her mind, rolling and twisting and diving in the waves of pain, making her want to scream at the intrusion. The syllables splinter apart and divide and reproduce, filling her head with random, meaningless noise. The letters dance behind her eyelids, taunting her. There is no sense, no order.

The outer limits of her body have dissolved; she can't catch her breath. The pain doesn't come and go anymore, it just keeps coming. She's drowning in it. It keeps pulling and stretching and it's beyond the breaking point and this one will never end and she twists her face into the pillow and realizes that she's suffocating but even when she turns to breathe she's still suffocating she can't get air and she's going to drown it won't end I can't I can't ithurtsithurtsithurtsohmygodohmygodohmygod.

CHAPTER 20

It stops.

Maggie finds herself panting, wrung out, but suddenly aware of the room around her, Sam murmuring in her ear, Tracy gripping her hand.

Just like that, she is back in the room, here and now. The crescendo of pain has simply stopped. She takes stock and finds that, while she's no longer on the threshold of death, she is still pregnant. Her awareness expands and she realizes that her mother has disappeared.

"What happened?" she asks, interrupting Sam's running monologue in her ear. This one question will have to stand in for all the things she's trying to ask.

"You must be complete. Do you want me to check?"

"What?" She and Sam blurt in unison.

Tracy chuckles. "I imagine you're fully dilated. Sometimes it can suddenly feel a lot better when you move from transition into pushing. You're lucky—you're having a pretty distinct break here. You should try to gather your strength a little bit."

"That sounds ominous," Maggie says.

She turns back to Sam, still wondering about her mother, as Tracy moves around to the foot of the bed. The question leaves her head when Tracy once again digs her fingers deep into Maggie's wide-open nether parts. She grimaces slightly, holding her breath until Tracy withdraws her hand and pulls off the rubber glove. "Yep. Just the tiniest little lip of cervix there still. Are you feeling any urge to push?"

Fatigue is now rolling over Maggie. The relief of the end of transition has faded, and she begins to feel the toll of a full day of laboring. "No. I'm so tired," she says in a small voice. She looks at Sam. She can see relief and anxiety warring in his face.

"What does that mean, a lip? And should she do anything now, since she's feeling better? Like go to the bathroom, or move, or something?"

Maggie looks at him, aghast. She's so tired she can barely speak, and he wants her to move? Has he lost his mind?

"I'm not moving." She doesn't need to hear what Tracy thinks. There's no way she's going anywhere, even the bathroom.

Tracy chuckles again. "I guess she'll be staying right where she is. A lip means there's only a tiny last little edge of cervix that hasn't pulled all the way back yet. Think of it like you're pushing a basketball out of the top of a turtleneck. You push the ball through with one hand, and at the same time you're pulling back on the shirt with the other hand. Right now, the very top edge of the turtleneck is still in front of the ball; as Maggie starts pushing the baby out, that little lip will pull right on back and disappear."

Maggie is amazed that she can both visualize and *feel* exactly what Tracy is talking about. That's what all that agony was. It was the turtleneck pulling back, stretching wider and wider until she thought she would turn inside out, or die, or explode.

This lip idea is worrisome; she ponders it for a moment, wondering why it sounds familiar, or perhaps even alarming. She remembers: there was a bit in one of the birth books she read. Something about how if you started pushing before the lip retracted, it could swell up from the battering, then refuse to retract at all. She can't remember what happens next in that scenario, but it must be bad. Is her body going to fail her now, after all this work? Tendrils of panic twist in her chest.

Tracy is across the room now, taking notes, speaking into the intercom. She doesn't look concerned. Sam pours a cup of water and holds the straw up to her mouth. Maybe a drink will make her feel calmer. She takes one sip, then stops.

"No. Yuck. I don't…. Uh, oh." Her voice drops an octave, and she doesn't recognize the guttural, animal sound that comes from her throat now, as if ripped out.

"No...." The word becomes a grunt. Pure release. No meaning, no import, no expectation of response or acknowledgement. She has gone back inside again, her modern mind hijacked by this primitive process that will not be stopped. This new phase is something different altogether. She's not sure what she's feeling, but it starts deep in her gut and seems to explode upward, out through her throat. It's not pain, exactly, but some-thing...*powerful*. She realizes that Sam is speaking to her.

"What the hell kind of noise was that? Maggie, what's going on? Tracy! What's wrong with her?"

It has passed. When she speaks now, her voice is her own again, no longer possessed by...whatever it was. "It's fine, Sam. I'm okay. Just tired."

Tracy is peering at her. "Are you sure you're not feeling any urge to push?"

Maggie thinks about this. What does the urge to push feel like? She's not overcome by desire to have a bowel movement. That's how one book described it. She mentally scans her body; nope. Bowels feel as fine as they can, under the circumstances. All is calm—relatively, anyway. Just so damned tired. "No. I don't think so."

Tracy looks skeptical at Maggie's shrug. "Okay. Let me know when you do. Probably soon, now." Tracy comes over to check Maggie's blood pressure and pulse again. Apparently everything is fine; she nods and sits back down to scratch in her file folder again. Sam is fidgeting in his chair; he gets up and walks to the window, then back to the chair again.

"What happened to my mother?"

His lips pinch into a tight line. "She went downstairs to find my mom and get some coffee."

"Are you serious? I'm giving birth, and she goes out for coffee?"

"Not out. Downstairs. I can call her back up here if you want her. But honestly, I think you're doing great like this. Tracy and I are here to help. We can handle it. Plus, if you're getting close to pushing, that means the doctor will be coming in soon, right Tracy?"

"Mmm. Probably so." Tracy sounds distracted and noncommittal.

"You're doing great. I don't think…." He's leaning back against a counter now, arms folded across his chest, ankles crossed in front of him. "I don't think we need an extra person in here, that's all."

He looks all rumpled and grungy. His jaw is prickly with stubble, and his hair is standing up every which way. His eyes are dark and indecipherable.

She's so wiped out. But something is nagging at her, an irritation in the back of her mind that won't be ignored. She scratches at the tape holding the needle in the back of her hand.

She frowns. Something is bothering her, nagging at her.

She'll only distract you," Sam says.

"That's not it. I'm just frustrated."

"What are you talking about?"

"The baby's coming soon, isn't it?"

"What does that have to do with your mother?"

Maggie stares at him, flabbergasted. "I thought she'd want to be here, that's all."

He pinches the bridge of his nose. "Fine."

Maggie closes her eyes again while Sam mumbles into his phone. Katharine is in the room almost immediately.

"What were you doing, waiting outside the door?" Sam sounds accusatory.

"Of course." She stands at the end of the bed, by Maggie's feet again, and surveys the room. "What's happening?"

"I'm not sure, but it's a little better." Maggie grimaces. "Only a little, though."

"All right, then. Good. Sam, what can I do to help?"

"Ask Maggie. She's the one who wanted you."

"Sam!" Maggie glares at him, but Katharine is unruffled.

"What can I do, dear?"

Maggie hesitates, surprised to be seeing this side of her mother. "I don't know. I just thought maybe you should be here. That's all." The words come out in a rush, and she squirms a little on the bed. She can feel the blush creeping up her face. "But you don't have to, if you don't want." Sweat is popping out on her forehead now; she closes her eyes and leans back against the pillow, a low rumbling noise building in the back of her throat.

"Maggie. Why would you say that? Of course I want to be here." Even through closed eyes, Maggie can feel her mother's sharp gaze. She's never been able to avoid it; it's as if this whole day, her entire life, even, she's been trying to find the meaning in those eyes. The rumble in her throat washes down and out, through her body. Maggie realizes it's now or never, so she takes a breath and jumps in.

"Mother—the baby roses. How could you?"

"What do you mean? Didn't you pick them up?"

"Of course I did—Dara said for me to—but why?"

"So you can plant them, of course."

"But why would you dig them up? That's…that's us you're digging up! Our childhood. It's—Jamie!" Something convulsive ripples through Maggie, and she groans. Katharine's eyes widen, but she grasps Maggie's feet with both hands and holds on.

"Maggie, honey. That's crazy."

"Nooo…." The word bursts out, low and loud, but Katharine doesn't budge.

"Maggie, look at me."

"Katharine, maybe this could wait," Sam tries to interject, but Katharine shrugs off his hand, not looking away from Maggie.

"No, Sam, it can't wait, and it's not like things are going to get any calmer around here any time soon. I'm not sure what kind of awful story you've built up in your head, Maggie, but let me be abundantly clear. I dug them up so that you could have them for your garden. I'm going to sell the house"—she raises one hand to stop Maggie's eruption. "Your father told me you called him this morning. I realize this was perhaps not the best timing, although I didn't exactly know you were going into labor *today*. I didn't realize you'd be so upset about it but I just don't need all that space. You girls are making your own lives, and that's the natural order of things."

Maggie stares at her mother, feeling as if she's been punched. It's too much to process. Even after worrying about it all day, she can't take it in, so she goes back to the question that has been bothering her.

"But I don't understand how you can dig up those roses. Don't you want them anymore?" Maggie holds her breath.

"Well, I didn't want to leave them behind, and I'm not sure what kind of garden space I'll have, so I thought if you plant them, they'll be together, and we'll all know where they are. Oh—but I forgot to tell you the best part! I've ordered a new one, for the baby. It was your grandmother's idea."

Katharine is beaming, rubbing Maggie's feet again with that steady pressure. Maggie's brain is moving in slow motion. This is not what she expected at all.

"That'll be nice, I guess. Thank you," she manages. "How did you, I mean, we don't even know if it's a boy or a girl. Did you get pink or white?"

"Neither! You won't believe it. It's called *mutabilis*—it's spectacular. The flowers actually change color. They start off sort of apricot and gradually turn pink, then red. And not all at the same time, so you get all the colors on the plant at once. You won't believe it."

"Yaya thought of that?"

"Yes, a while back, actually. When you were pregnant before. I took her to see the rose garden at the National Arboretum, and we saw one in full bloom. She said...." Katharine trails off, blinking. Maggie feels a lump rising in her own throat, but she needs to know.

"She said what?"

"She said it was like your baby. A new generation, with all the best qualities of the ones who came before blended into a unique new living thing."

Maggie can't speak. The steadfast, immutable realities of her life are crumbling—nothing will ever be the same. The sob comes from somewhere deep inside, convulsing her whole body. No one touches her, but she can feel both Sam and her mother hovering, ready to pick up the pieces when she finally shatters. It's Katharine who hands her the tissues this time, tears streaming freely down her face.

"Maggie, listen to me. You need to start looking forward, not backward. Your grandmother loves you to distraction, but she's going to want you to get on with your life. She's ninety-three. You can't keep depending on her. Your baby is going to be here any minute now, so you need to stop worrying about things like roses and ancient history, and start figuring out how to be a mother."

Katharine leans in to kiss the top of her head, then ducks out of the room before anyone can react. Maggie is too stunned to call after her. She looks at Sam, who is wiping his own tears.

"That's the whole problem," she whispers. "How am I supposed to do that?"

He sits down next to her, draping an arm over her chest, not speaking. Her tears subside into shallow hiccups.

She closes her eyes, and after a few minutes, she feels Sam stand up. Maybe she'll take a little nap. His shoes squeak back toward the window. She breathes as deeply as she can, still afraid that too much movement will trigger fresh contractions. The sounds in the room blur together. Tracy's pen, Sam's shoes, her own breathing, the clock on the wall above her head ticking off this endless day. She wonders what time it is, but only a little. She lets it all go, and sinks rapidly toward sleep. The squeaking is replaced by a regular, rhythmic scraping sound that wanders in and out of her consciousness. It crosses paths in her mind with a small wave of nausea, making her feel slightly motion sick, even though she hasn't moved in hours. How odd, she thinks. I'm seasick. She thinks of the seasickness bands she wore on her wrists in the early months, when she was always faintly nauseated. Why would she be seasick now, she wonders?

Chapter 21

That fishing trip was so bizarre. Maybe she's still sick from that. It's over, though, isn't it? She can't remember; she had to wear those bands all day, and they hurt, the tight grey elastic pushing those hard white buttons into the thin, tender white tissue on the insides of her wrists. She worries that she's got them in the wrong spot. If they push on a vein all day, will the circulation to her hands be permanently damaged?

She likes her hands. Her fingers are long and thin. Sometimes she likes to think they look graceful. When she's not on a dig, her nails can grow long. They're surprisingly strong. Every now and then she likes to get a manicure, and have them painted a shocking bright red. Just for kicks. They're good strong nails. They were red the day of the fishing trip. She remembers looking down at her hands. Her nails were so bright and normal-looking; it was incongruous, the elegant manicure, covered with slime and muck and fish blood.

She is in some strange limbo now; that fishing trip felt just as surreal.

§§§

It had been such a beautiful day—not a cloud in the sky. The air had that amazing clear autumn light that made everything stand out in sharp relief. After the haze of a Washington, D.C. summer, the sharp salt air of the Chesapeake Bay was bliss; the spray on her arms was a balm. She'd expected so much from that day—laughing, fishing, being adults together—the whole family-bonding routine. Maybe that was where she'd gone wrong, expecting it to live up to the picture in her mind.

They'd been going on this trip every year since she was—well, not very old, anyway. Dara must have been old enough to be safe on a boat, so maybe she had been twelve or so. It had become an annual Lambert family tradition, the only one that hung on even after the divorce. Yaya had tagged along for years, until the rolling motion started to throw off her balance. They all loved it. It was one of Maggie's few childhood memories that always involved Katharine smiling. Where was Katharine now? Hadn't she been here earlier? She hadn't been smiling; she was annoyed about something. Maggie wasn't sure what. She had been much more pleasant on the fishing trip.

Every year, late in September, Katharine would pack a cooler full of beer and pull out her rattiest old sweat shorts. She handled the fish with aplomb, never flinching. She'd wipe her hands on the back of her shorts and pull out the camera. She always insisted on documenting every fish they caught, even the ones that were too small to keep.

Maggie had loved the rolling of the boat, the smell of the salt water. Even the smell of boat fuel still brings back pleasant memories. The girls ran free around the boat; through their teenage years, they disdained the rod and reel in favor of bikinis and fashion magazines. But they never missed the trip. By the end of the day, they were all sunburned and windburned and happy as clams.

When Maggie and Sam were dating, she started dragging him along. He was usually content till lunchtime, then started getting antsy. By the time they were married, he had learned to bring along a week's worth of *Wall Street Journals* to catch up on while he waited for something to bite. Still, Maggie insisted they go. She had missed only one trip in all those years, the year she was working in Mexico and couldn't justify a plane ticket all the way home for a one-day fishing trip.

In the fall after the miscarriage, she had been particularly looking forward to being out on the boat. She was tired of feeling hemmed in by her sadness, tired of everyone tiptoeing around the subject. She set out that morning determined to look at it squarely, toss it overboard, and move on. Driving over to the marina in Annapolis early that morning, she'd told Sam what she was thinking.

"I'm sick of being sad. I need to move on."

He stopped at a red light and looked at her. "Okay. How are you planning to do that?"

"You're going to think I'm insane."

Sam chuckled, and patted her hand. "Well, you are a little odd. But that's okay—I love you anyway."

"Good. Because I want to have a ritual." She was watching Sam's face while he drove; he didn't take his eyes off the road, but pursed his lips.

"What does that mean, exactly?"

"It means…." She hesitated, realizing that what had made perfect sense in her head was going to sound very strange out loud. "It means I brought a bag of pinto beans. We're going to throw them overboard, like confetti."

Sam's lips twitched.

"Don't laugh."

"Pinto beans?"

"You said it—the baby was the size of a pinto bean."

"I remember." He reached for her hand again. "I couldn't possibly forget. But it's funny, when you think about it—tossing pinto beans into the ocean."

"I know. I think it's time to be able to smile about it, maybe, don't you?"

"And say good-bye?"

"Exactly."

"And you're sure you aren't going to want me to sing, or get naked, or hold hands with your dad or anything flaky?"

Maggie burst out laughing at the image. "You'd scare the fish. No, really—I just wanted to take a moment, and scatter the beans. For closure, you know?"

"I know, pumpkin. I was teasing. Whatever you want is fine."

"Thank you." She stretched across the console to lean her head against Sam's shoulder, optimism rising in her chest for the first time in months.

It hadn't worked out that way; nothing ever goes the way she plans. She wonders now if it'll be time for the trip soon; what month is it, anyway? Maybe Sam knows. She'll ask in a minute. She's so tired.

She hadn't been tired that day. For the first time in months, she had felt like her body was humming with energy. She drank a beer with Sam, early on. Then she had another with Ben. Then one with Dara, who had dumped a guy and was perfectly happy about it. Dara caught two striped bass in a row. Sam didn't catch anything, and Dara wasn't very nice to tease him like that. Maggie had another beer with Katharine. They started laughing at Ben, who had caught a spiny, roly-poly little pufferfish, but nothing else.

Out of nowhere, the wind blew up. It was the weirdest thing. A crystal clear blue sky, not a cloud to be seen, blew up all this wind, whipping the waves into a froth, wrapping Maggie's long, loose hair all around her head. She scraped it off her damp skin, restraining it with a scrunchie she dug out of her bag. The boat was rolling over the waves, up to a peak, down into a trough. Again and again. It was beautiful; she loved the exhilaration of pitch and fall. Hard to catch any fish, though. The boat had turned back early because of the wind, and they were packing up the fishing gear when Maggie remembered the bag of pinto beans.

She dug the bag out of her purse and sat holding it, the dry weight of the beans filling her hands. The Annapolis skyline was fully in view. Now was her last chance. Sam was leaning against the rail at the back of the boat, talking to her dad. She moved toward them carefully, the beer and the waves conspiring to make her sag at the knees.

Sam saw the bag of beans dangling from her hand and quickly looked down, studying the beer bottle in his hand. She lifted her chin.

"Dad, I want to do something before we dock."

"What do you mean?"

She looked at Sam, but he was peering into his beer, as if he'd lost something down the neck of the bottle.

"I want to have a…." She blushed, but forced the word out. "A ceremony. A good-bye, for the baby. So I can move on." Hearing her own words, she blushed some more.

Her father eyed her for a moment. "Okay. Whatever you want. What're the beans for?"

"I thought, since we don't have ashes, we could sprinkle the beans over the water."

Ben nodded, as though this made perfect sense, even though Maggie knew he couldn't possibly understand the significance of the beans to her and Sam.

"Do you want me to go up front, so you two can be alone back here?"

"No, actually, I thought maybe—I know this sounds kind of corny—maybe Mother and Dara could join us, and we could each sprinkle a few. I don't know—I sort of wanted a family thing."

"Shall I round them up?"

"Please. And Dad—thank you for not laughing."

"Of course." He patted her arm, and moved toward the front of the boat.

She leaned against the railing, resting in the shelter of Sam's shoulder, staring into the water. The boat slammed over every wave, shooting up foam. Droplets burst and fell, catching the sunlight, scattering rainbows in the air. Dara joined them at the rail, slipping an arm around Maggie's waist. They could hear Katharine's voice as she moved toward the back of the boat, and Sam and Dara both looked at Maggie. She frowned, but Dara gave her a quick squeeze, and Sam nodded, encouraging her.

She turned to face her mother, who seemed to be approaching with Ben prodding her from behind.

"What's this all about, Maggie? I'm trying to get things packed up before we dock."

"I know. It'll only take a minute. I—we—Sam and I—we wanted to have a little ceremony, to help us move on from…the miscarriage." It still hurt a little to say that word, but maybe naming it, saying it out loud, was half the battle. She forged ahead, in spite of the expression on her mother's face.

"I brought a bag of pinto beans, and I thought we could each throw a few out into the water, like sprinkling ashes."

Her mother looked perplexed. "What in the world? Maggie, honey. You lost a baby. I know you're sad about it, and I understand that–really, I do–but maybe you need to stop dwelling on it. Do you really want to memorialize that?"

Maggie faltered, but Sam stepped in. "No, of course not. But it did happen, whether we like it or not, and we have been sad about it. Maggie thought this might help us get some closure."

"I hate that word," Katharine mumbled, turning to look out to sea.

Maggie put both hands on her hips, annoyed. "What is that supposed to mean? This is what I need."

Katharine didn't turn around. Everyone else looked at their feet, or off toward the horizon, awkwardness hanging heavy around the wind-battered little group, until Ben spoke up.

"Maybe we should just go ahead and do it, Maggie. Not make a big fuss."

The disappointment stung. Maggie didn't know how to explain that she needed her mother to stand beside her and say good-bye to the baby that should've brought them together. The words jammed up in her throat.

Katharine finally turned back around. "Really, Maggie. Listen to me. I've been there. I know exactly how you feel–hear me out." She raised one hand to cut Maggie off. "You know I do. I lost a baby and a son, in one day. You know that."

Maggie's cheeks flamed red. She did know, but she tried so hard, for so long, not to think about it. She looked down at the bag of beans in her hands, and swallowed against the lump in her throat. Katharine kept talking.

"Miscarriages happen—you know that, too. It was sad and frightening and very, very unfortunate, but there's no sense in making a big fuss about it now. It was months ago. You'll get pregnant again."

Maggie shook her head; her mother didn't understand. "That's not it."

"Then what is it?"

She shrugged weakly, and stared off into the distance, over her mother's shoulder. "I wish Yaya had come," she said, her voice breaking.

"What does Mother have to do with anything?" She could hear the exasperation in her mother's voice.

Again, Maggie struggled to explain, to bridge the distance between them, but the words wouldn't come. "Never mind." She shrugged, and turned toward the rail.

Dara spoke into the awkwardness. "Why don't you open the beans?"

Maggie nodded, and fumbled with the bag. She doled out the beans. Katharine took a few, just like everyone else, but her discomfort was palpable. No one spoke. One by one, they each sprinkled a handful of beans over the churning water. Sam stood next to Maggie and they stared out at the Bay, but she didn't feel the rush of peace that she'd been hoping for. She didn't feel much of anything other than emptiness.

§§§

Chapter 22

The crackle of the intercom interrupts her sad memory. Everything is clear again. The swishing sound is the rocking chair, not a fishing boat. She's in the hospital, and everything is fine. This baby is fine. She's fine. She looks around for her mother, not really expecting to see her.

"Sam?"

"Yes?" The swishing stops.

"Where'd my mother go?"

"I don't know. But she'll be back soon—she knows it's getting close."

Maggie absorbs this, but she still feels panicky. "I can't see you."

"Do you need me to move?"

"Yes. I need to see you. I'm scared to be by myself."

"I'm right here—you aren't by yourself at all."

He drags the rocking chair around the end of the bed with much twisting and shuffling. He strokes Maggie's hair. "Better?"

"A little," she says.

"Wow—the chair really is better over here. I wonder why I didn't think of this before."

"Glad you're comfy." The sarcasm in Maggie's voice is anything but subtle. But then, out of the blue, she is grunting again. That deep, primitive noise seems to come from somewhere deep in her solar plexus. Her stomach muscles contract violently, curling her more tightly in on herself. Something is forcing these noises up through her throat. The word *lip* surfaces, and she has a cold feeling that something is wrong. She needs to be careful; it's not time to push yet. She needs to relax so that her cervix can finish dilating. It's hard to relax when her muscles are—"Ooomph," she grunts again—all clamping in toward her center. It seems to be involuntary. This doesn't feel right; she's afraid that her body is going to hurt itself, now, after all this. She breathes out, but it sounds ragged and animal in her ears. When she inhales this time, the spasm has passed. Now she really can let go of her muscles.

Sam has stopped rocking next to her. She can't read his face. Worry lines furrow his forehead, but his eyes are almost dancing. His face is quicksilver, emotions warring for expression. "Is this it? Are you pushing?" He turns toward Tracy. "Now? Is it time?"

Tracy smiles down at whatever she's writing. "Yeah, it sounds like she's starting to have some pushing contractions. But it'll be a while yet. They'll pick up, and she'll have to work with them as they get stronger. Give it a while. Don't worry, this is normal. Sometimes they start kind of far apart like this. It's fine that she's getting a bit of rest. She needs it."

Maggie wonders why no one is addressing her directly, but the thought wanders away. She doesn't feel any urge to push. Push what? She never could quite figure that one out in birthing class. That crazy instructor had said it felt sort of like needing to push out a bowel movement. This made no sense. If she was supposed to spend the whole dilating phase relaxing those muscles (which Laura had been very clear about), why would she now clench up to take a shit? It made no sense. She couldn't feel the muscles, and therefore couldn't visualize it in practice. Besides, in class Laura said they shouldn't actually bear down anyway—apparently trying to push a baby out before it was ready could result in dire consequences. Maggie had wondered what those consequences might be—surely you couldn't make yourself go into labor simply by moving your bowels? If you could, why in the world would any sane woman ever allow herself to go past her due date? Realizing that her brain is getting all wound up in thoughts that don't make a whole lot of sense, she tries to quiet herself.

She opens her eyes to look at Sam. He still has that worried look on his face. She smiles encouragingly. He smiles back, slightly, but doesn't look particularly reassured. He pats her hand, then speaks to Tracy as if Maggie isn't there.

"Do you think she should drink something?"

"Actually, we prefer that moms not drink once they're through transition. An ice chip or two would be okay. But we don't want a whole lot of liquid sitting there in her stomach right now."

Maggie obediently accepts the ice chip that Sam deposits on her tongue. It melts almost instantly. She squirms on the bed, trying to rearrange the pillow under her shoulder to lift herself up a bit. Finally, she realizes that the bed can do this for her.

"Could I sit up a bit? I'm tired of lying down."

Surprise winks across Sam's face, but he jumps to fiddle with the buttons on the bed rail. The top half of the bed cranks into motion.

"Just a bit. There. That's good." She settles back against the solid support of the bed, and realizes that the room looks entirely different from this vantage point. But her legs don't feel right. Or maybe it's her stomach. Something. "I need...."

Sam is looking at her; she should complete the sentence. Somehow, it doesn't want to come out. She is distracted again. There—there's that spasm in her middle. It pushes up, through her chest, and out through her throat.

"Uuunph." Her breath pushes out, sounding as if she's been punched in the stomach. She tries to breathe, to remember the pattern that's gotten her through the last few hours. No pressure, no pushing. Remember that lip. Keep it all loose and easy. She breathes. It passes. She pants a little.

Sam is still looking at her. "What? What do you need, Maggie? Do you need to push?"

She brushes off his question. Does she *need* to push? She can't quite grasp this notion. How to reconcile *need* and *lip*. Two such different words.

"No, but something's not quite right." She squirms a bit, takes a breath, and starts over, trying to be more articulate. "Sitting like this is uncomfortable. It's pulling on my stomach, somehow. I need to curl up or something."

"Do you need to lie back down?"

He's not getting it. "No. I'm better up, for a while. But my legs. I sort of want to…." She puts her feet flat on the bed and draws her knees up toward her body. "But it makes my legs too tired. I can't do this."

Light dawns. "Oh. Here." He goes to a closet by the door, and pulls out three pillows. "Will propping them up help?"

Maggie's whole body sags with relief as Sam shoves all three pillows under her knees, then tucks the bed pillow behind her head. "Perfect." Even smiling is too much of an effort. "Almost human."

He fusses for minute, straightening and tidying and rearranging. When he dumps a pile of newspapers into the garbage Maggie has a pang of guilt that they should be recycled. He moves Ben's flowers two inches to the right, then back to the left again. He fishes out the long plastic stake that had held the card and throws it away. He pulls the tangled sheet out from where it has gotten wedged between the mattress and the foot of the bed and folds it, placing it neatly on the counter. He closes Maggie's overnight bag and tucks it into that closet by the door. She can't stand it any longer.

"What are you doing? Are we having company or something? You're making me nervous."

"The mess is making *me* nervous. I can't stand it. I can't sit still any more. Are you sure you're not ready to push?"

Sam's eyes shine. Maggie looks at him, but she's too tired to comprehend his excitement. It doesn't have anything to do with her. She shrugs.

"Where's Mother?" she asks. Sam rolls his eyes.

"I just told you—I don't know. She's here somewhere. She'll be back."

He gathers all the admittance forms and photocopies into a single pile, which he tucks into his briefcase.

She closes her eyes for a moment; she's so tired. Images swim in her mind: Sam's briefcase, a mackerel thrashing on the deck of a boat, Katharine's stern eyes standing at the end of the bed, a soft pink lip of flesh pulled shiny and taut against the end of a battering ram. None of it makes sense, but she can't escape from the swirl of smells and sounds and sights. She wants to stop the flood of memories, to slam the door on it, if only to still the cacophony. The reprieve of the last few minutes seems to have ended, and she's falling once more into the surreal fog of exhaustion. But before she can drift off to sleep entirely, another convulsive spasm punches her into wakefulness.

She wonders if maybe she has somehow caught a stomach bug. She has that cyclical sense of feeling better right after the fact, then increasingly hallucinatory as it approaches again. These whatever they are—they don't feel anything like the contractions she was having a few minutes ago—these *spasms* have that same involuntary muscular contraction that she remembers from an attack of food poisoning once (not in Mexico, or Egypt, or any of the sorts of places where sensible people get traveler's diarrhea, no—right here in Washington. A crab salad sandwich). She would sink deeper and deeper into hell, her brain playing hideous jokes on her senses, until she wasn't sure even of her own name, and didn't really care, and then suddenly her intestines would contract, so hard she felt like she had been punched. She managed to make it to the toilet every time, but barely. She'd sit there shivering and shaking while her bowels gripped and heaved and exploded, leaving her shaken but lucid. Then the cycle would start over, as the force behind the spasm seemed to slowly build back up, taking over first her body, then her mind, until it doubled her over on the toilet again.

This isn't diarrhea, though—not at all. As far as she can tell, it has nothing to do with her bowels. But it has that same odd cyclical quality: the building of misery, accompanied by the simultaneous loss of intellectual faculty, punctuated by a convulsive punch in the stomach, followed by a few moments of gradually deteriorating clarity and comfort.

She's all right at the moment, but by now it has become clear that it's going to come again. It's ridiculous—she's too tired for this. All she wants is a good nap. She can't get comfortable. Her body seems to resist curling up and relaxing. She can hear Sam chatting with someone; what are they talking about? She tries to listen, peevishly. It's hard to follow.

"Yeah, it's been her show. She's got the room all ready—there's a stroller blocking the back door. The diaper service has already made a delivery, and we don't even have a baby yet…."

Maggie thinks about those diapers. The cloth ones seem so much nicer than the disposable ones, but those Huggies are so darned cute. They're little itty-bitty, barely much bigger than her hand. She hasn't a clue what to do with them. She remembers the baby with a start—she's forgotten all about it. That is why they're here, isn't it? It doesn't seem very possible at the moment. She even packed a little infant outfit in her suitcase—it's some sort of a nightgown, with elastic around the bottom, and yellow ribbons trimming the placket and the sleeves. Where is it now? She starts to open her eyes to look for it, then realizes that she can't remember what she's looking for. Oh, well. Maybe she'll rest a little while Sam sounds so chatty.

"That's the one thing we haven't worked out—did you hear that business with her mother a few minutes ago? I think Maggie's feeling kind of torn about it, actually. She had a brother who died years ago—his name was Jamie. It's a good name, and it would be fine for a boy or a girl, but I worry that that's too much baggage, both for the baby and for Maggie. Maybe even for the whole family. I think …." Maggie can't quite hear, and misses part of what he says as he lowers his voice.

"But I think we'll know in a little while. We both kind of like Emma for a girl, but a boy's name is a little trickier. I don't have a strong need to have a fifth—something other than Sam would be interesting—but Maggie likes Benjamin. It's her dad's name. Nice name and all, but Benjamin Franklin is just unacceptable."

Maggie ponders this. How does Sam know Benjamin Franklin? For some reason, this is odd. Didn't he wear those funny little square glasses? And it seems like he was bald on top; Sam has lovely hair, and it covers his whole head. Wonder where he met Benjamin Franklin? He's dead. As a matter of fact, he's been dead for a very long time. Maybe it's the person Sam's talking to who knows him. She wonders who it is that Sam is having such an odd conversation with. He's been dead for—oh, several hundred years. Something like that. How peculiar that someone is gossiping about him like this.

"Unnh." There it is again, that punch in the stomach. She grunts, doubling over. Her breath oozes out in a low moan—she can hear the primal sound of it, but it doesn't fully register that those are her noises.

"Maggie? How're you feeling? Don't you feel like you need to do some pushing now?" Maggie knows that voice. It's Tracy. Tracy is so sweet. She ponders the question. She still can't really connect the words to what's going on in her body. She's content to let the process do what it will, accepting it passively, rather than trying to figure out how to be an active participant.

"Mmmm...not really. I think I'll rest a little more." She looks up at Tracy, who has a line etched down the bridge of her nose, and a tiny cream-colored crumb in the corner of her mouth. Perhaps she's been eating. Maggie doesn't feel particularly hungry, but perhaps she ought to. She can't remember the last time she ate anything.

Tracy pulls out a cuff and checks Maggie's blood pressure and pulse. Maggie has the urge to lean her head on Tracy's shoulder. Something tells her not to. Tracy seems so capable. She knows what she's doing. She won't let anything bad happen to Maggie. This is a comfort. She would like to take a break from this whole business for a while, to curl up and let Tracy hold her, keep this dreadful process at bay for a while. Maybe make it stop altogether. Tracy puts her stethoscope up to Maggie's belly, listening to the baby. It'll all be okay; Tracy's in charge.

"Baby still sounds good. Let's try some pushing. Aren't you about ready to find out if it's a boy or a girl? "

This is confusing. Maggie doesn't know what Tracy means. It's so hard to concentrate. The words don't make sense. And she isn't sure how to express her confusion—she's not even positive how to make her mouth work. She decides to try. "I'm not sure...I don't think...I don't know...."

But then her voice drops an octave, and that animal is growling again.

"Nooooo...ummmph..."she takes a breath. "Mmm...maybe...."she forces the word out.

"All right, Maggie. Let's push now. Take a breath and hold it and push through your bottom. Push to my count of three. Ready, now. Breathe, and one…two…three. Now breathe easy. There you go. How was that?"

That was perplexing. She wasn't really supposed to hold her breath, was she? Hadn't one of the books said something about never, ever holding your breath—because if you always keep breathing you'll be all right? On second thought, maybe that was scuba diving. She thinks she might cry. She had studied so hard, reading all those books, going to class, taking notes. Now it's all so confusing. She had even made some little flash cards, with condensed instructions for each stage of labor. She wonders where they are now. Wherever she left them, Sam has probably tidied up and thrown them away.

And she still doesn't get the pushing bit. What is that supposed to *feel* like? Isn't it supposed to be some huge uncontrollable urge? Wasn't she supposed to be overwhelmed with the need to bear down (whatever that means) and push her baby out? Push with what? Where? She doesn't know what to say to Tracy, who looks so hopeful. She shrugs.

"It's fine, I guess."

Tracy looks at her for a minute, frowning. "Was it? You don't sound sure."

Maggie closes her eyes in exasperation. Why won't everyone go away and leave her alone? She's too tired to play twenty questions. This is not interesting; it's enervating. She has no idea what the right answer might be. It is an effort even to remember the damned question. "Yes. I'm fine," she snaps.

Sam snorts, and she glares at him. He stifles his amusement. She casts irritably around the room for a distraction. Nothing seems like a good idea. She doesn't want water, or ice chips. She's way beyond reading; that's not even a plausible thought. The television would be annoying. Music— she can't think what she brought, or what might be soothing. Too much trouble to figure it out. Maybe another little rest now. The flowers are so pretty. She loves stargazers. Sam's mother calls them *rubrum* lilies, drawing the first syllable out with heavy emphasis, then drawing the second up short. The way she says it always makes Maggie think of crepe myrtles or mint juleps or mosquito netting or something.

The petals curve out and back, away from the throat of the flower. What a sensuous word for a plant part—throat. *Throat* implies submission and vulnerability. The physicality of the flowers is unnerving. Liquid oozes from their pores, gathering in clear drops, swelling and trembling as if the petals weep. They are paler around the edges, the pink darkening toward the deep scarlet throat. Each petal is thick, fleshy and substantial—voluptuous. Luxurious. She gazes at them, drawn into the heat at the center of each flower. There are twelve in the vase, a heavy, heady mass of pistils and petals and anthers and stamens. The words tumble in her head; she isn't sure which part is which, but even in their trimmed state, these flowers exude fertility.

The arrangement from Ben graces the windowsill; she turns her head to look at the roses, mostly the very palest pink ones, cool and elegant. Some sort of open, lacy fern—one that Maggie has never seen before— sets them off, casting them more in a spring meadow than the muggy Washington garden of her childhood. Even the vase is an image of simplicity. The glass is clear and thin, with a gentle curve that extends the reach of the flowers. The soft pink glows, nestled in among the airy greens. Tiny, tight buds of pristine pink close in on themselves, while the loose, open ruffles of the cabbage roses promise languid ease. They soothe Maggie's eyes, and she tries to convey the image of conscious tranquility to her agitated body.

It doesn't work. She doubles over herself, grunting again, the very center of her body convulsing against itself in a spasmodic ecstasy. Somewhere at the back of the sensation is exactly that—an ecstasy, or satisfaction of some sort. Completion, perhaps. She isn't sure; but her body seems to settle to this new pattern with an ease that reassures her.

Tracy is there by the bed again. "All right now, Maggie. Let's push. On my count. One, two, deep breath, now push. That's it. Puuush." She draws the syllable out, as if there is some relationship between that insignificant little word and this primal power that is bearing down now. When Maggie opens her mouth to speak, the voice that erupts from her throat is not her own. That brutal noise can't possibly be her.

It's the cry of raw fear, of passion, of the ancient power of the divine feminine. She hears clearly, cut loose from the shroud of time, all the women who have led her here, to this center of herself, this precarious divide between life and death. She hears it and feels it. It could go either way. This baby could rip her apart—her own body could work itself to death. Or crush and smother and break its own immortality. She could close her eyes now and let herself roll over the precipice, dissolve into the sea of fatigue that clutches at her.

But she calls herself back from the edge; it *is* somehow, her power, their power—even her mother's power. Language is irrelevant—the words stand in for the sounds that are the real meaning. She knows someone is talking to her, chattering; she feels the voice, feels the woman, but that's all that matters. The words are so much buzz, obscuring the reality. Her voice blasts out of her throat once more—it is no longer her own. She doesn't recognize it, or control it.

She sees, in her mind, once more, her necklace—the dominant belly, the legs thrown wide, the face taut with effort. She feels it now, knows it to be herself. The weight of it is strong in the hollow of her throat. This is all that's left to her now—this tiny lump of clay, dangling from a thin strip of leather, warm from her body's heat. She cranes her neck, trying to look at the amulet, but the cord is too short. What she sees instead is the rise of her huge belly, and above it, those swollen, blue-veined breasts that don't resemble her own even remotely. She sees the echo, though, of the ancient laboring woman, and the recognition prickles in her eyes. She blinks hard, and feels her body ease up just enough.

Chapter 23

Something is happening on the edge of her universe. She is on her side, facing the window, aware that someone new is in the room behind her. She is coming out of a fog and can't place the voice, but it's familiar. Wait—Samuel. Her brain is moving in slow motion. He wasn't here earlier—somewhere silly—an airplane—a football game—he must have caught an earlier flight home. Ahh. The storm must have let up. She looks over her shoulder and can see Samuel in the doorway, with Sam, but also with Katharine, who looks furious. She wonders what the problem is.

Maggie is suddenly aware of her own nakedness, and pulls the sheet right up to her chin as she heaves herself over onto her other side, so she can see what's going on. Sam looks up; stubble has grayed his chin, and his eyes are tired, but he is grinning like a little boy.

Katharine is scolding. Samuel is red-faced and almost as rumpled as Sam; Maggie recognizes his bullish look, the look that tends to steamroll right over people. She usually steps out of the way. She can't really do that now, beached as she is under this sheet.

"Well, it's your own fault for not being here to begin with. The rest of us have been waiting all day!" Katharine shrills.

"Sam," Maggie whispers. "What's going on?" He looks from his father to his mother-in-law, and rolls his eyes as he walks back to his rocking chair post.

He shrugs and stretches his neck. "Who knows. Your mother is furious about something. I don't know what. My dad is—I don't know. Drunk, maybe. Certainly difficult. Are you okay?"

"No. Stupid question. But what's the actual problem? And," she looks around, realizing, "where's Tracy?"

Sam's syllable of laughter is tinged with panic. "Hah! She leaves for two minutes and all hell breaks loose. I don't know. She went somewhere. Something about a cart. I don't know." He sinks into a chair and rubs the bridge of his nose. "Are you ready to push again?"

Maggie ignores him, distracted by the continued bickering, which has now moved out into the hallway. "But what are they arguing about?"

He takes a deep breath, and recites. "Well, he really is tipsy. A little bit. I'm not sure whether he was celebrating in Atlanta, or not until he got the phone call, but either way, Mom is mortified. She tried to send him up here so your mother wouldn't figure it out—apparently he faked it enough to get by security. But Katharine decided he shouldn't come up—she's gone all mama-bear over you—and got in his way and wouldn't let him by.

"Of course he saw that as the ultimate challenge, and nothing was going to keep him from this room. So in the process of trying to stop him, your mother got a whiff of him and realized what's really going on, and is apparently now sharing every nasty thought she's ever had about my entire family since our first date. And of course, they happened to storm into the room as soon as Tracy left, and you were off in la-la land some-where, and my head's throbbing.

"I give up. It's bedtime. Can't we get this show on the road?" He leans forward and rests his head on the edge of the bed.

"Sure. No problem. I'll just, you know, push really hard or some-thing—then we can go home." She blinks hard again. "Okay. It's starting again. Mmmmph.... Can't you...make them...go away?" The arguing in the hall recedes, then the room disappears. This time there is no Tracy guiding her, and she is lost, buffeted by her own body. She can't remem-ber what to do—how to breathe, which muscles she needs to feel—how to get to the other side. All she can do is open her mouth and let it all out, and she does. The groan tears at her throat; she can feel its rawness. She remembers Sam's odd phrase—mama-bear—and wonders if this is what her mother sounds like, out there in the hall. It's hard to imagine

Katherine, always so driven and focused, allowing herself to just *emote*. The sound comes from the very pit of her stomach, forcing its way up and out, into the light. She gasps, and groans, and stumbles through the contraction. When it subsides, her body droops with exhaustion.

She looks up to see Katharine storm into the room, followed by Tracy, who lets the door thunk closed behind them.

"Do you people always get along so well?" Sam snorts, but Katharine ignores Tracy and comes to stand by the head of the bed.

"The managing nurse is not going to put up with that in the hall—there are women in labor here. You'll have to keep the noise down, or take it outside."

"There's nothing to take outside. I'm perfectly calm." She shoots a look at Sam. "Samuel has gone to get a cup of coffee. He'll be fine."

Maggie hears all this, but is untouched by it. Their stress buzzes around her, but seems irrelevant. Her body consumes her attention. She is hot now, burning up. Sweat pops out on her forehead, and beads along her upper lip. She kicks at the damp sheet with her feet, and tries to push the loose strands of hair back from her face. It's so hot—she feels almost sick from the heat burning through her body. Then just as quickly, it breaks. She feels the clamping again; her gut seizes up and she doubles over.

The spasm passes. Her mother is still standing by the bed, watching.

"It hurts my neck to look at you," Maggie says.

Her mother moves to the end of the bed. "Better?"

"No. Sit. Please."

Her mother hesitates. "I don't want to take your chair, Sam."

"I'm fine."

She sits down in the chair, closer to Maggie's eye level. "I can leave, if you'd rather."

"No, stay." She pauses. "This is bad."

Her mother leans her head closer, as if to tell her a secret, and waits, not meeting Maggie's eyes. Frustration surges through Maggie. She wants something—*needs* something—desperately. But she has no idea what, or how to get it. She wants to shake her mother, shake the secrets, the answers, the magic solutions, right out of her. She blinks back hot tears. *Look at me*, she wants to shriek.

But something else pops out instead—her old fall-back. "I wish Yaya was here."

This time Katharine looks her in the eye. "Me too."

"You don't understand," Maggie says, but pauses, grunting, when the spasm grips her again. She hangs onto the thought, her indignation carrying her through until she's gasping when it subsides.

"What don't I …." her mother begins, but Maggie stops her, the words tumbling out before she can stop them, now or never.

"I don't know how to do this! I don't understand how I'm supposed to just *become* a mother! *What if I can't*?"

"What are you talking about? Of course you can—it's not the easiest job in the world, but you'll be fine. Women far less equipped than you manage just fine, every day. I did."

"No! You didn't—Jamie died! He *died*, Mother! That wasn't just fine, not at all. I've already lost one baby. What if I can't keep this one alive, either?"

Maggie can't breathe. She can't snatch back those catastrophic words, can't forget she spoke them, thought them, felt them. The silence in the room compounds her horror. She turns her face into the bed, unwilling—unable—to face the betrayal reflected in her mother's eyes.

She hears a shuffle, and Sam clears his throat.

"No, it's okay Sam," her mother says. Maggie still doesn't look up. Another spasm grips her, and she steels herself against it. She won't moan, won't even whimper—she has no right. This is only what she deserves, for saying such awful things.

"Maggie, look at me."

Maggie tries to bury her face deeper in the bed, to press herself into oblivion, but her body tethers her to the moment. Finally she is compelled to look at her mother. Katharine's face is pale; a bright, high spot of color burns on each cheekbone.

"And it was more than I could bear, but I did, because that's what you do. I didn't have a choice." Her voice cracks.

"*But I needed you!*" It's as if the words have been ripped from her throat, after she's held them in for all these years, and now she can't stop them. "I was so scared. I never even understood—what happened that day, Mother? *What happened?*"

"Oh, honey. Don't go there. Not today. Not now."

"I have to! *I can't remember.* I have to remember!"

"No—no you don't. I remember. I remember it all. I remember enough for both of us, and too much too."

"*Tell me.*"

"I don't know." Katharine's voice is exhausted. "I never did really understand why that baby died. I didn't get hurt or anything. It was like my body knew how badly Jamie was hurt, and couldn't cope. I started bleeding, and then it wouldn't stop. I thought I was going to bleed to death back there on that site, lying there on the ground, holding him."

Maggie remembers the sight of her mother at the hospital, after the accident. White as the sheets on the bed. The memory still makes her feel hollow inside. At the time, it had just been scary. Now it makes sense: Katharine had lost too much blood. She tries to calm down, but her traitorous brain won't let her. She has to know, has to hear it all. "Was it a boy or a girl? You never told us." Even to her own ears, it's more accusation than question.

Katharine sways a little, but her eyes never waver. "She was a little girl. I lost a son and a daughter, in one day." Her voice cracks. "They wanted me to see her. I was already six months, you know. They had to do an emergency C-section because of the bleeding. But I didn't want to see her. I think your father did, but I couldn't handle seeing her. We never even named her. I think that's the most cowardly thing I've ever done."

Maggie can't bear the naked grief on her mother's face. She smashes her face back into the bed, trying to escape the loss of a tiny baby sister, and her own baby that hadn't made it. This is more than she can take in. Her own miscarriage is still raw in her mind. There had been no baby for her to see, just a haze of fear and drugs, then weeks of anemic exhaustion. But Katharine—that baby had been fully formed, had quickened with life, moving and kicking. Maggie can't think about what that must have done to her mother.

Oh, God. Panic surges through her; her mother's grief and pain are still raw, too, after all these years. Maggie could never handle so much loss. She doesn't have it in her. She's not ready, even as her body relentlessly pushes her toward motherhood. She fights against another spasm, actively resisting the urge to push now. She's too scared—it hurts too much. She's having trouble remembering if there was ever anything that wasn't pain of one kind or another. She clutches at a hand—her mother's hand—and grinds out the words. "I'm sorry. I'm so, so sorry."

Katharine is all she can see. "Maggie. Look at me."

"No. I can't." She sobs. "I should've run faster. I should've tried harder." She can hardly breathe.

"*It was not your fault.* Listen to me, Maggie. Let that go. It was a terrible, tragic thing, but it was a long time ago. Your baby is almost here now. Focus."

Maggie feels Katharine's other hand, the one she's not holding, rest lightly on her bare belly, cool against the hot, tight skin. Her breathing settles as the contraction subsides, and she is still, resting in her mother's touch.

Then Tracy's voice comes through to her. "All right Maggie. I think you need to focus on pushing now." She whispers something to Katharine, then moves around to the foot of the bed.

Katharine squeezes Maggie's hand, then says, very gently, "I'm going to go wait in the hall. You're going to be fine—it won't be much longer."

"No—wait," Maggie starts, but Katharine has already extricated her fingers. She pushes the hair back from Maggie's forehead and gives her a small smile before she slips out of the room. The spot on Maggie's belly where Katharine's hand had rested feels naked now, exposed.

Tracy pats her on the foot. "Look at me, Maggie. You've got another contraction starting. Let's push this baby out. On my count. One, two, three—now push. Chin down. There you go—push against my hand." Maggie can barely feel the pressure of Tracy's hand between her legs. She pushes toward it, and there—that's it. She feels the push. That's all she needed, that direction to the specific muscle. It's deep, so deep. It's as if she's pushing her insides out. It's in her bowels, but not; deeper and lower. This is what they meant!

"I've got it!" she blurts. Finally, something she can get behind and put some effort into. This feels less like being run over by a truck and more like pushing the truck up a hill, but at least it's not so passive. Her whole body clenches around her middle, muscles straining. She can feel her face going red with work; she is trying to turn herself inside out.

She stops, panting, gasping for breath.

"Wow! Great job, Maggie. That's the right idea. You rest now. We'll do it again on the next contraction." Tracy pats her foot and pulls the sheet up over her legs. Maggie looks around for Sam, and she's grinning now. She can't read the look on his face. He looks pleased. Not excited, exactly—a bit green around the gills still.

"That's so much better. I didn't know where to push. But….."she turns to find Tracy again. "But what about that lip?"

"What lip?" Tracy frowns.

"You said I still had a lip of cervix. Is it okay? I mean, I shouldn't push too hard, right?"

Tracy's eyes widen. "What are you talking about? Of course you should push hard. That's the only way this baby's coming out. I'm not sure what you're worried about."

"You mean I didn't need to be waiting?" Confusion wells up in Maggie's chest. "You said, last time you checked, that there was still a lip of cervix."

"Yes." Tracy waits. Maggie tries to remember the logic that was holding her back.

"It said, in one of the books, that you shouldn't push against a lip, that pushing could cause it to swell and then it would be even harder for it to fully dilate."

"Oh, for Pete's sake." Tracy speaks slowly, as if to one who doesn't understand. "Is that what's been holding you back? Honey, you're going to have to learn to ignore those books. Yes, you did have a tiny little bit of cervix that hadn't slipped back yet. But that was a matter of minutes. I imagine you were fully dilated almost immediately after I checked you. It's been a long time since then and your body is plenty ready for you to go ahead and push as hard as you can. It's fine. I promise. You're not going to hurt yourself by pushing. It's part of labor. That's how you get the baby out."

Maggie's face betrays her lingering hesitation.

Tracy looks at her for a second, then reaches out and brushes the amulet still dangling from Maggie's neck. "It's okay. Your little birthing woman here? I think it's time to let her watch from a distance. You're getting into the part where we don't want anything getting in the way."

Maggie put a hand over the tiny stone. "But I don't ever take it off."

"I know. She'll be safe, right here. She'll keep an eye on things. You know what? She was pushing hard. That's why it's called labor. It's hard work. Your body knows what to do—trust your instincts." She reaches behind Maggie's neck to unclasp the leather cord.

Maggie nods, and mulls this over for a moment. Sam comes to the edge of the bed and pushes her hair back from her face. Without speaking, he reties her ponytail, then wipes her forehead with a washcloth. The institutional terrycloth is rough, but Sam has dampened it with cold water. She closes her eyes and lets the coolness wash over her.

"They've moved on down the hall, I think."

"Who? Oh. Them. Good. I can't cope. What's going on with her?"

Sam throws the cloth across the room, into the sink, and stalks toward the door, then back again. He looks pent-up, an odd combination of exhaustion and anticipation. His khakis are now rumpled in every possible direction, creased and wrinkled and floppy. He is an exclamation mark in the room—tall and emphatic. Maggie realizes, watching him, that she already knows the answer to her question.

"Nothing any grandmother-to-be wouldn't be feeling. She just has a little more baggage than most."

Maggie tries to reconcile Sam's words with the mother she knows. The overlapping images don't quite match up, but the jagged edges remind her of her own grief. She blinks back tears. "But what about your dad? What's his problem?"

Sam throws his hands into the air and turns back to the door. He opens it, sticks his head out, looks up and down the hall, then withdraws back into the room, like a turtle pulling back into its shell.

"Dad's fine. He might've celebrated a little too much in Atlanta. He didn't realize he was going to have to turn around and fly back in a hurry. He didn't even have to, really. He probably should've stayed put till tomorrow. I'm glad he's here, but I could do without the craziness out there." Sam opens the door and scans the hall again, in both directions, shrugging his shoulders as he turns back into the room to face her. "Maybe it's blown over for now. Are you okay?"

Maggie is beyond him already, grunting and panting. Tracy, who has been discreetly buried in paperwork in the corner, comes to the side of the bed and turns on the energy in the tiny little room.

"All right, Maggie. You remember, now, right? One, two, and push! Atta girl. Okay, Maggie, deep breath, and close your mouth. Try to push through your bottom, not your throat. I'll put my hand there so you can push against it again. One more. Great job! Okay. Take a little break now till the next one, and we'll do it again. Just like that, okay? Try and remember where you were pushing toward my hand; that's the right idea." Tracy pulls the sheet over Maggie and goes to the sink, leaving her panting and exhausted as the contraction ebbs.

Sam comes back to the edge of the bed and rubs the back of her hand. "Sorry," he says. Maggie finds this notable, but her mind has been wiped clean, and she has no idea what he's apologizing for. She nods and closes her eyes.

"How about some ice?"

"Yuck."

He leans down and whispers in her ear, "What about a butterscotch?"

"Ugh. No." Even the thought turns her stomach. She swallows.

Sam sits down and casts around the room. "Should I take some pictures?"

Even in her addled state, Maggie has the wherewithal to be horrified by this notion.

"You've got to be kidding. Don't you dare. Besides, that's bad karma or something."

Sam's grin twinkles, even through his stubble. Maggie feels another contraction starting—so soon!—and braces herself. She warns of its imminence with that low, rumbly groan. Tracy comes back to the bed, and this time Sam stays. Maggie is vaguely aware of his presence.

When it's over, Tracy pulls her stethoscope from one of the pockets in her flowered top and presses the end to Maggie's belly.

"Baby's doing great, you're doing great. You're going to be a mommy soon. But I want to help you get into a better position. I think this baby might move on down a little faster if we get gravity to help a little bit. I want to get you sitting up and see if that helps." She pauses, and Maggie looks doubtful. "Actually, you know what? Do you think you could lean up over the ball again? That would probably be even better—would you like to try?"

Maggie eyes the ball in the corner, and shakes her head. "No way." She is decisive. The idea of moving is inconceivable. The trauma is too much; she is curled in on herself, hanging on.

Tracy rolls the ball over, ignoring Maggie's dissent.

"Come on. We'll give it a try and if it doesn't work for you, we'll bag it. Sam, would you give us a hand?" She keeps a patter running as she and Sam work together to get Maggie into a more vertical position—not sitting, exactly, more like propped. She sways on the edge of the bed for a moment, then another contraction begins before they can get her into position. Tracy has another trick—she twists a lever, and the bottom half of the bed breaks away, leaving Maggie sitting on a ledge, with her feet resting on two steps angled back toward her at the right height so that she can wedge against them and—then she's pushing again.

"Okay Maggie! Use the steps, that's right. You've got some leverage now—let's work with it. On my count…"

It goes on, much like the last one, except that her pushing muscles now have an enclosed space within which to work. She feels like she's made a remarkable discovery. She holds a breath, and pushes hard, trying to pry the two ends of the bed away from each other. She tries to visualize the power of the push flowing up from her legs, into her back, out from her belly and spine, down through her perineum. She still can't feel that she's pushing a specific object out of herself. She had expected that it would feel like pushing a bowling ball out. Instead, it seems a bit pointless. But it's clearly stronger and more satisfying now. Somehow, Tracy has made it better.

As she follows through to the end of the third of this series of three pushes, the words come together in her mind.

"Thank you," she whispers. It is the loudest voice she can muster.

Tracy looks at her blankly.

"For the steps. It's better."

"Good. Let's try the ball. You'll like that even more."

She is panting from exertion. The ball looks insurmountable. "I don't think so. This is good. I'll just stay here."

"Come on. We'll help. I'll get you rolled over, and Sam will hold the ball steady for you." Suddenly the bed has gone flat behind her again, leaving her drooping without the support. Turning over, finding her center of gravity, bearing her own weight on her knees—this is all too much. Her body is pulled in too many directions, like one of those Indian sunburns she used to do to Dara when they were kids. Her belly seems to be ripping open. She cries out, more shrilly than she realizes, gasping at the discordant pain that shoots through her.

"No!" The pushing, while hard, feels *right*. It is her body's work, and she can bear it, because it seems to work through her, instead of slamming into her. This, though, is not *right*. Her body protests, and the difference cripples her. She is trapped, one knee on the bed, one leg dangling down behind her, unable to find the step to rest her foot on. She can't hold her head up, the weight of her belly sagging toward the bed feels as if it will tear her skin, and her vagina threatens to explode outward.

"Wait. Stop. This isn't working," Sam says.

She can hear panic creeping into his voice, and she moans in response. He bends down to look into her face. Her mouth is hanging open; her breathing is ragged. Drool gathers at the corners of her mouth.

"Are you okay?"

She shakes her head no; it is heavy, dangling loose on the end of her neck.

"Roll the ball up under her, Sam. It'll hold her up. She'll be better that way."

"I don't think so. This isn't working. I think she wants to sit back like she was."

"Just do it—here—like this." Tracy moves around to the other side of the bed, picking up the ball and dropping it on the bed in front of Maggie's head. Maggie sways; the round ball, the strange, upside-down droop of her head, the pain—she is disoriented and dizzy. Gravity pushes her toward the bed. Her arms are beginning to buckle. Above her, some-where, Sam is saying something to Tracy, but it's background noise. There is no world beyond this inch of rumpled white sheet. She presses her nose into it. The wrinkles are disruptive, but persistent. She wants to curl into a ball, but she's stuck—halfway on the bed, sinking downward, twisting and grinding. She wants to roll back over. This nonsense needs to stop. The great weight of her belly pulls at her. She takes a breath and hauls herself up on her hands and knees. She has a job to do.

"I need to push. *This* way."

Chapter 24

"How's it coming in here?"

Dr. Morgan's cheerful boom penetrates Maggie's fog of misery, and she lifts her head slightly to see her doctor suited head to toe in green scrubs. Dr. Morgan ignores Tracy and Sam. She is still tucking her hair into the cap—an elasticized number that looks exactly like a green shower cap. It gives her an air of frazzled distraction.

Maggie's peculiar stretch half onto the bed draws the doctor up short. "That doesn't look too comfortable," Dr. Morgan says, taking in the room, the stand-off between Tracy and Sam, the agony contorting Maggie's face.

"We're trying to get her into a better position, so she can get more leverage. She's pushing, but there's not much force behind it," Tracy explains.

Dr. Morgan squats down so that she can peer into Maggie's eyes. "Maggie, let's get the ball up under you so you can push a little better. It's time for your baby to come on out."

"No. That won't work—it hurts too much. I don't want it. It was better sitting up." It takes all her effort to get the words out, but fear has taken over. She feels like she can barely breathe face-down like this. She mashes her forehead into the bed, trying to brace herself as her body knots up again, pushing against itself. She hears Tracy saying something about goal posts, wonders again what rabbit hole she has fallen down, and loses herself as the pain rips through her body. She grunts, then whimpers as the contraction ebbs. Dr. Morgan is still there, right at eye level.

"Maggie, we're going to move you into another position—see if we can get you more comfortable, okay?" Without waiting for an answer, the doctor, all compact strength, gets behind Maggie and hauls her back around into a sitting position on the end of the bed. She resists; she is afraid of the pain that accompanies movement. But Dr. Morgan is stronger than she is.

Upright, she can breathe again, but the relief is short-lived; she sits, beginning to tremble, on the end of the bed. A very small, disconnected part of her brain notes that Sam looks like shit. She waits. The contraption that Tracy pulls out of a hidden cupboard truly does look like a goal post, except upside down. Two upright poles attach to the end of the bed, one on each side, connected horizontally at the top by a third pole, framing Maggie's view.

"All right. Now you have leverage, and you're going to use it to push this baby out. Ready?" This must be a rhetorical question. She's not ready—how could anyone be ready for this hell?—but she's more than ready for it to be over. Dr. Morgan raises the top half of the bed back up into its chair configuration. Now she is sitting up, leaning back against the mattress. The doctor lifts Maggie's legs, one at a time, and props her feet against the poles, so that her knees are pointed back toward her armpits. She can't imagine a more awkward feeling, but her hesitation evaporates as the next contraction gathers.

"All right, Maggie. You're going to bear down now. Take a deep breath and hold it, that's right, now push. And push. Good job—another breath. And push. That's it—hold it, hold it, keep pushing. And release. And breathe, and last time, push. Once more, push. That's it. Good job. Rest for a minute." Dr. Morgan's cheerleading is different from Tracy's. Maggie can feel it; the difference is qualitative, somehow. There is less wasted energy; the pushing goes straight through to her crotch.

Maybe it's the poles; the power behind this new position is amazing. Maggie's hands are behind her thighs, pulling them wide, opening her to the world. The deep breaths stop her energy from flowing upward, redirecting it down and out. She can put her whole body behind this position, and push from her shoulders on down. Something shifts and catches in her pelvis, then holds up hard. It's going to rip her open, she knows it is.

Her brain and her body are in direct opposition now—she has to push it out, but feels like she'll die in the process.

She strains and struggles. This is like trying to push a house off its foundation. Nothing budges. She is heaving against an immovable object.

"Okay, Maggie. Rest. You're doing great. Take a break." This is Dr. Morgan again. She moves around the room now, flipping through the chart, opening and closing drawers and doors. She rubs Maggie's foot as she moves past the end of the bed. Her unruly hair is a sandy sort of red, browner than strawberry but with enough flame to give her a faintly volatile air. It's wiry, like her arms. Thin and muscular, her arms are corded with veins. Maggie has spent the last nine months being slightly intimidated by Dr. Morgan. Her body fairly quivers with energy. At first Maggie found the ebullience off-putting, but she has come to expect it. Her doctor's straightforward efficiency today is disconcerting; even in her exhaustion, Maggie feels an aura of serious intensity around the doctor that is unfamiliar.

Maggie flounders a bit. Tracy has stepped back, out of her line of sight, and Dr. Morgan only partially fills the void. As the contraction fades, Maggie pants and relaxes. Her legs are heavy; she can feel, even through the soup of sensations that have overrun her body, that her hamstrings are being stretched beyond their limits. The contractions have been singing up and down the backs of her legs all day, and now her legs are practically wrapped around her neck. It's too much. The ache builds in her mind until she can no longer bear it, and lets go her hold on the backs of her thighs. Her legs immediately begin to shake violently, sliding down the poles. Her muscles have gone slack; she can't even control the descent toward the bed.

Another contraction begins.

"All right Maggie. Let's push some more. How about if we get your feet back up? Use these poles, okay?"

"Mmmmmm—can't. Too tired." The groan begins again, down in her chest somewhere.

"Okay, then I'm going to help you roll onto your side. It's not as hard to hold your legs up that way. But I want you to be able to use the poles. You really pushed the baby down with that last one." Maggie stops listening. She is trying to push again. It's what her body needs to do. But without the physical cues, the parameters, she can't take her limbs out of the equation, or focus her energy, or control her breathing. She flails, and pushes randomly into the cosmos. There is no satisfaction this time.

Dr. Morgan manipulates her body again, compensating for Maggie's fatigue with her own strength. She tips the bed back closer to flat again and rolls Maggie onto her side. She arranges her leaden legs so that the bottom one is hooked onto one of the vertical poles, and the top leg is up on the top pole.

"I can't hold it." Maggie feels the weight of her own leg pulling downward, and knows that if it slips off the pole, she will have no control over its crash back to the bed.

"Sam, stand there and hold her leg. She can rest it on your shoulder between pushes, or she may need to push against you."

Maggie lies inert on the bed. Somewhere in the back of her mind her overarching modesty has taken a beating, but she can't label the feeling. She's too tired. The word survival flits through her mind. That's all she's trying to do. Beyond that, even—she just is. She's not actively striving toward anything anymore, even something as basic as survival. This pain, this exhaustion, this little patch of white cotton sheet—this is all she knows.

With this contraction, Dr. Morgan is a bit more strident. Maggie is too tired to concentrate. Nothing happens when she pushes, anyway. She's straining against an immovable object. She can't remember where she is or why. She hears people, through a tiny little tunnel in her consciousness, from very far away, calling to her, telling her to push. She tries. It goes nowhere. It's too hard. All she wants is to sleep. Her face rubs up against cotton. All around her is dark; she can't really see much beyond her nose. There seems to be a lot of activity somewhere very far away. She feels very warm; the warmth seems to flow out from her center, melting her body away. It's so warm; her arms and legs are dissolving.

Now they're yelling again. Calling her name.

"Maggie. Maggie! Look. Look here in the mirror. Look—you can see your baby's head! Look here. Maggie—look!"

She doesn't want to look. There's too much light. She squeezes her eyes shut against the brightness. Then she hears, through the noise, a voice she knows. Sam.

"Maggie! Oh, Maggie! There it is—push! There's the baby!" This pierces the fog, and she opens her eyes. When she gives them a second to adjust, she identifies a huge mirror, there, between her legs. Oh, God. It's horrifying. She gasps and screws her eyes shut again. She's not sure what she saw, but it was nothing identifiable. But she pushes again. Dr. Morgan calls to her, cueing her breathing, coordinating her muscles. She obeys. There are hands in her vagina. She doesn't care. Then—relief. So warm. Heat spreads through her pelvis, from her battered crotch inward. In a minute, the heat subsides, then again. The warmth is so good, so soothing. She relaxes into it, and then is brought up sharp by the searing pain.

"Oh, God. No!" She knows she's groaning again. She can't help it. She can barely breathe. "It's ripping me apart! Oh, no. I can't!"

"Yes, you can, Maggie. It's okay. I've got you. Let your baby come on out now. That's it. Relax your perineum. That's it." She's not sure what's happening, except that she is really being torn apart. She can feel flesh and skin stretching and tearing. It burns beyond comprehension.

"Okay, Maggie—stop! Don't push!"

Tracy is in her face. "Breathe, Maggie. Like me. Like you're blowing out a candle." Tracy pants very rapidly, short, shallow breaths, blowing them out in little puffs. Maggie does as she's told, and feels the panic subside a bit. She can hear Sam; he's holding her hand, squeezing it. She doesn't know what he's saying. But she feels the pressure of his thumb in her palm. She pants some more.

Then "Okay. One more push. That's it."

How bizarre. It's lumpy—hard, knotty bumps there, at the edge of the world, passing through the lips of her vagina, sliding through, slithering.

She gasps. Suddenly everything is over. Her body is still. Instantly, peace. That's it. She is empty and alert and Sam is sobbing.

Chapter 25

A baby appears right next to her on the bed, a tiny, scrunchy, angry thing, bleating like a lamb. It looks like a preposterous old man, with a little pink and blue striped knitted cap, pulled down almost to its eyes. Someone puts a blanket over them both, and she has to pull it back to look some more at this creature. Sam is there with her, hanging over them both. She looks up at him—he-who-is-real-in-her-world—and then back down at this mewling little, little, not-of-this-world-little baby. She bursts into tears.

"She's perfect. Oh, God, Maggie. Look at her. She's so perfect."

Maggie is beaming and sobbing and dripping tears on the baby. "Is she a girl?" she asks, laughter catching in her throat.

Sam is weeping as well. Tears are sliding down his face, his chin quivers, but his whisper reveres their daughter. *Yes, a girl, of course, a girl.* Maggie pulls the blanket down again, peering at the trembly little legs, soft and thin and slightly smeared. The little cleft between her thighs is so clearly a girl's, Maggie can't believe she didn't notice in her first glance at the child.

She's too much to take in. Maggie has to pull her head back slightly and tilt down her nose in order to see that this baby is here, in this room, with the rocking chair and the pile of newspapers and the anonymous pink drapes drawn against the chilly dark. She is real. There is even a cord, still, a twisted bruise of a rope that is part of this little belly, one seamless piece of flesh, yet she knows she can feel it still, resting on the inside of her own thigh, tying her forever to this little person. She tries to look at Sam, but can't tear her eyes entirely away from the baby.

"She's real." Her voice breaks and cracks and surges. "She's really real."

Sam is laughing. Maggie looks up. Tracy is laughing too, and so is Dr. Morgan. Maggie hasn't a clue what the joke is. She is oblivious. She props herself up on her elbow, feeling fabulous. It's beyond euphoria. It's pure adrenalin. The pain is over, it's finished, and she could move mountains. She wants to get out of this bed-prison. She wants to run and shout and—this baby. *My God.* This is exactly who she expected. She is precisely the person that Maggie knew all along, in her bones, without realizing. The recognition is staggering, and she gazes down in total amazement.

Maggie doesn't think or feel or know anything. The room drops out of her senses and disappears. Her blurry eyes consume this baby, through tears and pain and fatigue and joy. It's all gone, over with, the last twelve hideous hours. She feels like herself again, right through to the core. The little eyes peer out at her, dark and distant. So dark. She had expected icy blue, but these eyes are the sum of all color. There is no visible white; they are all iris. They are dark and deep and eternal, and she knows them. She is looking into herself. So solemn. There is no difference between them, no boundary or dividing line. Maggie knows that she is looking not at a part of herself, or a reflection, but the very essence of her own soul. She is lost in the eyes of her daughter.

Just as suddenly, the baby's eyes close, and Maggie blinks, returning to the hospital room. Tracy is fiddling with the bed controls, Dr. Morgan is occupied down by Maggie's feet, and Sam is leaning over her. Maggie begins to see the rest of the baby. She is not any one color, but pink and grayish and mottled and purple, all at once. Her hands are so tiny. Maggie uncurls a little fist, to examine the fingers. She can't imagine anything so small. They're nearly see-through. They have little fingernails, too tiny to even count as fingernails, just spots at the ends of her little fingers that look different from the long wrinkled bits.

A thin mat of very dark hair is plastered to her baby's skull. Maggie can see the pulse beating in the soft skin on top of her head. It seems so temporary, so random. As if it might stop working, after all. Memory flashes snapshots of her mother, propped up in a hospital bed, beaming down at a newborn Jamie; and her mother, ghost-like, withered by grief. The fragility of the fontanel is heart-breaking.

Maggie begins to feel something distracting her; the umbilical cord weighs heavy against her crotch. A sensation buzzes around her brain like a gnat. She isn't sure what it is, at first, and ignores it in favor of rubbing gingerly at the spotty, cheesy white flecks on the baby's arm. The stuff rubs off on her fingers and melts into her skin like lotion. But finally pain penetrates her fascination, and she gasps with the force of another contraction. She panics, and begins to shiver uncontrollably. Her whole body jerks violently; she's never been so cold. Her teeth chatter.

"Maggie? What's wrong?" Sam touches her shoulder.

She can barely get the words out. "I'm s-s-so c-c-c-cold!"

Tracy puts another blanket over her, but shivering has wrenched her abdominal muscles painfully.

"It's not over!" Her breathing is ragged and sharp. Words get caught in the tangle of fear that washes over her. Her eyes claw at Sam, and she moans. Mercifully, it's over in an instant, and she pants.

"What's wrong?" she pleads, tears welling up again. "Oh, please, let it end. I can't take this anymore. Why does it still hurt?" She is crying now.

Tracy rolls her over to half sitting. "It's the placenta. We're going to help you push it on out now. It won't take long, just a few good pushes. I'm going to massage your uterus a little to get it going. After it's out I'll go get some blankets out of the warmer."

With that warning, she plants both hands on Maggie's belly and bears down. The pain ruptures her consciousness and she knows she must die. This is more than she can survive. She sobs out loud, not hearing Dr. Morgan's exhortations to push, or Tracy's mumbled apologies, restricted by the effort of her massaging. Later, Maggie will conclude that the phrase "fundal massage" is a malicious euphemism perpetrated on vulnerable pregnant women.

When Tracy stops pounding on her stomach, she breathes again, a deep, raking breath. She feels a snap, and peers down between her knees. Dr. Morgan has cut the cord. For a brief second, the memory of which will fade almost instantly, Maggie feels her oneness with the baby severed. The loneliness keens through her whole body, and she vibrates on the edge of unbearable grief. But only for a split second. The moment is imprinted on her cells, but passes unnoted by her consciousness.

Something warm slithers from her, and she squints down at Dr. Morgan, who seems quite preoccupied.

"Was that it? Is it all out now?"

Dr. Morgan doesn't even look up. She is very busy with the ominous-looking instruments on a tray by Maggie's feet.

"Yep. All done. But you're bleeding a little bit, so Tracy's going to massage your uterus a little more so it'll contract. And you need a couple of little stitches. Only a few more minutes, and we'll get out of your way so you can rest, and nurse your baby."

Nurse. Oh, that's right. Damn. She meant to do that first thing. She remembers reading somewhere that breastfeeding before the cord is cut is really important. She's not quite sure why. Damn. This thing is screwed up from the very beginning. Oh well. She's not sure what to do; the baby is still there, curled on the bed beside her. Her brain homes in on the idea of breastfeeding until she makes the connection, slowly, that she must attach the baby to the breast. But about the time she formulates this thought, Tracy scoops the baby up and hands her to Sam.

"Let's let Daddy hold her for a few minutes, while we get you straightened out." Without warning this time, she throws herself again onto Maggie's stomach, pressing the life out of her. Maggie gasps, but has the presence of mind this time to breathe as if through a contraction. When it ends, she is moaning. If there were bile in her, it would rise into her throat, but there's nothing left, just the nausea of utter exhaustion. Shivering rattles her very bones.

"Please. Give me a minute. It hurts so much."

"I know, honey. It won't be much longer, I promise. It'll help when you get started nursing."

That was it. Now she remembers. Nursing helps with afterpains, or whatever it is that's supposed to happen afterward. She nods.

"Can I try?"

"One more push." And Tracy kneads that flaccid belly again, mashing its emptiness into a small ball of dull misery. Maggie is certain she can't take any more.

She sinks back against the pillows and breathes for a moment. As the pain of the massaging and contracting slows and fades, her minds clears a bit, and the room comes into focus again. Sam is standing right by the bed, rooted to the spot, with the baby in his arms.

He holds her cautiously, as if she might shatter. Maggie looks at him, and his expression is inscrutable, but feelings are flashing across his face like lightning. She puts one hand up, afraid to lose physical contact with the baby. Her fingers are touching the fragile curve of the back in Sam's arm. The baby's skin is softer than air; it feels transient, insubstantial against the hairy coarseness of Sam's forearm. The little head is cradled in the crook of his elbow, the spine curves down to the tiniest little buttocks fading into the palm of his hand. The legs are extra, somehow; they flop until Sam props his other arm up under them, his arms crossing to hold his daughter like this forever.

Chapter 26

Maggie is on her back now, sitting half upright, draped with various blankets and sheets. Stirrups have appeared at the end of the bed, but she doesn't pay them any mind, not really. Now that the breastfeeding issue has arisen, she's anxious to get started; her self-doubt about her ability to do this mysterious thing has plagued her for months. The moment of truth has arrived—it is no longer enough to theorize. She is the mother now.

She doesn't know where to start, or how. The pictures in the books looked manageable enough—all those diagrams of nipples and holds and cross-sections of the baby's tongue position—but now that she's faced with attaching an actual person to her actual breast, it's all a mystery. She waits, but Tracy doesn't tell her what to do.

"Tracy? How do I do this?"

Tracy chuckles. "All right. I'll get you started. The lactation consultant will come around in the morning to make sure it's going all right, but in the meantime, your postpartum nurse can help tonight. I'm leaving in a few minutes." She grabs a couple of pillows from a closet and puts them in Maggie's lap, then takes the baby from Sam, who backs away from the bed, looking a bit stunned.

On top of the pillows, the baby is right at Maggie's breast, which looks, placed on a pillow next to that tiny head, oddly huge. Maggie can see the baby's little mouth opening and closing, the tiniest bit, like a kitten whose eyes haven't opened yet, crying soundlessly for the mama cat's teat. Tracy unceremoniously shoves the baby's face into Maggie's left breast, and wiggles it around a bit, and suddenly Maggie feels the mouth clamp down, like a vise. Nothing much happens. Tracy looks at her. "How does that feel?"

Maggie squirms, a bit uncomfortably. "A little pinchy, that's all."

Tracy frowns a bit, and pushes her pinky finger into the corner of the baby's mouth, and the nipple slides out. "It shouldn't pinch. You should feel a strong, steady suck, but not a pinch. Better to take her off and start over. You don't want to hurt your nipples. And always break the seal with your finger like that—don't just pull her off. That would hurt you."

Maggie nods and looks up at Sam. He is peering over Tracy's shoulder, riveted.

"Are you taking notes? I can't remember all this."

He nods, unable to tear his eyes away from the baby, whom Tracy has once again jammed into Maggie's breast. This time, however, her mouth is on better, and all of a sudden Maggie feels the suck, pulling her nipple deep into the baby's mouth. The power takes her breath away.

"Oh! It's so strong!" She peers down at this little vacuum, pulling at her with its turbo-strength suction. The second suck establishes a rhythm. Maggie stares at the tiny pink lips clamped on her own skin, marveling at the outline of the perfect little jaw. The baby is outside of her body now, but this sucking connects them still, their bodies still working in tandem.

"How bizarre! I can feel it!" Her breath catches in her chest, and she stifles a laugh, afraid of upsetting the precarious balance of belly and breast and baby. Tracy nods, and goes back to help Dr. Morgan at the end of the bed. Sam pulls the chair back in by the head of the bed, and sits back down, fixated on the baby's mouth, working away. Maggie is barely breathing. She looks down in amazement. Sam seems as blown away as she feels. Their eyes meet, and he kisses her.

"I'm proud of you," he whispers in her ear. It's the nicest thing she's heard all day, she realizes. She smiles back at him, then looks down as the sucking stops.

"Oh, no! Tracy! What do I do? She stopped."

"That's okay," Dr. Morgan responds. "I'm going to do your stitches now, anyway. Take a break, and try her on the other side in a few minutes.

Okay, a little pinch." Maggie's torn flesh shrinks from the needle, but the pinch hurts like hell anyway. She grits her teeth; Sam puts two fingers into her palm for her to squeeze. Every sensation is heightened by fatigue. She can feel the thread rub as it is pulled through that sore, soft tissue around the edge of her vagina. The needle pierces again, then again. She feels cut open, flayed, and helpless against the bite. Again.

"There you go. All sewn up. You only had a tiny little tear, but I wanted it to heal up neatly. Those stitches will dissolve in a few days. Be sure and keep them clean."

Maggie nods in a daze.

"Can I please be finished hurting now?" Her voice is very small. She can't do any more. She lets Sam's fingers slip away. The baby is still lolling awkwardly on the pillows in Maggie's lap, and Sam lifts her, cradling her into the crook of his arm again. Dr. Morgan lifts Maggie's feet out of the stirrups, and she gingerly draws her legs together and curls up around the pillows. She is afraid of any more pain, any at all. Her crotch is battered and shredded and broken; her stomach is bruised and limp. She is afraid to let down her guard against her body's misery. If the onslaught were to begin again....

She looks at Sam holding the baby. Her euphoria has faded to a pale, glimmering joy that cloaks the room. Sam and the baby glow. Her emotions are too big to comprehend, so she lets them wash over her. For once, she feels no need to compress and compartmentalize and label her feelings, in order to gain control over them. Exhaustion has obliterated the filter that separates her mind from her body. She is a jumble of fear and pain and fatigue and joy; anxiety and pride and love. That's it. She pinpoints the undercurrent, and relaxes into the mattress. That's the bit she wasn't expecting—the intensity of this huge wave of love. Something inside of her has broken open, and she feels a bright, humming wire of ferocity connecting her to the bundle in Sam's arms. She feels like she might burst.

The room is warm and pink and quiet for a moment. Dr. Morgan is examining something disgusting in a basin, and Sam has very intentionally turned his back to her. Tracy is jotting notes again. There's a soft knock at the door, and she stands up to answer it rather than hollering, like she's done all day. It's another nurse, with a pile of blankets. They confer for a brief moment, then come to the bedside.

"Maggie, this is your postpartum nurse, Annie. We're going to help you get cleaned up."

Maggie nods. She's still so cold she is shaking. She can feel the skin of her thighs sticking together; the bed is rumpled and tangled. She is content to be cleaned.

Annie introduces herself to Sam and coos over the baby while Tracy runs warm water into a bowl and brings a pile of cloths and blankets to the bedside table. Together, Annie and Tracy swab Maggie's legs and crotch, very gently. They pat her dry, and carefully maneuver her arms into a clean, soft gown, one that snaps all the way up the front. With an efficiency that Maggie can't even understand, they roll her to one side, then the other, and when they're finished, she's sitting in a neat, orderly, well-made bed, with hot blankets over her legs and around her shoulders. She can feel crinkly pads under her butt; she doesn't question why. She is toasty and tidy and Sam puts the baby back in her arms. All is right with the world. Maggie glances up to see that the clock on the wall reads exactly 11 p.m. The shift will change soon—Tracy will leave, Annie will stay, and the world will go on revolving around the still center of this room.

Tracy comes to the edge of the bed and touches Maggie's shoulder. "I'm going to go, honey. You did good work tonight. You have a beautiful baby."

Maggie feels a mild stab of anxiety. Tracy has been here from the beginning; she's in charge. "When are you coming back?"

"I'm off for New Year's, so not until Friday. You might be gone by then. You're doing fine, so you'll probably go home pretty quickly. But Annie's here tonight, and I'm not sure who's on tomorrow. Anyway, you'll be fine. Annie will take good care of you, right Annie?"

"Absolutely. Plus there's a crowd of folks out in the hall that are dying to get in here and help." Her grin is cryptic; Tracy's eye-roll is much more transparent.

"Oh, I had forgotten about all of them. Sam, who's out there?" Maggie asks.

Sam is communing with the baby, smiling down at her without even looking up. "I don't know. Your mother is definitely there—last time I checked, she was guarding the door."

"Against who?"

"I'm not sure. Maybe she needed to feel useful. You kind of made a lot of noise."

"Who, me? No I didn't. Did I?" Maggie looks at Tracy for back-up, but is met with a rueful nod. She can't be bothered to blush.

"Is Dara still here?"

"Probably. I know my mom's still out there. I don't know who all else. Maybe my dad finally settled down. Or maybe not. Who knows. Don't worry about them. They'll wait, or they'll go home and come back tomorrow. We're busy."

Maggie shrugs, relieved to postpone the onslaught as long as she can, but oddly comforted, knowing they're all out there.

"I'll tell them when I go out, then, shall I? That you're still getting settled, and Sam'll be out in a bit? What about the baby? They're going to ask—do you want me to say it's a girl, or do you want to tell them yourselves?" Tracy is moving toward the door.

"Umm…I don't know. Sam?"

"I don't care." He is making faces at the bundle in his arms now. "Tell them whatever you want. I'll get to that in a while." He raises his eyebrows, his mouth forming a small round O. Then he smiles and nods, lost in a conversation that no one else can hear. Tracy shrugs at Annie, and heads out into the hall. The room feels empty without her.

Annie sits down to look through Maggie's chart. Sam sways in the middle of the room, completely engrossed in the baby. Maggie watches him, noting with mild interest that she's fine with that. It looks right, and she's so wiped out. She is finally warm enough, and her body is still, and she closes her eyes for a minute. The room is peaceful now—someone has dimmed the lights, and everything sort of glows pale pink. Sleep creeps up on her, and she dozes.

Her eyes open of their own accord, calmly, without panic or pain. She looks up at the clock, surprised to see that she's slept for only ten minutes. Everything is exactly as it was when she drifted off, except that Sam is now sitting in the rocker, holding the baby-lump curled against his chest. How odd, that a cat-nap could make this much difference. It was like some kind of super-sleep, dreamless, and utterly restorative.

Dreamless is good. For the last nine months, Maggie has been plagued by wild, Technicolor dreams, full of severed limbs and lost children and dead-end mazes. None of it made much sense, so she chalked it up to hormones. But blank, empty sleep is definitely good. She stretches a bit, hesitantly, afraid to move too much, and cocks her head, listening to her body's complaints. Everything aches, but she seems to be intact. The stitches are worrisome—how does one walk, or sit, or move, really, without hurting?—and her bladder is beginning to feel full. Now there's a thought. She looks around the quiet room, and realizes that Annie has left. Well, she definitely can't pop up and have a pee without some help, so she shifts a bit in the bed to relieve the pressure, and stops thinking about it.

She looks at Sam, and his eyes glow.

She smiles, then glances toward the door. "Don't you think we need to let them in?"

"Who? Oh, them. Yeah, I suppose so. She's asleep. You should probably breastfeed her again soon."

"Why? I thought you said she's asleep."

"Well…I don't know. Aren't you supposed to do it a lot?"

"I don't know." They look at each other. Maggie snorts. "This is going well."

Sam grins. "We'll be fine. All right, baby girl." He stands up, cradling her tight to his chest, like a china egg, "It's time for you to meet your insane family. The barbarians are at the gate, and we're going to let them in. Brace yourself."

CHAPTER 27

He hands the baby to Maggie, then opens the door. Maggie is still trying to situate the baby in her lap when the hordes descend. A wall of faces presses against her, pushing her back into the bed. The air of the small room fills up with their breath, with perfume and food and body smells, and Maggie feels that perfect moment slipping away. Katharine is there, and Ellen and Samuel and Dara and Melissa—no children, she notes with relief. Annie has come back in; and is moving around the room with calm authority. Maggie relaxes, and relinquishes the baby. They pass her from hand to hand, cooing and babbling. The baby looks at them with wide, sober eyes.

Sam is beaming and telling labor tales to anyone who will listen; his audience varies, depending on who isn't holding the baby, or hanging over the shoulder of the person who is. Ellen chatters and gushes. Samuel booms; he avoids Katharine's eyes, and they orbit at a distance from each other. Katharine's earlier stiffness has relented, and she hovers while Dara welcomes the baby with goo-goo eyes and secret, whispering smiles. Maggie watches it all, amused.

She feels generous and expansive. This moment feels right, as if all the pieces have slipped into place. She realizes with a jolt that she's been waiting for this all along. This is the moment she had tried to visualize, and couldn't: the coming together of all these complicated people, to create a place in the family for her daughter. It seems to be working.

Melissa wants to hear about the birth. Maggie gives herself wholly to her sister-in-law's attention, and tells as much as she can remember.

"It hurt. It really, really hurt. And I didn't think it was ever going to end. Oh, my God. Never again."

Melissa laughs. "Never say never! That's what I said. I was wrong!" she crows. Maggie laughs along with her. Now that it's down to the moment, she's glad they're all here, in this tiny little cozy pink room. It's late; they must've been waiting for hours. Ellen kisses her on the cheek, and Maggie knows that this time, she means it. Samuel is holding the baby now, and he's rock-steady on his feet. He looks around the room. "What's her name?"

Everyone stops talking. Sam looks at Maggie.

"It's up to you, pumpkin. You know what I think."

Maggie contemplates her daughter, the small, tidy bundle that has brought this noisy group together in the middle of the night. Samuel holds her tight in the crook of his arm, beaming as if he'd brought her into the world himself. Maggie fights back a bittersweet lump in her throat while they all look at her, expectant. Her family—her daughter's family. Katharine comes to sit on the edge of the bed. Her cool hand brushes Maggie's hair back from her face, then she reaches in to wrap her arms around Maggie.

"Her name is Eliana," Maggie announces over her mother's shoulder, sure now.

"It's Hebrew," Sam says. "It means a gift from God. I think it fits."

Maggie smiles. She watches. Ellen opens her mouth, but Dara is suddenly next to her, handing her the baby. Ellen melts, visibly. Katharine squeezes Maggie's hand.

"Good choice," she whispers.

"I know."

Melissa is the first to go, worried that her husband might have had trouble getting all of their children to bed. "Michael swore he was going to stay up until midnight," she worries, by way of apology, as she fumbles with coat and bag and scarf. She slips out, and then Samuel begins to fade.

He plops down in the rocking chair, scraping one of its rockers against the wall. "Sorry." He doesn't look terribly concerned, but Ellen suddenly remembers her identity, and squawks into project management mode.

"Oh, my gracious. We need to get you home. Here, Dara, you hold the baby. I'm exhausted. Sam, honey, would you walk us down to the car? Your father's exhausted. Katharine, you'll be here a few more minutes, so I can borrow Sam, right? She's a beautiful baby, Maggie. We're very pleased. Her crib is all ready at our house, so bring her soon. Happy New Year, everyone!" She is still chattering as her son and husband bustle her out the door.

"What crib?" Dara asks. She is, as everyone else has been, grinning foolishly at the baby in her arms. Annie's tight, neat swaddling is starting to drag and unravel.

"Don't get me started," Maggie groans. "She's convinced we're going to drop the baby off at her house all the time for her to babysit. I don't think that's going to work so well with breastfeeding. It's a problem."

"She has a name. Eliana," Katharine reminds her quietly.

"Who? Oh, right, the baby." Maggie remembers. She reaches her arms up to Dara, who hands her the bundle of blankets. "Eliana. Do you like it, really?"

"I think it's lovely. And it's her name—so call her by it. 'The baby' is not a very dignified thing to call a person. She needs to hear her name. It matters." Katharine is emphatic. Maggie is surprised at this insistence.

"Okay. Hello, Eliana. I'm your mother. It's nice to meet you." She stares at her daughter, memorizing the curve of her cheek, the slant of her nose. The baby gazes back, and Maggie has that flash of recognition again, so powerful it takes her breath away. The baby—Eliana—blinks, then yawns, a squeaky little sound. Maggie turns to her mother and sister. "I don't know. It sounds weird. 'I'm your mother.' I'm not sure I can be anyone's mother. Well, I mean, aside from the obvious fact that I can't possibly be old enough. But do I want to be called mother? Maybe Mommy, or Mama. I don't know. What do you think of Ma?"

Dara laughs. "From what I can see of children lately, you'll be lucky if it's not 'hey, you.' "

Katharine's cell phone rings. She glances at the number, and hands the phone to Maggie. "Speaking of parents, it's your father. It's the crack of dawn in London."

"Uh, oh. We should've called before now." She opens the phone. "Hi Daddy. It's Maggie. I had a baby."

"Maggie! Are you okay?" He sounds static-y and distant.

"We're fine. She's a girl."

"I was worried—are you sure everything's okay?"

"I'm sorry—she was only born a little while ago. It took a long time, but she's beautiful and perfect. I'm tired, though. God, it was so hard. I think she may have to be an only child."

Ben chuckles. "It's hard work. But you didn't have any problems?"

"No. I think I threw up. Otherwise, no."

"What's her name? What does she look like?"

"I don't know, really. She's little, and kind of mushed up. Her eyes are mostly closed, but they're really dark when they're open. She has a tiny bit of black hair, but she's pretty much bald. And Daddy—her name is Eliana. Maybe we'll call her Ellie."

"Oh—I'm glad. That's a perfect name."

"Yes. It is. It's perfect for her. It turns out she's her very own person."

Maggie can only imagine her father's smile, but she can see her mother's.

"I thought she might be. How much does she weigh?" Ben wants to know.

"Oh, I'm not sure, come to think of it." Maggie looks down at the baby, in awe of this child who is already her own being, with her own name and weight and secret self. "I don't even know. Here, I'll let you talk to Mom. I'm tired. I'm glad you called, though. I miss you." She hesitates, remembering, and suddenly unsure. "Come home soon, so you can meet Eliana."

Ben pauses. "I love you, Maggie. I'm proud of you. And I will be home soon, I promise. Don't worry about me or your mother, sweetheart. Just enjoy your baby."

The exhaustion hits Maggie like a ton of bricks. Even her bones hurt. Her questions hang in the fuzzy cellular silence, unasked, unanswered. Sadness nudges at the edges of her consciousness. She looks down at the baby, touches the soft spot on her head. The wonder in her chest swells up, pushing the sadness to the side. It's still there; she knows, somehow, that it's here to stay, a part of her. But it won't get much space, now. Her heart is filled up with this baby.

She holds the phone out to Katharine, who looks at it warily, as if it could bite.

"I'm finished. Just take the phone."

"No, I don't want…."

"I don't care. It's your phone—take it. Talk to him." Maggie holds her mother's gaze until Katharine looks away, and reaches out a hand to take the phone. She turns toward the door. Maggie can hear her voice, but not the words.

She smiles down at the baby, then looks up at Dara, who is silent in the rocking chair. "Do you think I need to feed her now?"

"You're not really asking me that, are you?"

"No. I guess not." They grin at each other.

"She'll be fine, you know." Dara glances toward the door; Katharine is standing in the hall, still talking to Ben.

"She's not the one I'm worried about."

"Dad's fine, too."

Maggie thinks for a minute about her father's slim frame and his tidy silver hair. "I don't know. Maybe I'm not worried about either of them. Maybe it's us—maybe we're the ones…."

Dara comes to the side of the bed and gazes down at Eliana. "No. We're all going to be fine. She's here now. You and Sam have to be parents, and I have to be an aunt."

"Is it really that simple?"

"You know, I think it is. We're not them. We're us. End of story."

Maggie nods, and squeezes Dara's hand. "I still don't know if I ought to try and feed her. Can you hold her for a minute while I get ready?"

"Can I hold her? What kind of silly question is that?" Dara coos at Eliana as she gathers the baby into her arms and settles into the rocking chair. Maggie tries to remember how Tracy had arranged the pillows on her lap.

Katharine, finished on the phone, steps back into the room and begins slipping into her coat.

"I'm going to go now. I'll come back sometime tomorrow. And … I'll do my best to bring your grandmother, if she's up to it."

"I'd like that. But only if you think she's well enough."

Maggie thinks of Yaya, frail and insubstantial, and knows in her bones that her time is drawing to a close. She takes a breath, gazing over at her daughter, and peace edges out the flutter of sadness. She smiles up at her mother through tired eyes. "Thanks for being here."

Katharine shrugs shyly. "It's what mothers do. You'll see." She stands behind Dara and touches Eliana on the head. "Your father is very excited. He…he hates that he missed it. He said to tell you."

"I know. Thanks."

"All right then. Sam will be back in a few minutes. Do you need anything else before I go?"

"I don't think so—did the baby fall asleep?"

"Eliana, remember?"

Maggie rolls her eyes at her mother. "Really, Mom? Is this how it's going to go?"

Katharine chuckles. "Do you mean am I going to be a meddlesome grandmother? Probably. When you were born, I thought Mother was going to drive me up the wall. She wouldn't leave the hospital—she slept in the waiting room until I was discharged, then she stayed at our house for two weeks. She was convinced I was going to drop you, or forget to feed you or something."

Maggie's throat tightens, but she half-smiles, thinking of Yaya's scolding voice. She is surprised to find herself rolling her eyes again. "I don't intend to drop her. And how could I forget to feed her? I've got these gigantic boobs to remind me."

Katharine laughs again. "I think you're going to do fine."

"You know, I think so too. I just realized it."

Katharine stops by the end of the bed and squeezes her foot through the blanket. "You should send Eliana to the nursery so you can get some sleep."

"Like I said—we'll be fine. We've got this."

"Oh, you're so sure? Okay. I'll see you tomorrow, then."

"Thanks for coming, Mom."

"I wouldn't have missed it," her mother says, and slips out of the room.

Dara is ready to give Eliana back. As she leans over to put the baby in Maggie's arms, the porcelain scarab on a chain dangles from beneath her shirt collar. Maggie smiles when she sees it.

"Thanks for wearing that today."

"You're welcome. I figured we could use some healing or protection or whatever it can do for us."

"I think it worked." Maggie smiles at the idea, and touches the bare spot at the hollow of her own throat.

"I was wearing my Mayan birth-woman. She's here somewhere; they made me take her off at some point. I think Tracy was worried I was going to get it caught on something. Thanks for wearing the scarab for me. Maybe between us we warded off the mean evil spirits." She smiles up at Dara, then down again at the baby.

Dara grins. "Yeah, she's pretty damn cute. Not that I want one or anything. I think I might like being an aunt. Maybe I'll buy her lots of dreadful stuff that'll drive you crazy. Obnoxious toys. Or trashy clothes when she's a teenager."

Maggie rolls her eyes.

Sam has come in on this last statement, pushing a roll-away bed. "Not my daughter," he pronounces.

"Hah! Watch me!"

Maggie grins, happy to see them rib each other. "You *would*, too."

"Of course I would. What're sisters for?" She rubs Eliana's head. "I'm proud of you," she says, her voice lower now. "We couldn't hear much out there in the hall, but it took so long. And she's a real live baby. That's pretty impressive. You're going to be a great mom."

Maggie blinks back small, quick tears. "Thank you. I'm glad you waited. It was important to me that you meet her." For a second, they're best-sister-friends again, like they were sometimes when they were younger. Then Dara stands up.

"I have to go, honey. I've totally blown New Year's Eve, but I think there's a party at my neighbor's that I need to drop in on. I'll come by tomorrow, after I sleep in very late. Call if you need me to bring champagne or something." She grins, and in a rush of kisses, she's gone.

Sam has unfolded the cot, turned down the lights, and is now getting into his cot. He kisses her on the forehead, and takes the sleeping baby from her. "I'll put her in the Isolette, and put it between us. If she wakes up, we can both reach her. But you should try and sleep."

"I know. I will. I'm tired, but I'm kind of wound up, too."

"I'm past wound up. I'm going to fall over if I don't sleep. You're really going to regret it if you don't, too. Everything's quiet now, and there'll be people in and out of here all day tomorrow. I love you. Go to sleep."

He lies down, then reaches up and adjusts Eliana's blankets so that he can see her through the clear plastic of her box. Within seconds he's snoring. Maggie smiles at the familiar sound, and presses the button to lower the head of her bed. She curls on her side, so she can see both her daughter and her husband. Hanging on the bedrail, right in front of her eyes, is her amulet. She unhooks it from the rail and puts it on, rubbing it once more for good luck.

She reaches over and pulls the crib blanket up a little further over Ellie. It doesn't matter anyway. That's all ancient history. She chuckles to herself, pleased at her private little joke. It is ancient history, after all. She cautiously calls up an old memory of Jamie, swinging in the backyard, and is pleased to see that no sharp pain accompanies it. She wonders if she's ready to bear the weight of her memories. Maybe they're not so heavy, after all. Or maybe she's strong enough. She's too tired to sort it out now.

Maybe later. Out in the hall, voices are singing. She gazes at Eliana for one more moment, listening, then closes her eyes.

> *Should auld acquaintance be forgot,*
> *And ne'er brought to mind,*
> *Should auld acquaintance be forgot,*
> *And auld lang syne.*

EPILOGUE

A small child fidgets, tired of waiting. "Now, Mama? Read to me now?"

Mama looks up from her computer. "Come here for a snuggle." She gives Ellie a hug and kisses the middle of her forehead.

"Not yet, Ellie. Mama has a little more work. Play for five more minutes and then we'll read."

Her mother's eyes are looking back at the computer. Ellie looks around the back garden for something to do—something close to Mama—and spies a red string curling out from under the deck. She tugs, and pulls out the brown and white doggie with the red wheels that she couldn't find at naptime. He is muddy. She fusses and murmurs over him, making sh-sh-sh noises and rubbing off the dirt, like Mama does when she falls down.

"Let's go for a walk, little puppy." He bumps along behind, his wheels making a clacking sound. They go all the way around the garden. When they get to the special stepping stone with Ellie's handprints on it, she stops and says, "Here are the baby roses, little puppy. That one's mine."

She picks up the plastic dog and holds it up to sniff an apricot-colored blossom. Just then, she hears a familiar voice, and drops the toy puppy with a clatter.

"Grandmama!" The little girl runs back toward the house and clambers up the four steps to the deck, so she can wrap herself around her grandmother's legs. Her grandmama squats down to give her a big hug. Her pretty white shirt is soft and silky against Ellie's cheek. Grandmama holds her hand, and they sit down in the chair next to Mama, who closes her computer.

"Hello, Mother. How's the packing going?"

Ellie doesn't like to think about Grandmama packing, so she twists around to whisper up in Grandmama's ear.

"Grandmama! What's in that big box? Is it a present for me?"

"No, honey, it's for your mother. Maggie, I found one last box from Yaya's house. I'm not sure how I missed it, but I brought it for you to go through. I don't think it's terribly interesting—just pictures and papers she'd hung on to, but I thought you might want to see it."

"Thanks. I'll take a look at it later. Maybe after the Peanut goes to bed."

"Mama, I'm not a peanut. I'm a…." Ellie casts around for ideas, knowing they're both watching her. "I'm a bunny. Watch!" She wriggles out of Grandmama's lap and hops. Her shoes make a satisfying *clomp* on the wooden deck. She hops some more, counting.

"One, two, three, four, five, seven,"

"Don't forget six, Peanut."

"Oh! One, two, three, four, five, SIX."

"Okay, that's enough Ellie. Go play in the garden for a few minutes while Grandmama and I chat."

"Then will you read to me?"

"I'm not going to stay long, Ellie," Grandmama says. "I have to go home and pack."

Ellie remembers about Grandmama and her big trip—Mama showed her on the globe, tracing one finger all the way around, but it just looked blue and green and not very interesting—so she stops hopping like a bunny.

"When are you going to mail me presents?"

"Soon. Before you start preschool."

"Okay." Ellie hops down the steps to the garden, holding on to the rail so she doesn't fall down. She hears Mama's voice get quieter, so she listens harder.

"I'm going to ignore that," Mama is saying.

"She's only two," Grandmama says. "She's too young."

"She's bored out of her mind at home, and so am I. It's time. We're both ready for it."

Mama smiles and nods when Ellie looks back at her, so she hops some more, around the edge of the deck.

"It's harder than you realize, walking out that door and driving off every day, leaving your baby behind. I hope you don't regret it—you can't ever get these days back, you know."

"Nonetheless, our minds are made up. Thank you for the advice, Mother, but Daddy's busy, when he's in town, and now you're not even going to be here to pinch-hit anymore. Wait—that didn't sound right. It's great that you're going to travel—we're happy for you. But Sam and I have decided Ellie is ready for preschool, regardless of where you're wandering off to—or Ellen and Samuel, for that matter. This is the best thing for us."

"Whatever you say, dear. She's your daughter."

"Yes. Yes, she is." Ellie can tell her Mama's voice is happy again, but she's getting bored with this talk and her legs are tired of hopping, so she wanders back to the rose bed.

A few minutes later, she comes back to hang over the arm of her grandmother's chair.

"I have a surprise for you, Grandmama. Hold out your hand."

Katharine obliges, watching as Ellie uncurls one small fist, dropping a shower of multicolored rose petals in her grandmother's open palm. Some flutter into her lap.

"Oh, Ellie, honey—you mustn't hurt the roses."

"Mama said I could." Mama confirms this with a nod.

"But the thorns might scratch you."

"I was careful. Aren't they pretty? They're like fairy wings. Don't worry, Mama, I only touched my butterfly rose, like you said."

"She's fascinated by the fact that it's hers," Mama says. "I think she's much less interested in the others."

Ellie picks up the petals that have drifted to the floor, and carefully puts them in her pocket. Then she kisses Grandmama on the cheek and goes back out into the garden to find her doggie on the red string.

www.ingramcontent.com/pod-product-compliance
Lightning Source LLC
Chambersburg PA
CBHW021004120726
47905CB00009B/2850